T0355020

# AMERICAN SECOND
# CIVIL WAR

James Hendershot

Order this book online at www.trafford.com
or email orders@trafford.com

Most Trafford titles are also available at major online book retailers.

Print information available on the last page.

ISBN: 978-1-6987-1776-0 (sc)
ISBN: 978-1-6987-1775-3 (e)

Trafford rev. 10/04/2024

 www.trafford.com
North America & international
toll-free: 844-688-6899 (USA & Canada)
fax: 812 355 4082

# CONTENTS

# CHAPTER 01

# THE BEGINNING OF THIS MISERY

My name is Josey Henry for this account. Naturally, this is not my real name, which I cannot use any existent names in this report, because most of these demons and angels were still alive as late as 2017. I was born in July of 1957; therefore, fortunate to have enjoyed a sadly Affirmative Action victim life. My government sold out my life, nevertheless, I was intelligent enough to find a method to join the bandwagon and live above the low level our government assigned to those such as myself. My loophole offered a surprise raft as the United States fell; my family and I escaped to a new home that had the technology to finish this account. As an adolescent, I understood the opportunities available for me in the Eastern Mountain foothills, therefore, required me to leave my hometown. You will not find this on a map, as most locations must be given false names. I will attempt to give enough clues for those with a need to know can discover the truth. Please remember, this account refers to events after the account is released. Accordingly, I left everything and flew off for four years in the Air Force, foolishly leaving it to return to the disappointing a prejudice family and hometown. I was engaged to a beautiful colored woman from Atlanta. This woman notified her family about this engagement during a visit at her home, only to be beaten by her brothers. This was shocking to me, as I never heard of the colored being prejudice. I was constantly flooded that whites were the sole race that was prejudice. This was reinforced when I traveled in military uniform, and received the hateful glares and snobs from the people of my race. Eventually, I traveled in civilian clothes. I entered the military after the United States left Vietnam. I was terrified about Vietnam, and was thankful it ended after the United States left Vietnam. The fear began while I was in the sixth grade ridding on a school bus seeing a high school boy crying on the bus because he was drafted for duty in Vietnam. For so many young men, this meant an injury-filled life, mental illness, death, or if fortunate labeled as baby killers, and rejected the remainder of his life. I remember, over twenty-five years later, a person who selected me for a sales position expressing his concern my veteran status, claiming the perceived extreme danger in hiring veterans. Fortunately, since his family had purchased my grandfather's farm, he took a chance on me. I was never able to shake that from my status, combined with an Asian wife; I left everything once more and moved into the Seattle area in Washington. Afterwards, here my family shared with me the prejudice as Asians they suffered in Ohio. My children attended in an Elementary school that my Grandfather's cousin help founded, and name was on the top of the plaque as they entered that school. It has once served as a high school, with their class pictures posted on the cafeteria walls, which included their grandfather in one such picture.

Consequently, I was so busy denying my great educational experience and scrapping day to day to make a living, that combined with my military retirement barely made ends meet. The military instilled within me pride in leadership and my nation. I believed in following the law. Nevertheless, the United States changed during my just over eight years in Asia. Half of these years were with the United States Army, serving until my retirement in 1995. The initial shock came with my attempt to bring my wife back with me. Both our children were Americans, both in Korea on United States passports, son born in 1993, and daughter in 1998. Upon my application, we were married about eight years. Additionally, I purchased a home in Ohio prior to the application. The American government agency in South Korea would not grant my wife entry. Unfortunately, South Korea does not neighbor the United States, as does Mexico, where my wife could have walked over the border and gone straight to the welfare office. In addition, South Korea hosts the United States military with over eighty such sites, unlike Mexico, which does not.

I had to write my congressional representative, who later became governor and an Ohio senator. The representative and BOTH Ohio senators wrote the American immigration administration in South Korea to grant my wife of eight years entry into the United States. This was my first experience where an American administrative agency, openly defied the Congress. I also wrote the President who ignored my request, only to have his wife later defend those who illegally enter the United States. I later discovered the President was eating pizza and smoking cigars while receiving sexual pleasure with his interns in the Oval

Office. I, therefore, brought my two children back to Ohio, setting up our home, without a driver's license, as my state would not renew my driver's license. I would have been fully qualified to drive if I paid the renewal fee the years serving in the military in Korea, even though I did not drive in Ohio. Consequently, since Ohio had no intention of thanking me for my service, even though they taxed my military pay while in South Korea, I went through the permit and driver's license tests and of course paying the additional fees, became qualified once more to drive over the Ohio roads. This license qualified me to search for work, as the Demon Federal Government agency operating in South Korea required copies of two paychecks before allowing my wife entry into the United States. They finally granted her entry; interesting enough her plane ticket was paid for by the United States Army under my transportation-benefits post-Retirement. She equally important arrived as we began the re-bonding of our family. Our son had suffered disappointed in so many promises his mother was returning soon, to no fault of his parents, went unfulfilled. Our eight-month daughter, whose first birthday cake was baked by her older white American half-brother, had completely forgotten her mother. A few days of her mother's tender loving care, revived this memory, even though no mother should have to suffer this pain.

Our plane trip back was met with a few challenges beginning with a lazy flight attendant that pretended not to understand my son's request for some orange juice. I finally stood up, looked at her straight in the face, and said orange juice, which by some miracle turned on her slothful brain, and the light came on, with an okay response. The sad result was the total destruction of my youngest son's confidence in talking with daddy's friends, which he called all English-speaking people. Once in the United States on our trip from San Francisco to Pittsburg, I got a taste of the American people, which left a pleasant taste in my mouth. I was asked by many passengers where I got such pretty children. They were willing to go to where I got them and enjoy these sort of children the remainder of their lives. I disappointed them when I told them I did it the old-fashioned way and made them. They were not paying attention to my daughter who tried desperately to pull the hair of the man who sat in front of me. I was even more shocked when the same man told me he had never seen such well-mannered children in his life. My shock was resultant from my ignorance that American parents were not monitoring their children, on in spite of such basic things as not pulling a stranger's hair even though your hands can reach such a person. My son came through for me, as we had to make a mad dash from customs, in one building to the next building. We had a lot of luggage, with of course the important toys. I took the heavy boxes and my daughter in her cart, loading the lighter boxes for my son, with a height almost twice his size. He followed me, staying within about one-hundred feet, which was close unless going around corners. I was fortunate that another American passenger would signal me that he was safe and following me. We made it to check-in with one minute to spare. I later learned they had canceled this connection, most likely tired of having to reschedule stranded passengers.

I understand that those wanting to understand how the United States fell may not see the connections I have started with in this report. I am showing how my ignorance did not catch the obvious signs, even as early as 1999. The government was two-faced, in that I would take two Ohio Senators to beg an American Federal Agency to allow a retired United States Army veteran, with his foreign wife of eight years, in a marriage that created two children. After I submitted two paychecks, requiring me to find childcare, my wife came to the United States, plane ticket paid by the United States Army. I had to bow to them, and play their Mickey Mouse game. The previous administrations were negative about the military. One President, that I will call Bin Laden, even stripped the military budget placing the military to such a despicable strength, that a former command Sergeant Major for a four-star general with CINC power, told me the Army had been stripped so paltry they could now only throw stones at the enemy. This was even complicated by the fact our enemies knew this, many of which did not show him any respect when he visited them. Air Force One sat neglected on the landing strips. The United States was so close to a foreign invasion; nevertheless, to Fake Press ignored these warnings and twisted the fact at the point the people did not understand.

America regained its last breath with the election of President Hiplinger, who brought the economy back to life, providing riches, for those who voted against him, regained international respect, visiting the Arab's speaking to a large group of Muslim leaders, subsequently flying directly to Israel, receiving praise from their Prime Minister, then flying to visit the Pope. The Fake Media, planting their seeds to destroy America, down played this historic visit, as they did with his Asian visit. They forgot that President Hiplinger was a billionaire, with a worldwide empire, notwithstanding his opposition party, the Patricians disregarding he paid for his candidacy, that he might gain some money through his empire, even though he donated all paychecks to charity. Donating your paychecks for President was merely done by one previous President, who also is my sole Patricians hero, JFK. If only his son lived, but as so many others who possibly could interfere with Corrupt's goals, who would play as dirty as they come in her presidential bid in 2016. It still amazes me that JFK's plane mysteriously crashes, killing him while at the same time giving Corrupt the perfect chance to become a Senator for New York. Someday the truth will become known, as it eventually does, but not before so many innocent people suffer while laying a foundation for the fall of the nation she helped bleed.

So many factors lead to the death of the United States. These included religious battles, as the Americans began to disregard Christianity and passing religions with indifference, while in broad daylight the Muslims were preparing to make all American's Muslims and live under Sharia Law, with of course the penalty of execution if they refused to serve. There was a complete loss of national identity, with no more pride in the United States. This began by refusing to stand for the anthem and burning flags in riots. Another reason for this was the method's President Bin Laden praised Muslims and went after Christians, notwithstanding making an organization of Catholic Nuns provide contraceptives for their employees. Moreover, this demonic leader, even made Christians approve wedding certificates for gay marriages, and for Christian owned bakeries prepare cakes for gay marriages. The purpose was to punish the Christians at every juncture, mocking Jesus and the Bible, while promoting the glory of Muslims. Corrupt had NBC leak a private recording, recorded without consent or knowledge of those they illegally attacked, a recording in which Candidate Hiplinger engaged in male-only locker room talk. I was so shocked when all the men criticized it, claiming they would never talk such talk. To be honest, I have been in the locker rooms, and that is the main thing men discuss. I have never met a man whom I could testify claiming they never talked like this. It is just two-faced, hypocritical shameful rhetoric. I have talked much worse and in the same braggadocio's tone. Men must create a great benefit for having sex with women, which many times results in a pregnancy and marriage thereafter, giving up many enjoyable activities to provide care for his new family. The testosterone forces this male; the women love me, competition. Leaving that to the side, President Bin Laden spoke publicly at the Cambridge Public Library about having ribs and pussy, in which he mentioned pussy several times. Even though this went viral on YouTube, the Fake Media ignored it. Even though I boasted privately among men, I would never use such a word with my mother. I am thankful no one did, as she used this term for her cats, at no time understanding why our faces turned red when she called out for her pussies.

The use of Racism to create political division by the Patricians also led to the fall of America, when the colored races realized the Patricians had used them as political pawns in their quest for power. How they kept them so blind, so long was a great mystery. The Patricians termed anything divisive as they could with a phobic ending. The phobic made this seem so horrifying; nevertheless, they did much worse in secret. Notwithstanding, the public discovered the truth, and began the destruction of the United States. Employers became so feeble, fearing anything they did would become a phobic. One such example was how frail the

NFL owners were over to kneel during the national anthem. Corruption ran wild in the United States, from multiple Attorney Generals and FBI directors. This too was discovered and exposed. The American justice system was so corrupt that, as I learned, you may in no way plead not guilty unless you want to spend thousands of dollars, and run the risk of a lazy cop falsifying his report, and the jury believing that cop. Stay out of jail by paying a stupid fee, such as a monitoring fee, and then go free. Freedom for a fee, and the hell with justice. Additionally, they created a concept of 'Politically Correct,' to justify corrupt concepts. This spurred the Silent Majority to go into action and put President Hiplinger in the White House. Unfortunately, the Silent Majority became quite while the Washington swamps unleashed their illegal anti-constitutional massacre against him.

The Fake Media joined the Patricians and People Party in name only politicians as they constantly tried to cause problems. He said you are bad, what you will want to say about him. Well, I think he is black-hearted as well. Bammo, you have a fight, in which they will continue stowing the coals and watch it burn and destroy the people fighting. The Patricians used their memorized talking points to promote the belief in their utter lies. They would add little zingers among these talking points and watch how they were perceived, and later use these zingers as absolute proof. I was constantly amazed how these meathead Patricians spoke these talking points as if they were not falsehoods. The Fake Media search for lies to cause them troubles. Sometimes they did not have to search hard, as the seventh floor of the FBI hated the duly elected President of the United States. The FBI leaked protected information to the public, causing public chaos. This became so routine that a fired Director confessed to leaking confidential information to Congress with no concept of being punished for doing so. He was correct in that is corrupt behavior would proceed unpunished. The police were under constant attack with many of their methods of discovering criminals coming under attack as being racial profiling. Many of these situations demanded criminal profiling; nevertheless, having to abandon this actually caused more harm to the race they were struggling to protect. Instead, they had to stand by when these lawless citizens mowed down their innocent neighbors. The blame for this was naturally the other race, even though the victim's race was reluctant to give the police the information, they needed to remove these killers from the street.

Another critical failure in the United States government was the politicization of the Intelligence agencies. They are absolutely corrupt, and sadly greatly inaccurate. They presented a report against Russia claiming it was considerably probable that Russia interfered in the election. They had nothing to say about all the other nations interfering with our election. A Director of one of the primary agencies claimed on TV that he had no evidence to prove this claim. The false media ignored this and actually reported the probably interfered as proof and attempt to tie President Hiplinger's hands in his attempts to have a favorable relationship with the Russians. They had to keep this President away from the Russians fearing the Russians would reveal all the bribes, they paid the Patricians in such activities as the Uranium One deal, which saw twenty percent of our Uranium flow across our borders, creating a shortage of this Yellow Cake. Notwithstanding, this is needed for the hundreds of thousands of cancer x-rays costing Americans so much more to get this needed health care product back into the United States. Another of the get rich quick at any price and let the Americans pay for it. Corruption ran rapidly, until the divided United States fought, and just as in the first Civil War, brother killed brother and father killed sons. This time it has expanded to sister killing sister and mothers killing her children. There were no borders as this war was one on one guerilla still killing. Search for the weak and go for the quick kill. Many times just opening your front door would result in a bullet in the head. The Patricians regarded the People Party as non-human causing the People Party to fight back at all costs. They had to exterminate, or be killed. There was no opportunity for discussion.

The attacks against the American foundation came into full force with the disregard of Marriage being between a man and a woman, which dated back to Adam and Eve. Marriage could now be between members of the same-sex. If you objected to this family unit-killing concept, you would be labeled with a phobic and face harsh punishment from the government. Even agnostic churches appeased this new law, created by the Supreme Court. No more laws created by the Legislative Branch as the Executive and Judicial branches started creating the laws. One law illegally passed by President Bin Laden was allowing children who were smuggled in by their parents illegally into the United States to remain in the United States. It continually amazed me how the blind Patricians pushed so hard to allow people who invaded the United States to jump in front of those who were attempting to come in legally. Their love for anti-social behavior created their thirst for blood, which later the Patricians could not turn off when it drank the blood of the Patricians leaders. The death of Justice created the lawlessness that finally created the near-future blood bath. As Pascal (1623-1662) claimed:

"Justice without force is powerless; force without justice is tyrannical"

Another great thought came from William Gladstone (1809-1898) with claimed, "Justice delayed, is justice denied."

The stripping of Justice's force helped add fire to the brutal killing that spilled to every street in America. Justice was slow for so long, with even innocent people tossed in prison for years, while lying prosecutors mislead judges. The victims were treated equally as the criminals in the courts. The law-breaker would tie the case up in court for years preventing the victims from receiving their just compensation. Everyone who killed knew justice had died first.

Just as in the first Civil War, a state threatened to leave the Union. This pitiful state passed laws directly in conflict with Federal Law. Their leaders claimed they were serious about the environment and would do anything to save it, yet allowed sewage from Mexican cities to flood our beaches. As Thomas Huxley (1825-1895) quoted, "It is not who is right, but what is right." It is not accurate that Americans must swim in the sewage from a foreign nation and at the same time, grant them open access through weak borders. Even Horace (65 BC to 8 BC) claimed, "Justice, though moving with a tardy pace, has seldom failed to overtake the wicked in their flight." This summed up the Death of the United States; with no justice, nothing could overtake the wicked Patricians in their quest to strip the wealth from its citizens hoarding the wealth for themselves. The Patricians lived from other peoples' money, hating President Hiplinger's hard work that created thousands of jobs for Americans, creating his over ten billion-dollar Empire. The concept of earning your living died from the Patricians' concept of the government more entitled to your income than you are, leading so many to give up, and become supported by the government. The Patricians considered this buying their votes, the conflict arising when many of these people supported the People Party. The Patricians did not take this lying down, spawning their hate for anyone who did not follow their false doctrine.

The war lasted for just a few years, as it was guerrilla as they carried out harassment and sabotage. The Patricians identified themselves with bright yellow hats. Their ignorance did not detect they were making their people easy targets. They also killed each other by accident when a member forgot their hat, receiving a bullet through the head by their comrades. The Riots began as early as 2015, with the race baiting tying the police's ability to protect the innocent, while advancing their sick agenda. One such example was in Charlotte, where the police herded the opposing Parties into each other, and then refused to protect those injured. Anti-fascists continued their bloodthirsty anti-social behavior, hitting anyone on the other side with their clubs. Anti-fascists started the fight, as shown on national television. Afterwards, the Patricians claimed the President was supporting the lawless side, when, in fact, they had broken no laws, and were beaten so badly that one member killed an Anti-fascists supporter with his car. That was sad; nevertheless, we must remember that when justice fails, tyranny prevails. This Virginian city's Patricians leadership created an environment where people were put in danger, and the blood is on their hands. They believed they had got away with it, only to have bullets kill them during the

Civil War. Such is their way when the blind lead the blind; they both fall into the pit. The anti-Americans used this as an excuse to begin destroying or defacing public monuments. In Chicago, they even defaced a statue of Abraham Lincoln. When the Racists actually destroy an image for the man who divided a nation and fought a bloody four-year war, the first American Civil War, and freed them from slavery, is nothing more than biting the hand who feeds you.

These led up to the socially acceptable belief that being white is bad. The whites have a cultural privilege, regardless of being more than sixty-seven percent among the population. Just because these whites came from Europe, fought the British for their independence, and then later side by side with the Racists killed innocent American Natives stealing their land should give them no privilege. This belief was installed early when the Federal government removed qualification for a job and discriminated against the white people under the name of Affirmative Action. What a reverse discrimination tool, that only led to more of the Racist complaining about how bad they have it. Their situation was made worse by the Patricians, who lied to them, getting their votes and keeping them on their plantation for the next round of voting. They would create their lying talking points and drill these into the heads of their blinded supporting brainwashing them into believing their lies. Another effective tool was to open the borders so drugs could pour into the country. Pocketing their share from the profits, they would then stand at the corners crying how terrible it was for so many innocents to die, while their blood was pouring from their mouths. How easy it is to control drug addicts with the hint of preserving their habit. They have decreased their ability to comprehend, detect lies, and understand what is truly happening around them. They will even follow a socialist who promises a free college education. The Patricians do not believe in letting those who work for their money keep it. Those who become rich must instead support the remainder of the society, and the riches income is ripe for the government to redistribute it. They did not realize how easy it was for them to close down their factories, move overseas and accumulate their wealth in a considerably more appreciative and productive environment. Even though the Patricians created government jobs through over taxation, these jobs became too much for the government to afford, especially when President Bin Laden accumulated more debt than all other Presidents combined did. He unleashed a shovel ready one trillion dollar infrastructure bill that witnessed those funds mismanaged and through corruption, creating merely a few temporary jobs and left the American infrastructure in crumbles.

Subsequently, the newest generation was not properly equipped emotionally to handle even the most basic of issues. Universities created safe areas, where these snowflakes could go to recover themselves. The universities provided these snowflakes, hot chocolate and play doe for the road back to their deranged sanity. The Patricians flooded them with their anti-social beliefs. This was coupled by insane professors, with the vast majority advancing the destructive policies advanced by the Patricians. They fought with violence when anyone from the People Party challenged these sick beliefs. This even included burning university buildings and openly destroying public property. They were willing to die to provide sanctuary for illegal aliens, while making their fellow legal citizen victims of their attacks. This generation was lovers of pleasure more than any concept of earning and paying your way. Not all are that way, as my sons and daughter earned their way and were financially responsible, even to the point of scolding their parents when we purchased things we did not need, but wanted. Due to laziness on my part, I did not raise them in the church. Notwithstanding, they do hold a solid moral base, and actually keeping me in line. As I discovered what the succeeding generation was up to, destroying the foundation of the United States, I was caught off-guard. I blindly assumed the ensuing generation was as my children were. Factors' attributing to this was my concept of the many technologies available for them to challenge. I built computers for them, and purchased a wide assortment of game consoles. My belief was they were active, thinking, with a coordinated sensory response. Their computers had the Internet, which gave them everything they wanted, not only for their education, but also for the information from the world at their fingertips.

My children had parents that properly bordered by compromising and understanding parents. Unfortunately, we were an island in the middle of a raging storm. Children were ignored by parents who were too deep in their personal activities. Too many homes had solely one parent. The pressure on the economy dropping while prices were raising forced many parents to work more than one job. Many communities had gangs that were hungry for the young and innocent. These children would become armed and many actually killed to gain status. Accordingly, the drugs locked them in these social dungeons. Subsequently, new refined deadly drugs hit the nation. Parents were outliving their children, watching their children locked into the eternal rest as their caskets to resettle six feet below the surface. These death demons were killing young people throughout the entire nation, leading President Hiplinger to declare it a national emergency. I made myself available for my children and supported their social activities, even treating their friends with respect. I operated with the concept that the more challenges they were provided enveloped in a concept of pleasure to keep them from drugs.

The nation appeared to support the irrational riots and destruction of public property. They were immune to these activities, not acknowledging the illegality of it. Massive riots destroyed their communities reacting to comprehended Racism, fueled by a Fake Media and mysterious injustice of the Judicial System. Stories were falsified and amplified to make the criminals appear as angels. A belief that white cops were killing minorities and being acquitted for what they perceived as crimes. Not all cases were based on the same events. The Racism fever created the perception that violence was justified, and they could destroy anything around them. Unfortunately, they destroyed the innocent businesses located in their community. These businesses were privately owned, leaving the owner bankrupt and out of business. These owners relocated in safer neighborhoods, leaving their previous residence without the products and services they once provided. This mentality of instantaneous destruction laid the foundation for this response to anything. The Racism labeled minorities, promoting their greatness, while declaring the whites who promote their race as Racists. They would burn your house and destroy the public places that were needed for their survival. This fire did not stop the destruction and misery, as those victims from these areas, had to go into other neighborhoods to obtain the scarce items they needed to survive. This led to more violence and killing. The perception of Racism was a hot keg that filled the streets with want to be killers. Much of their plight was established by the Patricians, who created the economic dumps where these people lived, fostering the belief that those who had must give to those who do not have. Any person who 'made it' and became rich owed them. Sadly, when one of them made it, that person got the hell out of Dodge.

Many adolescents found they could not learn from the schools they attended. The students ruled the schools, and the teachers had to obey or pay with their lives. Violence was everywhere around them and had been for many decades. The foundation of this Civil War was not so much a sudden change in beliefs and views. It was the gradual progression and societies ignoring and accepting that ignited this powder keg. These random actions became planned and implemented for strategic purposes. The ability to run over the teachers provided the confidence needed to challenge other authority figures, including the police. They would watch and provoke the police into some response and then claim Racism, igniting their fellow villains into a full-on caponized fight. Those injured were paraded as heroes and the law enforcement officer who responded to their attempt to slay them, were branded as the outlaws. False stories about these events were spread by the fake news demons, in which they harped on it repeatedly creating a pugnacious population, who slowly lost their ability to ignore. Therefore, rushing into their negative warlike mode and kill those innocents the Fake Media branded. The anti-social behavior became incorporated by respected public officials, actors, and entertainers. These entertainers began by attacking any person trying to maintain a socially secure society. They went after ministers to an unusual extent. Christian religious beliefs were challenged and if that Christian did not abandon his or her belief, they were punished by the government. Contrarily, disloyal Americans would call for the acceptance and enforcement of Sharia's law. These lamebrains demanded acceptance of same-sex relationships and equal rights for women. They were so ignorant, not realizing Sharia Law forbids same-sex activities and would never recognize equal rights for women. Ironically, there were enough combatants to prevent the rampart spread of Sharia Law.

Notwithstanding, blindly these women supported this anti-west rogue version of the law, which even supported genital mutilations. This mindless supporting philosophy that they know nothing of is so sad. It takes little imagination when the woman, who claimed she would fight until the death for women's rights, experienced her genitals mutilated would be screaming for justice. She would want to crucify the idiot who authorized this, not knowing when she stares into a mirror, she would be witnessing the idiot. We had a similar experience in our state this current year. Our state, as does many government levels and licensing agencies simply tacked on an additional fee to the yearly fee. Even though we complain consistently about these nasty techniques to steal our money, while these unelected tyrants had the gall to say they are increasing revenues they generated, they tacked it on your once-a-year "permission fee". Our state's Department of Licensing whose entire fee created money for the government to spend, for merely giving citizens' authorization to drive on their roads. The greedy got greedier and tacked on an additional $200 per vehicle making the car sticker cost around $300. We have four drivers in our house, costing our family nearly $1,000 a year to drive our vehicles. This is on top of the practically ten percent sales tax paid when purchasing the car, which the salesman explained the state made more money from the sale than does the dealership. The government was doing no work, except for mismanaging the public's money, nevertheless, making more money than those who were working. Another tax where the government loves to steal their citizens' money is the property tax. This is a tax on a product the citizens were paying with funds that had already been taxed for Federal, State, Local, Social Security, and Medicare. This tax is payable each year, even if the property is owned. The float the rate using their tricks to make it sound like nothing, nevertheless, if you do not pay this, they will send the sheriff and take your home and kick you on the street.

These were just a few of the methods the government was using while stealing and mismanaging the public's money. The Patricians and sadly, many in the People's Party (PP) enhanced by a ton of greedy, corrupt demonic bureaucrats' strong belief that they were entitled to the income from the citizens. They secretly held to the belief that the citizens were too ignorant to understand how to spend their money; therefore, this was the government's money. The psychological impact of constantly working only to allow incompetent idiot civil servants to put their hand over the wage earners when receiving paychecks planted the seed and need for revenge. The middle-class was overburdened with taxes, notwithstanding the same government agency declaring they needed no financial assistance. Nevertheless, the low-income earners paid little or no taxes, and received a ton of public assistance. There were so many lower-income voters than middle-class voters, making their votes easy to buy. Moreover, if the Patricians kept them close to starvation, their votes would remain cheap. The one thing they forgot was something my Behavior Psychology Professor taught me while in college was that a hungry man has no laws. Compound a Fake Press, corrupt Justice System, lying Patricians and the fire is stocked enough to burn.

Notwithstanding the fire did burn, even though it still could not ease the rage that Americans had for each other. The Fake Press praised anything that destroyed the American infrastructure. The West was in ruins, and so shameful when compared to the East as the Asians held on, as best they could, in the heart of their rich heritage. They took responsibility for their actions and need to contribute to their government, even the Communist in China knew their future depended upon their support of the communist party. Compared to their past, they were now on a perceived gravy train. The act of so many flooding to their deaths in the Korean War, as if human life was of no value. America got a taste of life with no hope of living, such as so many young Chinese's men in Korea experienced. Waves of Chinese's men were mowed down. The second Civil War had the same massive numbers killed each day, notwithstanding rather than in one concentrated area; these kills were dispersed from sea to shining sea. Snipers would pick off mothers as they were leaving their homes, or children return home from school. Even though the home residents called the protectors associated with their party affiliation who would attempt to neutralize the sniper. The Patricians went after the People Party members. There was no middle, as the Patricians wore yellow hats. Naturally, when they forgot their hats, their party would execute them if possible. Accordingly, the People's Party attempted to execute anyone they saw wearing yellow hats. Many of the executions were from neighbors who knew who was in each party. The hate was intensive. It was almost impossible to remain secluded, and venture outside, even just for groceries or medications. Notwithstanding, those powerless to get out had to send others out to get their necessities incapable to know if they returned. Ugly and so bloody. Many housebound people had their homes burned, bombed, including hand grenades tossed in the windows or into the home after a door was compromised. Additionally, smoke bombs force the hidden people out of their hiding places and easy picking.

Subsequently, the availability of destructive weapons was massive, as in many cases weapons, fatal chemicals, and abundant ammunition, were as available as cigarettes and milk. Young boys, around eight or nine were trained in weapons and fighting in their Party's training center. Attendance and enrollment were mandatory, no exceptions. Failure to train could place their family's security support. Everyone had binoculars and moved from tree to tree or building to building, striving to obtain maximum concealment, which was just as effective to the same degree as cover when considering strategic or tactical maneuvers, notwithstanding simple daily life-sustaining activities. The Parties gained control of their television networks and web sites on the Internet. This insured their members could keep up to date and prepare for infrequent attacks. The security benefits of these networks additionally had some snakes in its garden. Hackers and other digital geniuses monitored the opposing party's networks for valuable intelligence and vice versa. They were experts at sabotaging each other's data and important military missions. This led to unsuspecting people walking into preplanned deadly ambushes. Consequently, this destroyed any form of social security coupled with party protection, creating a feeling that even the trees were ready to kill.

This report will continue to define the elements responsible for this cultural decay. Accordingly, even if a citizen could bypass all the psychological and social environmental variables they could still end up with a bullet into the head from a weapon of a social defect who fell prey to these contributing factors. When a member within a community group was slaughtered, the community immediately activated into a full war mode attempting to destroy anything from the opposing party. Each death, from either side, elicited more deaths and a full-blown community war. The combinations of the contributing elements could manifest its destruction in as many possible modes as the stars in the sky. Subsequently, a migrating factor that created additional terror and increased stress were drifters that lived from the land and would target suspected opposing party members at random with a fresh perception of establishing targets with a totally unknown strategy. A migrant may scroll through an hour during odd hours and pick off unsuspecting targets through unprotected avenues; a common one is during the night hours hitting their targets through windows in lighted rooms. Communities usually had established safe times or zones, which were open for slaughter by migrators. The bottom line was every possible thing could happen every conceivable time. Naturally, there was no dependable source of supply, considering truck drivers would be shot while driving, or if wanting the products being delivered, pop them off during rest stops. Social protection was just about impossible to provide to provide for people traveling between communities. Naturally, individuals employed a myriad of techniques to increase their chances of survival during these high-risk journeys. This reduced the frequency of the trips, which placed critical supply shortages driving up prices, with actually deadly encounters while fighting over the small amount of available resources. Naturally, people ate whatever they could that would not immediately kill them. Grass was eaten so much that it was considered wasteful to mow your lawn. The best grass eating time was at night, when a person could dress in black and crawl over the ground having planned where to eat by scouting the areas through their windows during the daytime.

Notwithstanding, the crumble of any social force and cohesion mechanism promoted the decay of the American society and blistered the family unit. This forced the morally strong citizens to forgo many traditional customs. One such custom was marriage, no matter if it was between sexes or same-sex. Not only was it unsafe to assemble that many people, but also rare to throw together most friends and family located in other communities, even if they were still living. A young bride was expected to go through multiple spouses through sadly short periods. The communities accepted their daughters engaging in numerous relationships. Each time they visited the daughter, which was most likely at frequent small funeral services, fresh partners were expected, when considering the service was most likely her previous partner. Funeral homes were using new chemicals and techniques to dispose of the bodies employing modified methods of cremation, because a follow-up at a graveyard was too dangerous and easy pickings, even though the grave stones provided excellent cover and concealment. The sole enjoyment factor in these frequent ceremonies was an update on who was still alive as friends and family updated their family trees. Moreover, the population growth in the United States was negative if merely considering new births. Naturally, week borders welcomed illegal immigrates worldwide as foreigners would select areas, build new forts and secluded communities. They were planting seeds, which provided a foundation for future anti-American independent locations. Most communities preferred to ignore these areas using them as buffer zones against their opposing party's forces.

A precipitous review of several compounding issues that established the quicksand the United States existed upon precluding the destruction of stars and stripes leading to the war and blood bath in the streets, in each other's homes, and back yards. This war did not adhere to the conventional front line unit style. It was a guerrilla clandestine, kill by any method possible. Things as low as fishing lines to trip and hammers to bash in heads were routine. Riots tended to be the sole community greetings, although all the members did not survive, as they were popped off by snipers. The rioters enjoyed the destruction of public and privately owned property, not caring who would suffer the financial loss. They failed to recognize that repairs would not come as it did previously. The race baiting press and public officials stirred fires flooding the streets with blood. The public became so tired of the Fake Press that they turned to social media. Public officials who previously called on the public to resist ran like chickens when the people they abused turned against them. Thank God for small miracles. Freedom of religion only applied to those religions that had nothing to do with our founding and the horrors of devout persecutions of Europe in the 17th century. The European religious wars concentrated and Christianity against the Muslim, then later evolving into a war between Catholics and Protestants, migrating into Protestants moving to the new world so their people could worship God in freedom, not for them to bow in the future to Muslims.

The people became ignorant to the truth, deceived by the Fake Press. Drug abuse destroyed the backbone of the nation's future generation. The Patricians blindsided the Stock Market and Wall Street with the constant threat of unleashing their puppets in mass demonstrations. The Blind will lead the blind, and they both will fall into the pit. The Stock Market was controlled by those who knew nothing concerning economics and business, as President Hiplinger turned the Stock Market around raising their value by over twenty-five percent in just nine months. Sort of answers they question how President Hiplinger as a businessman built a billion-dollar empire that fell and afterwards came back and came back hard to a ten billion-dollar plus Empire, turning into becoming the first President to win without ever serving in the military or government previously. This was the awakening of the Silent Majority. They awoke, then fell back to sleep, as their establishment attempted to crucify their savior. The Russians gained control of the American public through the Patricians, who were helpless puppets in their hands. The Patricians, as puppets of the Russians, brought Congress to a massive slowdown with obstruction. The passive press had their nose up the Kremlin as Americans could merely shake their heads and say, "oh my God." The churches were attacked, with many not returning alive; notwithstanding, cities and even states abandoned the security of their citizens and provided sanctuary to illegal aliens permitting them to rape and murder. The elimination of the borders flooded American schools with non-tax paying Spanish-speaking unlawful aliens.

Accordingly, the United States became immune to violence, with the real-life killing of a human being matched the excitement and equivalence of killing in a game console. Later, they discovered real-life killing left bodies to rot and not vanish as in game consoles. The Racism was too one-sided with the minorities bashing the whites. Any white person praising his or her race was branded as promoting white supremacy. White was branded as bad. If fact, anything white was a target for attaching. The terrorists who laid the seeds to destroy America struggled to destroy American history, denying the past and changing from corrupt into saintly. No matter how much perfume you put on cow poop, it is still cow poop. Sex scandals shook the nation's fabric as the Patricians supported their pedophiles, even attacking the victims of their perverts. They searched, many times far back as forty years to find anything embarrassing. Then a holier-than-thou public, ran by atheists pronouncing judgement. What continues to amaze me is the self-hypocrisy, as men would openly criticize opponents, and if the opponent dared to respond, declare them has bullies, claiming I would never do that, when, in fact, them doing it are what created the need for a response. Nevertheless, President Hiplinger met them head on and did not back down, as the opponents expected. They looked for twigs in his eyes, while they had logs in theirs. Either way, they betrayed Americans and cried like babies when the people rose and took everything down. When you take the bottom out of a trash can, all the trash flows out. Now is the time to examine several of the areas and how the blood flowed in their streets during the Second American Civil War.

CHAPTER 02

# ORANGE GROVE TEXAS
# (MÉXICO, VETE A CASA)

The story continues now coming to you from Orange Grove, Texas. Notwithstanding the non-stop guerrilla warfare, flooding the United States was controlling every city in the perishing USA. Orange Grove's racial makeup had just over fifty percent Latino or Hispanic. The Mayor of this tiny (1.1 square miles) understood the ramifications of this makeup, especially with Mexico so close. Another challenge facing this small city was that 40.2% of the homes had children under eighteen in them. This report now moves to the Williams, a Pacific Islander family. Their race (8.07% of the city) puts them between the whites and African Americans. Their locality sat between W, Mendoza Ave, W

Pundt Ave, S, Metz Ave and S Hammond St. Their ten homes were tasked with securing St John of the Cross Catholic Church, which now sat vacant. Several bordering neighborhoods stored supplies in the Church. The quarter accepted responsibility for securing this Church. It was simply too dangerous not to secure it, considering the carnage that needed to drive out any enemy forces. Two of the homes were vacant, well actually cleared through a bloody battle, executing the Patricians families that previously occupied them. The community cut the water supply to these homes and then chained their dogs to the home's openings. Eventually, the two families surrendered and were guided to the recreation area in the middle of the homes, tied and executed with arrows. The bodies were fed to the dogs, thus cleaning the vicinity. The small sub community believed the execution of the two Patricians families in their area was mandatory for their future. Allowing them to survive in the neighborhood would provide the Patricians an attack base leading to the death of all People Party residents. Patricians could not exist beside anyone who did not pledge absolute allegiance to them. They called for the death of all members of the People Party global, with the slogan, 'we will go worldwide, so you cannot hide.' Patricians patrolled the area continuously for People Party homes. They were not as successful in the southeastern area of Texas, excluding Houston. The rural residents who lived outside Houston blocked roads entering the city attempting to barricade the city. Most barricades were set up with mines and secured from concealed positions by snipers. It they attempted to secure it openly; Patricians snipers were executing them.

The community labeled themselves as Freedom. Freedom would send several archers in the neighboring rural area to harvest wild game. They preferred using crossbows because the rifle fire would alert any rogue Patricians snipers operating in the area. Another precaution needed was detecting any amiable hunters from neighboring communities operating in the area. It was extremely laborious coordinating with friendly hunting parties from People Party in the vicinity. It was too strenuous physically to contact them, and the risk of the Internet or Walky-Talky's of being hacked, leading the parties into an ambush. Each home had two families, with the owners get the master bedroom. It was so important to vacate homes that could not easily be protected. The exiting owners would burn their homes to prevent the Patricians from using the house. It is easier to protect an area with open space as compared to flush them out of a vacant house. Having two families in the house increased their ability to protect themselves, and it provided more continuity for the children when one of the adults did not return. The concept of move slow and only take what you need is the goal of external operations. Within the first two months of this war, resources started to deplete. Orange Grove was fortunate to be a little over twenty miles from the Gulf of Mexico and Corpus Christi. San Antonio, Austin, and Houston were a conceivable source, although extremely risky. It did not take long to learn that anything in the city, unless manufactured within it, had to come from an external source. Routes 35, 37 and 10 were potential sources of this highway commerce.

Hollywood closed and movies vanished, as did many of the actors, appreciations to the Peoples Party. Several stations provided limited shows, with the news channels prevailing. The news was strictly divided between the Patricians and the Peoples Party. The anchors tended to rotate, as they were considerable targets representing their party. The living face that could stare at their enemy and enter their homes. The news they had ordinarily come in from their satellites, which were currently within high walls and as concealed as practical. Usually, the household would catch the news on TV during a meal. The primary source of news was with a radio, usually including earphones, providing noise discipline. The radio news from a neighboring city provided intelligence needed in the local area. The news would report the names and numbers of casualties for the previous day. This was the prime reason to listen to the radio news, considering it might be the verification of a suspected death of an acquaintance or loved one. When their people become missing, they must hope they are dead and not suffering, especially as a Prisoner of War. The Patricians were consumed with the concept of morality, nevertheless, could not figure the complete situation. They consistently attempted to capture their opponents, afterwards taking them to their Prisoner of War camps. If they believed a person had the potential for indoctrination, they would attempt the conversion process.

The tricky part is when a People's Party (PP) person converts to Patricians; the Patricians eternally attach their yellow cap to their head through a surgical process. With a yellow cap on, the PP's would immediately execute them on the site. The radio would also present another local news, such as a retailer having certain items. The communities would calculate the risk and the items' cost and decide if they were going into the store that night. Consequently, stores solely operated at night and no longer had large windows, but now solid walls. The Williams family is the current leaders' Freedom. Their house was directly parallel to the Church, the first in the three building cluster, except for a long house beside the Church. The house beside the Church was previously used as a Church school. Freedom remodeled this building easily putting three families in it. The building behind Williams's quarters was remodeled as well, housing three families. Naturally, all windows and doors facing the streets were covered with metal sheets. The Williams shared their house with another family that was considered deputy leaders. This was once more in the continuous flow of their leadership. This area tended to receive a lot of sniper fire, which at times penetrated the metal. Freedom, therefore, applied another strong sheet material, which was highly effective against penetrating bullets. Freedom installed some little squares for sticking out their rifles. These tiny windows had small medal doors. These doors opened from the bottom when opened to provide cover from above the window. Additionally, the windows were coated with a sparkling metallic spray that produced blinding effects on snipers attempting to zoom in with their scopes. Freedom was effective in controlling the traffic at the corner junctions of W Pundt Ave and S Harrod St. Freedom secured the intersection of S Metz St and W Mendoza Ave. The PP assigned intersections to the various neighborhoods in an attempt to control any possible Patricians invasions. By not controlling every juncture, they hoped to draw them, whereas the next intersection they could defend with twice the firepower. Of course, they had guards on every corner. The guards on the crossings with no house firepower were assigned to notify the housing units; the enemy was en route.

Freedom enjoyed this time during the year, because the leaves were changing color, while those that fell upon the ground became crispy sounds when people walked on them. Freedom always provided their teams with snow shovels to clear the leaves before walking on them, and a broom for the last person to sweep the leaves back disguising their trail. The disadvantage to this season was that it additionally served as the hurricane season. Previously, Texas always had confidence that most would hold onto their homes during this season, until the floods of 2017. If they were to be hit with the same floods once more, it would be their death ticket. The floods would now be their death tickets, in that it would force them out into the opening. Many believed to worry about such future possibilities, when making it through the current day was a challenge great enough. This day began with a radio warning that a Patricians family of six was in the area, with only the male adult wearing the yellow cap. This was against the rules, and against the informal code of conduct agreed by the nonpartisan war council for the former United States. This code provided the unofficial punishment of public execution through intense torture. This was to be recorded and posted online. Gaining entrance through false party association could easily destroy a community.

Later in the morning, a guard reported a woman and four children walking down the street. The woman was identified as PP, with no yellow markings. The lead guard called for a stand down, allowing the family to enter. As a precautionary measure, the guards remained at their positions, and the welcoming committee remained in their secured position. Freedom got a break when the guard in the Church steeple noticed some movement through the woods on the other side of W Mendoza Ave with his scope. About twenty minutes later the guard clarified the woods had an intruder with a yellow hat. The male most likely was running cover for the female and children accompanying their mission. His yellow hat would provide protection from other Patricians. The two best Freedom snipers rushed to the steeple. They scanned the woods intensely waiting for a movement. Their dogs were released. The woman and four children were accepted into one house held under gunpoint in the waiting area. All electrical devices were removed, as well as all clothing and body cavities searched. Afterwards, the five people were tied and bound. Their clothing was searched looking for any proof of their Patricians affiliation. Additionally, they had no PP identification. The dogs flushed the man out from behind a tree, as the two PP snipers could execute the Patricians invader. After the dogs verified the woods were clear, the sad but solemn responsibly of Freedom to enforce the law laid upon the neighborhood. The children were assembled in the Church, placed in rooms facing the metal reinforced street side. The adults did not want them to see what would be happening, although these children witnessed it in other neighborhoods and on TV.

Freedom had an execution to perform while their dogs feasted on the Patricians shot in the woods. Consequently, for the initial part, the men asked the women to go inside and not look. The women tended to freak out when they saw children being executed; nevertheless, the execution was needed to preclude the Patricians from sending children to enable the death of PP, who, by the way, under those circumstances would witness their children executed as well. The initial part of any torture began by cutting out the tongues. These were removed to prevent loud screaming that may alert any rogue Patricians and thus complicate the process. The ideal process was to stage the executions to keep their flesh from spoiling for their dog's enjoyment. The four tongues were stored in a bucket, as the dogs were still chomping on the sniper in the woods. The adult female would be tortured after the children were executed, as her response to witnessing this would be an added element to the recording of the event. They hoped this would deter other women from accepting missions with children. At least for the minimum, they would not take their children, which could add to confusion and difficulties in coordination. Any small thing could turn the tide for a successful neutralization of the attack. With the four tongues removed, they now use pliers to remove the fingers and toes. Afterwards, just as before starting from the youngest child to the oldest child, the hands and feet were removed. Most times, after these removals, what remained of the bodies went into shock, if not; they would remove the legs and feet. Once the torso went into shock, the remainder of the body was chopped into small pieces. The flesh was then placed in garbage bags and buried to stay fresh for their dogs who knew where to dig up this flesh. The woman was raped by all the Freedom men. Naturally, they used protection; being suspicious, the Patricians would send disease infested women. The video included these rapes, and then her dissection. Once complete, the video was uploaded to the Patricians social media page. Another threat neutralized buying a few more hours or maybe even days of life.

Accordingly, no matter how hard the people tried, most suffered from some sort of psychological damage. The new socially accepted extreme was just as dangerous. The ability slowly to execute another person and feel no regret is abnormal and will eventually explode. These explosions if not controlled, could backfire on the applicable party. The radio news anchors have been always concerned about this underlying stress and would announce coping strategies each day. This amounted to creating a cold-hearted bloodthirsty society. You either killed or were killed. Another slogan was either you drank their blood, or they drank yours. It did not take long for the lines to be drawn. The problem was for those citizens who did not live in the same district as the party controlling it. Some regions became settled such as New England, northern Virginia, and the West Coast. Nevertheless, pockets did exist within these areas. The pockets tended to congregate around the state borders. The PP controlled most of the Midwest and rural areas. This was the key to the war winding down, until foreign nations began running the naval blockades. These were hit and miss; as the Eastern coast from below Virginia was controlled by the PP. Submarines were the demons of the seas. The West Coast had many strong PP pockets, especially in Washington, which except for Seattle-Tacoma area, the remainder of the state was PP.

Another psychological dilemma is the inability to depend upon an agency to provide protection and security, especially during emergencies. Many described it as falling with no ground in your future. I am sure that those who have fallen would not consider the absence of a ground as their greatest disappointment. Disposing of dead bodies was consistently a challenge. The human body creates so many gasses and odors as it begins to decay. Humans are not as equipped as animals in dealing with this decaying process. The dogs became in high demand, as packs of them would roam throughout cities, feasting on the humans who did not move. Wolves, foxes, and bears, began to roam in the open throughout cities. Notwithstanding, bears would in turn go after the living as well. Rats and other rodents began to over-populate. This terminated any social neutering and spading of cats. Accordingly, they were now permitted to populate at will, and forced to survive as barn cats, hunting rodents to survive. For the most part, cats for forced to stay outside, as was dogs. Dogs were given much longer chains, or placed inside fences. The dogs were the saving alarms for most communities. When they began barking, their owners would be rolling out of bed, grabbing a weapon and rush outside. Most owners knew their dogs well enough to know which direction the dogs were causing the dogs concern. This would cause the owner to begin his search in that area, which fortunately vacant because of the dogs barking. Either way, if an intruder or Patricians were in this area, they would brand this area as risky for any future scouting. Notwithstanding, this was an issue that was more and more occurring on the outer borders, as the small city was working hard to kill off the Patricians residing in their city.

Orange Grove selected the area between S Leona St and S Eugenia St citywide to clean this night. Lowe's Market and Orange Grove Area Museum were currently under PP control. The PP also designated Bella Mia Hair Studio and Boutique as the launching area. The City equally important placed guards on the route 359 exits to protect from any attempted escape. Freedom would launch from the United States Postal Service on S Eugenia St. The goal was to work towards Orange Grove Mobile Home & RV Parts. Once complete they would work south clearing any Patricians out of this area. Once cleared, they would return to the skeleton crew that remained at the Museum to establish a solid base line for when the city did their final clearing drive. Freedom gathered thirty-eight shooters (twelve of which were female). Twenty-two of the shooters would begin as archers. Freedom elected to begin their attack at 3:00 PM, needing the daylight for their archers and wanting to get their final strong line in place to push the Patricians north, concentrating them so Orange Grove would have a more concentrated target for easy kills, with Orange Grove approval. Their drive from the post office began with clearing the buildings with windows facing S Eugenia St. The Patricians retreated to the Orange Grove Mobile Home

& RV Parts area, permitting Freedom to pick off many of the snipers while exposed during their retreat. Freedom was also able to follow this retreat making it easier to concentrate on the new quickly selected fighting positions. Freedom had an ample supply of smoke bombs provided by Orange Grove. Children, advancing under cover provided by Freedom shooters, worked up to the windows where they tossed the smoke bombs into newly opened windows. The windows were shattered by shotgun fire.

Subsequently, Freedom launched a squad of archers to the opposite side of S Leona St, which proved highly successful massacre of Patricians that retreated from Orange Grove Mobile Home & RV Parts. The smoke prevented the Patricians from maintaining their foothold, and was eliminated during their frantic attempts. Freedom stressed shooting only from positions that provided excellent cover. They did not want to lose any citizens. Freedom declared a great bonus, as it became known that the Orange Grove Mobile Home & RV Parts was a food and a supply storage position for the Patricians, as they were preparing for a strong invasion center on Freedom within the next few weeks. The supplies were left in place, for mutual distribution by Orange Grove upon successful completion of the mission. Either way, the Patricians lost a prematurely stocked warehouse of military supplies. Freedom also recovered seven advance rifles converted to automatic fire, and a solid stockpile of ammunition. Freedom received authorization to use these rifles and ammunition for the completion of the campaign. This freed the archers to redeploy as hidden guards to concentrate of guerrilla warfare. The absence of sound enhanced the continuous flow of targets. Freedom secured the Museum, afterwards cleaning out the lone snipers who were scattered throughout the southern portion of their mission. An additional threat to the recovered rifles was the silencers that accompanied them. Their southern sweep was silent, except for their dogs that barked when a target was located. The cleaning was effective, as Freedom deployed several of their adolescents to guard this territory, much to the displeasure of their mothers. The adolescents used dogs to verify the cleansing of all territories between Freedom, W Pundt Ave and their newly secured positions in the mission area. They could now employ sniper fire any movement in the Orange Grove Municipal Court. Freedom elected to use archers with burning arrows when shooting into the Municipal Court. The building was not of any future benefit if obtained; nevertheless, shooting fire inside might ignite any weapons or ammunition storage.

Accordingly, in the southern sweep, Freedom secured the Orange Grove School District and Woodmen of the World Insurance building. Freedom eyed these buildings for some time; however, believed that if they took these potential Patricians sites, the Patricians would launch a strong counterattack. This fear was not practical during this current campaign. The Patricians pulled most of their lone guards back to the main line of the northern mission. The northern mission was strongly effective in their fighting, completely defeating the Patricians and providing a solid security buffer for the PP in Orange Grove. Lowe's Market provided a new secure PP headquarters. Unfortunately, as they did in all things, the Patricians had completely stripped the Lowe's Market, hoarding the coveted building supplies. Nevertheless, they stored many supplies needed for a long mobilization. This puzzled Orange Grove as they forwarded this intelligence to Austin, as an activity that did not fit the current situation. The northern campaign lost twenty-six people, whereas the Patricians lost two-hundred and thirty people. The factor that the PP suffered much fewer casualties was attributed to their positions have cover and or concealment, whereas the Patricians ignorantly attacked through unprotected open areas. Freedom lost one male who broke the mission plan and went pass a tree without first ensuring it was clear. Freedom executed seventy-eight Patricians, the vast majority through surprise ambushes and smoke bombs forcing them into open.

Orange Grove's PP was motivated, and enthusiasm was high. They realized the Patricians were preparing to reconsolidate and move back a few blocks, which would permit them to reemploy their sniper activities. PP elected to flush Orange Grove and push the Patricians out of the city. There was another issue they had to face, and this was the overwhelming majority of Hispanics were Patricians. The council decided the risks associated with allowing Hispanics in the city was too great; therefore, when they swept the Patricians whey would do a 100% sweep of the Hispanics. They announced this policy while attacking, allowing any Hispanic that had proof of PP status an opportunity to exit the city. No proof existed. It took twenty-one days to do the sweep, costing seventeen casualties and executing thirty-one Patricians. A contributing factor to the successful sweep was the number of PP pockets throughout the city. These provided excellent launch positions, as most of this fighting was guerrilla style. The PP employed one-half of its force in providing an effective barricade. Accordingly, when the Patricians when out to hunt at night, the PP picked them off with their archers. Consequently, with their hunters not returning, the communities, elected to hunt in large parties, which backfired significantly, allowing PP units to engulf them in the woods and push them against each other promoting complete execution. The control over the water supply added to the effectiveness of the extraction, although not as good as if it were deployed in the summer months.

The nights were getting colder, which caused some hardship on the hidden Patricians, which most figured were currently women and children. This was a time-consuming process now of walking the dogs through all the communities and then a total flush on any house the dogs alerted their masters. Considering, most homes kept their dogs chained outside, the first security tool was to release these dogs and feed them some human flesh. Once the dogs were fed, with the absence of their owners, they tended to become loyal to their new masters. PP secured these houses by breaking into a door, or carefully opening any windows that were not locked. A common practice was to use a ladder and check second-floor windows, which most people did not lock. Once inside, they released their dogs, keeping any Patricians dogs outside. The dogs were extremely effective in identifying the hiding places, which were for the most parts highly creative. A crucial part in this cleaning process was to execute immediately, with the preferred method of a knife in the skull. This is not as bloody, and reduced the threat of a response. Once stabbed in the head, it was always best to tie the hands. The bodies would be pulled out into the hallways, for removal, to get them outside and start the harvesting process for the dogs. Once the blockades were established and largest hunting groups executed, water turned off, it was a waiting and flushing game. The important thing was to prevent the community from congregating, which could lead to mutual casualties. Immediate execution, and prevent any dialog, considering the lines was drawn and the concept that no one would change was instilled. Death was the sole answer. Within just over three weeks, the city has completely controlled by the PP.

Accordingly, Orange Grove contacted the PP notifying them; they were accepting new residents. The goal was to add at least two-hundred fresh people.

The PP sent members from San Antonio and Corpus Christi, considering these cities was continuously receiving PP fleeing their pastoral areas because of Patricians attempting to establish footholds in their area. The PP was always seeking to solidify settlements between San Antonio and the Mexican border. Orange Grove was excited about gaining residents from Corpus Christi, considering it was a port and excellent opportunity for sea trade. Large cities were constantly in demand for meat. All animal flesh had to be packaged with the animal's head or feet. This was for the quick lab tests to verify the flesh came from that animal, and was not combined with human flesh, as some greedy traders would attempt. Knowing the strategic places to trade and the markets that would produce the greatest benefits was common knowledge for the city dweller, nevertheless, a mystery for the country residents. This new wave of blood would provide Orange Grove an advantage, as it also would Corpus Christi, being able to add trust in this trading arrangement. Trust additionally included confidence in each other. The city's market needed sources they could depend upon, when knowing that empty shelves did not produce income, rather it creates angry customers who do not blame the source, which is hidden in a place outside the city, and instead to the retail owner who promised this source. Naturally, during this period, no product source was dependable; however, compatible substitutes were. An example would be chickens in lieu of turkey. Orange Grove gained new blood, thus less dependent upon observing local rural residents, since each bucolic resident added, left a vacant area in the rustic for potential Patricians occupation. The additional city residents naturally provided supplemental forces to deploy when supporting PP needing assistance in their rustic operations.

Astonishingly, additional small cities were cleaning out the Patricians, an activity not pleasing to Houston, a Texas Patricians stronghold. The PP did not attempt to liberate Houston, but instead enjoyed raiding their supply routes for desperately needed necessities. The PP controlled Galveston, which proved beneficial in controlling sea trade with Houston. This process has produced diminishing returns as the Patricians were attempting to move supplies inland to Houston using land lanes. Accordingly, the PP struggled to challenge these routes. Orange Grove participated in the coordinated attack on Mathis with an eye on the 359 and 37 intersection. This intersection directly affected the Orange Grove supply sources. This victory also included serious fighting in Lake City acquiring a solid footing on Lake Corpus Christi, a wonderful source of inland seafood. Orange Grove successfully cleared their neighboring K-Bar Ranch. The PP was not prosperous in completely clearing Alice, a coveted city controlling the southern flow for 359, east-west flow of 44 and north-south flow of 281. They did; notwithstanding, establish successful blockades, chocking Alice, while at the same time able to transfer needed supplies into the PP communities currently much stronger than before within Alice. The PP elected to cease the Alice invasion, deciding instead to clean the areas between Mathis and Corpus Christi. They accurately believe this geographical emphasis would effectively choke Alice within one-year at the tops. The overwhelming need reestablished mobilization procedures and took advantage of any modern opportunities from the new territorial gains, and route controls needed population relocations. These relocations were essential to prevent the tendency to form emotional bonds that are too deep that if lost, could severely put in danger the desire to survive and ability to fight as part of the team with a purpose.

Mary, a young twenty-two-year-old extremely religious southern Texas woman, as so many other young adults missed the socialization skills needed to form intimate relationships. She grew up on a small farm between Mathis and Lake City, spending time with nature on one hand and a long razor-sharp knife in the other. Killing was a way of life, nevertheless; she considered herself fortunate in that most of her killing was harvesting meat that would work its way to Corpus Christi. She had one sister and one male cousin, while she lived with her parents, an aunt and her family, plus Grandmother. The remainder of her family and relatives simply did not return from hunting expeditions, causing the family not to ask any questions and erase them as best they could from their daily lives. This was the best way, as her Grandmother would consistently remind her. Her mother and Grandmother petitioned the PP to relocate her to the newly consolidated Orange Grove for future mating purposes. She was exceptionally beautiful, which was a primary reason her family kept her safe and secure, as best possible. The Patricians preached morality, notwithstanding, would brutally rape and torture the PP women. On the other hand, the PP immediately executed them using the most human process available at that time. Nudity would be used for shaming and Psychological Warfare videos, especially when executing children. The argument was to create a strong enough deterrent to prevent future executions, thereby reducing the overall suffering. It was not for immediate anti-social sexual gratification.

There were issues that Mary's adult superiors shielded her from as much as practical. Mary would spend much of her time under the surface of Lake Corpus Christi, becoming an expert at snagging mud turtles, snakes, and large catfish. She was extensively successful with underwater fishing that she was able to make a hefty financial contribution to her extended family's care. Considering that her fresh seafood was competing with wild grassy vegetation, traders found themselves extremely eager to trade. Just as in the Middle Ages, except for some forms of weeds, if it was green, people ate it, to include grass, leaves, and corn stalks. This was not only in Texas, but also across the dying United States. Mary swam fast under the water and for minutes at a time. Her family claimed she was half fish. Actually, she enjoyed the perceived security of being under water. Other defensive skills included tree climbing, running, and Archery. Similar to many rural girls growing up in America during these times, she did not wear dresses. The overall fear was that if seen by a Patricians, she would be of a higher risk of being raped.

Moreover, many females cut their hair the same as boys. Having hair was too much of a hassle, especially to maintain for no survival benefits. It was much easier to spot potential dangers with short hair and removed the risk of having the wind blow the hair in their eyes. Bras faded into history, except in situations with a large group of males. Females simply wore heavier and dark-colored shirts.

PP reluctantly approved transferring Mary to Orange Grove. They felt her underwater skills in Lake Corpus Christi were not replaceable. Mary's parents assured the PP that her brother usually accompanied her on their submersed scavenging trips. Mary would be placed in an all girl's residence. The eight girls were aged eighteen through twenty-six. The practice was to give her an introduction, show her, which bed she would sleep, and collect the material, so she could make her uniform and cold-weather jacket. Everyone at Orange Grove wore a uniform. An elderly woman took Mary's measurements and gave her a sewer and instructions while Mary created her uniform. Once completed, the aged house governor took her to the other girls, so she could train with the girls. These girls were being assigned as night resource collectors. They would carefully roam the woods, looking for gold or anything of survival value. Mary also began her Archery training, which she was already highly accurate from years of roaming her woods. She felt this would be a wonderful job, even though she may have acquired it during an unfortunate period. The Patricians were scouting this area heavily, while readjusting their homes in this area. Many knew these vast woods well and therefore, wanted to keep harvesting the local game. Mary shoot two men her first night. She consistently aimed to center on the head always making complete kills. Orange Grove currently collected these skulls of the executed invaders, leaving any arrows in them if that was the source of execution. The skulls were anchored on ten-foot poles and anchored in the ground, as deterrents or scarecrows against any other hunters. Mary discovered the remaining girls in this group were recruited in the same fashion. It was actually their availability, which motivated the PP to create this group.

Notwithstanding, a new danger began to appear nationwide for those who worked in the forests, and this was the starting of large wildfires. The lone method to prevent this as to permit pockets of Patricians to live within the PP's areas. This was not acceptable for the PP's, who began to train a new group of fighters, called the PP's Fire Starters. This was a force of volunteers of approximately 200 people spread throughout the dying states. They were not a full time force, with selected members being activated for a mission and then released. The initial ones were in Seattle, San Francisco, San Diego, and Los Angeles. These would be burned one by one, and only after evacuating the PP from these locations. The PP expedited this process, since they desperately needed some additional ports on the West Coast. Likewise, they needed to hamper the mass importing by the Patricians in these large cities. The PP was also hampered by the Mexicans who were working closely with the Patricians in the distribution of these imported products, especially providing support on the open highways that ran in California, Arizona, and New Mexico. A serious challenge facing the PP was the Patricians supplying operations in Texas. Accordingly, the PP planned some small burnouts along the New Mexico border, especially desiring the ensure Patricians had to devote additional resources along the Texas border and not devote greater reserves against the Colorado-New Mexico border where PP planned to push hard. Mary chose to start her PP's Fire Starters earlier, considering she was still in the early training stages at Orange Grove and therefore, would not hamper operations with her early excusal. Orange Grove was excited that Mary would receive this training, considering they wanted to implement a fire-burning attack force for smaller-scale operations, especially with Alice in mind.

Consequently, Mary heard many stories concerning the Hispanics while training in Salt Lake City. She gave it not much concern, notwithstanding enjoyed the tales her classmates revealed. A few weeks later, as they roamed from desert bush to bush, at night while sleeping noticed many small campfires spread throughout the land below her. She traveled across the hillsides when possible and constantly slept on hills or high in trees. She adopted this technique as a result; she could study the ground action among the animals she was hunting. Accordingly, after returning to Orange Grove her small talk hit the ears of some elders who called her in for a hearing and casually questioned her extensively updated a map during their meeting. When they finished an elder asked Mary if she understood what was happening. She had no clue, and conveyed this message to them. They informed her they expected this revealed an indication that Mexico may be planning to attack the dying states. The council added some information they had from local operations and sent the information to Austin. After a short review and intensive questioning of some captured Hispanics in the area and sent these reports to ten southwestern States, which conducted their own interrogations and included this in their reports. Soon, the consolidated reports were sent to all States west of the Mississippi. The consensus was clear. The time came to present this information to the Patricians. A massive meeting was held in Salk Lake City, where a ceasefire was agreed, as the States committed to the armed forces. The units would not be mixed, and would remain with their party affiliation. This was to ensure a complete and the unhampered team spirit and to prevent the possibility of new party commitments.

The training and mobilization would be in Broken Bow, Nebraska. This location was selected as it was far from route 80, and had established low Hispanic population, and the total Hispanic ban in this area should not alarm many, considering it was a PP stronghold. Patricians areas would require relocation Hispanics, which would set off some alarms. There were also numerous Reservations (Pine Ridge, Rosebud, and Yankton) to provide an additional safety buffer above them, and the Cheyenne River Reservation north of them to solidity that buffer zone, as it was not yet known if the Canadians provided intelligence to the Mexicans. The training would merely be five weeks, as warnings were being posted the Mexicans were preparing to launch their missions, wanting to begin fighting in early spring, especially prior to the hot summer months that could cause problems in the southwestern desert areas. The Native American Reservations agreed to provide hunters and scouts for the three Army's when they moved towards the southern border. Each Army had ten thousand men, not counting the Indian support. The First Army would push down from the California-Arizona border. All Armies would approach from Texas, which, along with Arizona and New Mexico, were relocating their Hispanic population to Nevada, claiming the Patricians wanted to provide an additional buffer zone in California, a state they claimed was too valuable for the Patricians's future. Special Indian scouting units were placed along the southern parts of the southern border States monitoring Hispanic activity. Their activities had to be closely monitored, as concealment was mandatory.

The First Army would attack on the Arizona-California & Mexico border. Arizona has been engaged in an extremely bloody area war, considering Arizona was purely PP, and crazy California was home to the dingiest Patricians. Mexico did not expect any attacks from that area, believing California would push from behind. Even if not by official deployment, they understood a call to activation of the Hispanics living in the States. This is why the PP considered the Hispanic living in the States as a cancer that had to be removed. This angered the Hispanics, who fought back against the PP. Consequently, the PP snipers would execute the Hispanics on sight. Either way, they would never expect a force this large, or even half this size. The coolness of the southern border this time of year-hosted temperatures still low enough to keep the birds further south. Birds were dangerous for military operations, in that they respond to ground movements, giving away positions to enemy forces. Half of this First Army would clear the California border and then drive south seventy-five miles in Baja California, afterwards working east clearing the land and hampering any resupply attempts of Mexico. Every grocery store was completely stripped, and cattle added to the Army's herd. Horses were immediately taken for riding, and dogs were released. Chickens were cleaned and eaten at once. Pigs and hogs were released. Homes were searched for any needed supplies. Mexico still had a functioning society where goods were distributed equally throughout their nation. This provided a source for badly needed supplies to keep the Armies moving.

The current wars did not resemble previous wars in any manner. There were few doctors, if any. Moreover, field medical supplies were depleted early in the battles. Their production for resupply was believed to be non-essential. Several men carried small razor blades with them, so if they were seriously injured, they could cut their risk and die quickly. These were pretty much standard for both the Patricians and PP. Moreover; without adequate concentration camps, prisoners of war were out of the equation. Therefore, any prisoners captured after the battle were instantly beheaded. The Patricians actually tried to maintain social prisons when the war began. Naturally, the prison had to be in a Patricians controlled area. As supplies became extremely limited, the Patricians released these prisoners into their public. This did not work out well, as many returned to their criminal activities, especially the sexual deviants. Accordingly, when these deviants were captured in PP territory, their future chance of survival ranged around zero. The PP would publicly burn any rapists or child molester. The argument was they could satisfy these urges in the other party's lands, and afterwards return until the urge returned, and subsequently repeated the exodus. The PP handled the prison situation extremely differently. If a prisoner was on death row, they were immediately executed. Drug offenders were executed as well. Even though many believed they could be rehabilitated if the appropriate facilities were on hand, no such facilities were available, therefore, they removed the problem by removed those prosecuted for the problem. Theft related non-violent crimes were pardoned. The PP needed experienced thieves to appropriate resources from the Patricians territory. The prisons were given back to the government for emergency housing operations. These same rules were applied to any Patricians refugees, if discovered. These situations were extremely rare, because after the first six months of this war, virtually no one relocated across the borders. There was; however, one category that was excused from the immediate execution rules and this was infants. Infants when captured, on both sides, were taken back with the invading group and blended into their community, their secret never revealed. This was needed because of the extremely low birthrate among the general population.

Unfortunately, the infant rule was not in play by the American invading forces in Mexico, nor was these infants executed. They were simply ignored, which sadly may have led to their premature deaths. The First Army would clean and clear the California and Arizona borders and engage in any Mexican forces staged for entry into the United States. This Army cleaned the border with ease and then ran into a 50,000 Mexican deployment force. Even though the enemy greatly outnumbered them, the First Army launched the guerrilla warfare with both the Riflemen and the Archers. Their comprehensive goal was to be like sand in the trees, and be spread everywhere. Using silencers and arrows, they kept their positions confidential. The Americans also shot fire arrows into the enemy's fuel vehicles, causing massive explosions and reducing the force penetration range. The roads were planted with nail pads causing flat tires. The goal on the flat tires was to get the people outside of the vehicles, so they could pick them off with sniper fire. Consequently, by engulfing the enemy and preventing those soldiers from moving provided a rich source of stable targets. Ammunition trucks were hit hard, salvaging and stealing as much as they could, along with weapons. This was essential for the successful repealing of the Mexican invasion. It was incorporated in all three Armies being deployed, plus the Fourth Army that was currently garrisoned in the Cibola National Forest just above Albuquerque close to the intersection of 40 and 25. This would permit them to deploy in all four directions if needed.

The massive Mexican force was stopped on 2 heading North between El Sahuaro and Quitovac, less than twenty miles from the United States border. Both parts of the First Army joined this fight, while the Americans kept this force trapped in a long open convoy. In order to make time, rushing back from the Mexican side of the Arizona border, the second part of the First Army returned to the United States and rushed non-stop to the North of 2 and then pushed southward. The first part of the First Army detected this convoy through their northern advanced scouts. They extensively scouted their seventy-five-mile mission south of the border, ensuring that any form of danger to the dying states was neutralized. When the scouts alerted the main force, additional scouts were deployed in the second part of this Army, and then the force was immediately deployed. Their goal was to stop them in Mexico, although that part of the American side of the border had nothing of value to the Mexicans. Catching them in Mexico simply provided an opportunity to inflict side damage on Mexican soil. Moreover, Mexicans were members of a society that still had a commerce economy, whereas the dying states had a few trucks fighting their way through multiple ambushes to trade damaged supplies. Within the first day of fighting, the Mexican Army lost over twenty-five-thousand people, whereas the First Army lost three thousand two hundred people. Notwithstanding the First Army broke through the convoy securing forty-seven positions, and stripping the equipment, while doubling the original firepower of the First Army.

The first night in this fighting saw massive panic and loss of command control in the remainder of the Mexican Army. There were merely two breakout attempts throughout the entire crippled convoy. These were repelled by the Americans, using the grenades, bombs, and Artillery stolen from the Mexicans. The American command was close to determining where the breakouts would be launched. Actually, they believed the Mexicans would attempt to break out in four positions, which were located within one-half of a mile in the convoy. The reason the other two did not deploy was mass desertion among the Mexicans. The Americans cut the electricity along the convoy, preventing any buildings from having light in the night. Then they used two hundred generators to power ambush locations. The Mexicans followed these lights believing they were moving to safe havens, merely to march into dead-end locations of no escape. The acceleration of their exit placed them in large congregations, that when trapped provided the Americans easy targets for fast massive kills. Actually, the initial total destruction took mere minutes; the verification of each kill took almost two hours. The mission objective claimed that any Mexican who survived this fight would someday revenge this day. Considering the States was in a Civil War, this war had to end on this crusade. The Americans did not dispose of the bodies, hoping their decay would endanger the health of the Mexican residents; likewise, show them what happens when they attempt to invade the dying states. The First Army completely utilized all the Mexican equipment and brought all the large trucks for additional scavenging operations along the Mexican side of the border.

The First Army continued the scavenging operations, while also running convoys back across the American border delivering domestic supplies for distribution to people of both parties. All military equipment after this war were stored for future wars against foreign invasion. All cattle and horses discovered were transferred across the border and released to the open southern ranges. To survive, these animals would follow the water and grazing, which became richer as they moved north. The Second and Third Armies were tied down in extensive fighting along the Texan border. The Rio Grande provided a buffer zone, forcing the Mexican forces to concentrate, making them easier targets for the American snipers. The comprehensive military and mission resupply provided by the war bounty of the First Army enabled the Americans to launch extensive artillery into the trapped Mexican forces. These forces were much smaller than the giant main force First Army destroyed. Nevertheless, they could still cause trouble in permitted to deploy within the States. Apparently, the Mexicans considered the West Coast and California as the rich bounty for this invasion and merely desired to tie up American forces in Arizona, New Mexico, and Texas, securing their hold on the West Coast. The First Army came in behind these Mexican forces attempting to engulf them and reduce their punch on the Second and Third Armies. The game once more was Psychological Warfare, in creating the feeling of helplessness and teasing with possible escape-points. The Americans were taking full advantage of the Mexican gas stations, running fuel and food back to the States. They also deployed one brigade from the Fourth Army for this massive scavenging mission. The first three Armies wanted as much military force as they could muster to squeeze out the six five-thousand man Mexican units, with the goal of leaving no survivors.

Accordingly, First Army was watching their southern positions to monitor any additional Mexican forces, which might deploy. Mexico truly believed the forces they had deployed would ravish the western part of the segmented States. No one in one thousand years believed the divided States would unite to drive out foreign invaders. It was later discovered that Canada was preparing to invade the Eastern States; nevertheless, upon hearing the absolute defeat of the Mexican Invasion, the Canadian forces immediately disbanded. To reduce the number of American deaths and to demote the possibility of a large stockpile of destructive ammunitions landing in the hands of the opposing party, the three Armies blasted the paralyzed Mexican forces with the stockpiled Artillery. The main kill force remained the guerrilla soldiers, hiding behind the trees and hilltops picking off any Mexican soldiers attempting to desert. This was not completely a time issue; nevertheless, the Armies realized that if they stayed, Mexico would need to remove this cancer. They believed that a Sherman raid sort of mission, moving East and West, staying within a certain range from the border would entice the Mexican government to lay back and wait until this force retreated. An important factor would be the continue extracting of the expendable resources from within one hundred miles from the border, avoiding leaving any large force or unit without an immediate path back across the border. All cities and houses within ten miles of the border were to be burned and destroyed. All women and children were permitted to exodus, as long as they settled beyond the no settlement zone of thirty-five miles. All men remaining would be executed. In total foolishness, several men stayed and burned with the neighboring buildings.

Accordingly, the States issued the thirty-mile security zone bellow the border and an additional thirty-mile permission zone for scavenging non-military resources such as fuel and food. Mexico complained they wanted the same deal above the border. The Army Commanders suggested this deal would best be settled with a full-scale invasion of Mexico City. The Army's began to move south, executing every Hispanic person, male or female, claiming that since Mexico had not accepted their peace deal, they did not have to comply.

Within two days, an official Mexican delegation reported to the Army Commanders accepting their original deal. The Commanders altered the deal to include the additional three miles they conquered during this new campaign. The delegation accepted the deal. The deal will also include a promise not to attach the States in the future. The Armies agreed to divide into parties and then into States once they were within ten miles of the US Border and a ten-day ceasefire once the Armies have all turned in their weapons. The soldiers were permitted to keep any non-military bounty they had 'collected.' Not only was the world shocked at the way the States west of the Mississippi united to push back Mexico, but also the Eastern States. A short-lived hope the fighting would end filled the future upcoming Christmas air of peace and goodwill on Earth. Unfortunately, the Eastern States could not agree to a ceasefire, and the bullets and knives began killing once more. The Western States were soon killing again as the War Between the States returned.

Mary's life changed or temporarily postponed because of the war. During the initial mobilization, most of the men in Orange Grove either went to join one of the Armies or a special reserve force in the border States. Mary sent a request to her mother and

Grandmother for a temporary vacation with her small family. She feared that with her brother joining the military, her family would suffer. Her family agreed with her reasoning and agreed she could return home for a vacation. Mary rushed back to her hometown, although the weather had chilled, to a degree, her mother felt it not wise to swim in the cold lake water. However, she could enjoy other extended activities around the lake considering the statewide ceasefire in their war with the Patricians. Mary quickly discovered she could once more engage in an activity she truly believed she would never again enjoy once more, and this is fishing on a boat in the open water and daylight traveling across her favored lake without inhibition. She rowed her neighbor's boat from early morning to late night for her first two weeks upon returning home. She fished, catching many fish and smelled so much like a fish her mother feared the local cats would attack her. She joked about the simple solution was for her to grab the cat and dive into the lake's water. This, she laughed would divide them without hesitation. Her real solution was providing the cats with the byproducts when she cleaned her fish. This kept them on the lake's shores when she was on her boat fishing. Mary treated her homeland much different during this visit than when she previously grew up with her mother. She recognized this time was temporary, but also, that she was officially a part of another community. Ironically, her mother and Grandmother sent her to Orange Grove to find a male mate; notwithstanding, she lives at an all woman's home in which none of the girls wanted or were even contemplating a relationship with a male. Women did not want to have a legal relationship in an environment where becoming a widow was more probable than dying as a married woman, a situation that was not vastly uncommon throughout the complete American history experience.

During this age, there was little different in the work performed in rural areas between males and females. Mary soon curled back her fishing, as she believed her family had an ample amount of omega three proteins, since she worried about her Grandmother's heart. After this, she found some stones and sharpened her mother's scythe. Subsequently, she proceeded to clear the tall grass that was beginning to overtake the area around their house. She then raked the cut grass, saving most for their grazing animals and selecting a portion for a large vegetable soup, she was preparing for their evening meal. Yes, grass is classified as a vegetable, and actually eaten year round, dried in the winter. The dried hay was soaked in water, which regained a portion of the original texture. As a bonus, she slashed a large snake while cutting the grass. She cleaned the snake for the evening meal, and added the snake's skin to her mother's stockpile that was used for making shoes and other special projects. Mary was totally at ease with killing snakes. Usually, she would grab them from the back of their head and snap their neck. Her hands were not free this time, so she employed the benefits of her scythe, a quick response because the snake was on alert from the grass that she cut surrounding them. As the sweat rolled from Mary's body, and she felt her tired muscles beg for rest, she remembers how much she missed this wonderful experience. She felt it gave her a reasonable goal that could only be achieved through a lot of personal devotion. Mary believed this agonizing work gave her a break from the horrors of the current Civil War.

Consequently, even though Mary was exhausted, she decided that she needed a long-overdue pleasure with her mother and Grandmother this evening. Mary grabbed her ax and walked to a part of the forest where she had cut down some trees. She preferred to cut the trees down and chop them after they had some time to dry. Even though she had not given these trees her preferred time, she was merely cutting into logs from one part of cut-down trees.

Afterwards, she carried the logs into their small house and stored them beside their fireplace. Her plan was to enjoy a quiet evening after their snake and soup dinner. She ignited the lone fireplace in their main family room. It was not too cold, so she adjusted the fire to medium. Her primary goal was to hear a snap and crackle, as the yellow would dance through the flames. The quietness offered by this calm rural farm emitted a rare sense of peace. Mary's Grandmother recommended they enjoy this while they could, as the blood would flow again, although thanks to Orange Grove, not as soon as she originally anticipated. Mary decided this was an excellent time to ask her mother about boys and why they truly wanted her to live away from their peaceful home. Her Grandmother interrupted the questioning and told Mary that she was still at the beginning on the road in her life, while they were much further on that road. No matter how terrifying and horrifying this war would turn out to be, love would find a way to burn in the human hearts. It was a love that conquered all obstacles that have hindered humanity's pathway through the darkness and into the light, through the rain and into the sun, and through the valleys and over the mountains.

Accordingly, Mary confessed this truly confused her, and asked why none of her friends was searching for this thing called love. Mary's mother warned her of the dangers of following the blind, because when you do this, who made yourself blind. You may walk with the blind, as long as you keep your eyes opened. At this time, her Grandmother pulled out a jar from the bottom shelf of their bookcase and divided three cups among these three women. She poured some Dandelion wine into each of the glasses and recommended that each take a drink to open their minds to the issues being discussed this night. Mary once more asked for clarification why her family wanted her to live in Orange Grove. Mary's mother explained that Mary's life was as the garden they had down by the stream. She added that if they used only the seeds from this area and never added fresh seeds, they would never enjoy any changes in their per year yield. Notwithstanding, if they went away and collected some new seeds from other areas, then their yearly harvest would bring forth some new foods. Others, living elsewhere might trade their seeds with our seeds so that both could enjoy new things and a richer harvest. They were hoping that Mary would bring those new seeds back to their humble home and thereby give their farm some new hope for a wealthier tomorrow. Mary's Grandmother stressed that if we become too stiff to change, we will become brittle and break. Her Grandmother brought up an additional argument explaining this farm was not her or her mother's farm and homeland. Her father's family owned this farm and her father who invited them to live here. It is the way of women to follow the one that she has given her heart, because a body will die without its heart.

Accordingly, Mary's Grandmother cautioned Mary that you cannot accept unconditional love or, even worse, demand love from where love might be is the same demanding water from an empty well. They further told their youngest member. they simply wanted her not overwhelmingly reject or exert her energy towards fighting it. "If you fight love, you will die full of hate," warned her Grandmother. They reassured Mary that she was not in a situation to find Love or face their music. They wanted her to know that Love exists and that it can be both good and bad. Nevertheless, with patience and endurance the good can outlast the bad. Good can come from bad, notwithstanding the bad cannot come from good.

This is the test if the source is decent or terrible. Mary, who was now expressing interest in this subject, asked why anyone would ever want Love when it could turn to bad. Her Grandmother answered because the best things in life come from love. Mary asked what good thing has ever come from love. Her mother pointed at her and said, "You," while her Grandmother was pointing at her mother. Mary, who for the first time in so long thought about the possibility that someday she could have children, understood she needed some time to think about this. Her Grandmother reported that Mary could merely think about this now, as the war was not yet finished and that children usually are not given in marriage during wars. This could get much worse before it got better. Mary, now appearing disappointed, asked them why they would even get her to start thinking about something this serious. Her mother reminded her that wars do end and that one of the greatest things about life is that hope makes the impossible possible.

Mary asked them that since they are talking about the impossible, how she would know she was in love. Her Grandmother confessed this was a true question of the ages. The mystery of love has even the wisest believing they are fools. Love must have faith and dedication. These are such as is sun and water to the seeds in the gardens. At this time, Mary confessed, as she was pouring another glass of Dandelion wine that even the thinking about this made her want to drink. Her mother, also pouring some wine, acknowledged she was not the lone one experiencing these feelings. Mary asked how she would know she had found love. Her Grandmother explained that if the reasons for outnumbered the reasons against each day, then she had found love. Mary argued this was too much agony and hard work. She now believed life without love was much easier. Subsequently, her mother explained that the definition of War is life without love. Love can conquer all, and if this nation accepted love once more, the war could end, and families could raise children, rather than burying their friends and relatives. Her Grandmother began to cry, claiming to fear that young Mary might live a life without love. Her mother further explained there were many sorts of love, such as the feelings she had for her wonderful daughter. Mary then asked why sometimes she had ill feelings towards her mother, especially when they sent her to Orange Grove. Her mother explained this was normal; the key was to love more than not to love. Additionally, her Grandmother added to Mary's confusion by adding the reason they sent her to Orange Grove was based in love.

Consequently, initially Mary was both confused and angered by her Grandmother's statement. Her mother jumped in order to clarify this by adding they painfully gave up their lives with her, so she could enjoy her life with those she loved. Mary quickly responded she wanted to be with them because they are the ones she loves. Understanding this was creating so much more confusion, and if they continue to debate this, they could lose and Mary remains, they each gave her a kiss on her cheeks and said Goodnight. Mary kissed their checks as well and wished them a good night. Contrarily, Mary decided to stay with the peaceful fire and dance inside the yellow flames in her mind. She wondered about the issues her elders shared with her. Subsequently, her deeper reflection began to question if this was related to the emptiness inside her. The barrenness inside her vanished when she was around her elders. Notwithstanding, this emptiness grew fierce when she was in Orange Grove, ferocious enough to bring tears to her eyes. She often would release a fake sneeze, and quickly wipe her eyes as she pretended to wipe her nose into her handkerchief. This mysterious consideration began to reveal some peculiar sneezes from the other girls she knew as roommates. They gave up their previous lives to begin anew such as she did. Unfortunately, she could now understand she had closed herself from them. Consequently, strangely Mary was beginning to miss her roommates. Notwithstanding, she understood her time to return would be soon in that Orange Grove merely gave her one mouth claiming they needed her currently far than before. Mary would deal about these issues when the time came, for now she would enjoy what could before the war was to return.

Accordingly, her remaining time with her family ended and Mary jumped on her horse and began her ride back to Orange Grove. She was the last woman from her residence to return. She was extremely shocked when all these girls cheered her return. They all appeared so happy. Afterwards, one of them told her our soldiers were clearing the border now and that the war with Mexico would soon end. Mary decided she would approach Betty and begin a conversation. Betty was quiet such as Mary. She began the conversation as they talked for one complete day. Neither knew how to end nor wanted to end their conversation. That night something new began to grow inside Mary, and this was her fresh friendship with Betty. The following day, Betty and Mary requested they be permitted to work on the same projects, a request quickly granted. Orange Grove consistently promoted friends working together, believing it makes their days quicker, and gave them confidence. They also believed friends would watch each other's backs during combat missions, or even when it became necessary. Mary and Betty worked well together, helping clean the firearms for when the men returned. Within a few weeks, the men returned, with Orange Grove merely losing twelve men. Mary felt extremely sad as they watched the families who lost loved ones. It would take time to process, but they could not take long, because the ceasefire was quickly ended and the killing for all would return. Betty complained she could not understand how men could live and fight together and afterwards kill as if nothing had changed. The actual meaning of life was in serious question, along with the question of why continue living, if life is nothing more than killing, both humans and animals.

The elders wanted the young people to attend all these funerals, hoping to get their base fired up and create a deeper hatred against the Mexicans. They were close enough to the border, and strategically placed between major cities, whereas their position could provide an important position to hold and launch Mexican operations. Considering that Houston was the only great city in Texas with some Patricians stronghold, it would be practical to hit this area, considering the PP might not rush to their defense. The city finished their ceremonies for their lost citizens quickly, as there were no bodies involved. The bodies were destroyed in Mexico. The new superstition held that burning the bodies on the battlefield released their spirits over the killing grounds and thereby watched over their living friends. Many things, especially weapon malfunctions were attributed to these spirits. The Mexicans also adopted this superstition, as a result every evening; one hour was dedicated to burning. The belief equally important held that any who fought during this time their families would suffer a great misery. All weapons were put down during the hour. Additionally, the superstition held that Commanders could not give orders to fight during this hour, nor did any try. They believed the hour rest was productive in the long run and the importance of battlefield hygiene and psychology to remove these decaying corpses from the battlefield. The Americans did not know for sure yet if they were going to occupy the newly conquered territory, nevertheless, they did know at the minimum some sort of patrols would roam this territory and that civilians would be scavenging here, and the last thing they wanted was to have the landslide plastered with corpses. The Americans wanted the dead Mexican bodies disposed since they believed they would be occupying that land in their continue squeezing operations. On the other hand, the Mexicans assumed they would eventually break free from the barricade, and did not want to trip over decaying corpses in the process.

It did not take long for the American Civil War in the West to resume. Orange Grove wanted to make a hard push against Alice; considering their intelligence believed they suffered great losses in the recent Mexican War. Corpus Christi, Ben Bolt, and San Diego (Texas), were providing control of S281 and 44. Orange Grove pushed through Alfred, which was simple because the PP in Alfred had forced the Patricians into pockets, which Orange Grove cleaned out easily. The battle for Alice raged quickly as Orange Grove gained the vital positions vacated by the forces deployed south against the incursive Corpus Christi militaries. Orange Grove began by gaining control of T Texas Blvd and the Walmart Supercenter, while the second part of their invading force gained control of the Alice Air Port. These positions proved fruitful, as the closed Walmart Supercenter was a strategic deployment position for Alice, where they also stored their foods, fuel, and fighting supplies. The control of the Air Port was to prevent the Patricians from deploying additional reinforcements by air from Houston. The PP wanted this position, especially prior to and invasion of Houston, hoping to keep their air power pinned down. While the fight was blazing on N Texas Blvd and Alice Airport, the female Archery guerrilla forces bleed into the residential areas and picking off the citizens as they prepared to support the front line activities. In fairness to the Alice's sacrifice in the Mexican War, they gave the women and children a chance to leave the area and proceed to Patricians positions in spread out in the neighboring Patricians rural holdings.

Unfortunately, only one hundred women and children elected to take advantage of this escape opportunity. Those who remained back found their bodies burned with all who remained to fight. Upon taking total control of Alice, Orange Grover pushed south and west to meet up with the Corpus Christi forces. When they met, Orange Grove provided support for Corpus Christi as they returned to their homes. With the reduced threat from the Patricians, Orange Grove could spread their population and occupy many of the empty houses in Alice. This proved beneficial for Mary and Betty, allowing them to select a nice large home in the center of this much larger city. The elders Wanted Betty in the middle of Alice because of her outstanding Archery skills and with Betty, they made a deadly guerrilla one-two punch, exactly what they wanted in the middle of this city. The elders assigned some Orange Grove boys in the same neighborhood. Betty and Mary greeted these former neighbors as they worked out a foundation for their new home. Mary explained she felt it strange that these two men, whom they never previously spoke with, were now a part of their new family. Betty explained to Mary, these two boys were among the stronger ones from Orange Grove. Mary added they were not as ugly as most of the boys were as well. Mary, Betty, and these two boys were assigned one boy and one girl to city recon patrols. They were given horses or were able to get the horses from a nearby farm for their duties. They only used the horses on certain parts of the established routes and walked the remainder of their routes, changing their routes mixing it up randomly. Betty explained the Patricians scouts would study the area for days looking for patterns and any opportunities. Mary asked how she knew this, and Betty explained, because they had watched the PP and always copied the PP. Betty remarked how sad it was the Patricians were so stupid they could not think on their feet. Mary said that was good, because at least this allowed Orange Grove to burn their bodies instead of them burning Orange Grove's people.

Notwithstanding all obstacles between boys and girls, these boys put up with and got along fine with Mary and Betty. There was something wrong in the manner they treated these girls. Mary's mother and Grandmother came to visit, which her mother expressed disappointment that the boys treated them as their sisters. It was time to take these girls how to snag a man. Mary's elders decided to do the same for both girls, as leaving Betty lonely would not be fair. They began with hair grooming and fundamental hygiene and then showed them how to outline their faces with basic makeup they were saving for her. Finally, they altered their shirts and pants to ensure there were no mistakes, they were female. The results worked quickly, as Mary's elders taught the girls about charm and signs to watch in the boy's behavior, and most of all get a solid commitment while they burned prior to allowing them to enter the candy store. The elder relatives used the bait of children to entice these young women to seek the public commitment, as marriage was suspended until the war's end. Notwithstanding, infants were treated better than kings until they reached age ten, when they would learn the art of war. Mary's mother and Grandmother had to work quickly, as they did not want to leave Mary's brother alone too long. They told Mary and Betty that their son loved to indulge on candy at as many candy stores he could find. Mary did not understand; nevertheless, she did not want to appear ignorant; therefore, she pretended to recognize these words. Even if it was bad, she did not want to know.

Mary's neighbor boys divided the two girls among themselves and began their moves. One would pull Betty from the house, while the other would work his way into Mary's heart. Their strategy was to keep them independently; not knowing Mary's mother told the girls, they must keep the boys apart as well. Soon, the four reassigned their duties into two teams, one team per couple. Mary's elders returned to their new farm, in which they moved closer to the Lake Corpus Christi, feeling much more secure now that the Patricians were removed. Mary's male friend was called Mike, and they became extremely efficient in their scouting techniques, bringing in hands each day. After each kill, the scouts would cut off a hand and turn it in for a kill credit. These handprints would have the fingerprints pulled and sent into the national database, which was available to both the PP and the Patricians, so the names could be listed as killed by the war. The residents of Alice felt much more secure with Mary and Betty's teams roaming the woods surrounding their community. Betty's team was swiftly matching Mary's team skills. Betty and Mary still eagerly shared their knowledge and love, quickly scolding their male friends for any ill feeling towards their sister team. To the elders living around them, they represented a new generation, and even though their duties put them in harm's way, their youth and energy brought them home each night.

Eastern Texas had one large Patricians concern in its territory, and this was Houston. Even though the PP was steadily expanding their pockets and support lines into Houston, they knew Houston would need to be cleaned. The tighter their blockades hit the city, the fiercer the raids against their inside the city pockets became. The initial cleansing process would be officially to disrupt the supply lines, which would also dismantle their intelligence loops. The faster they could take Houston, without alerting the large Patricians Armies in other States, the quicker they could build a strong enough defense network that could force any reinforcement forces into the open for easy executions. The second cleansing process would be to swoop through the city, building by building removing the Patricians. This would initially involve massively reinforcing their already established pockets in the city, allowing them to push towards each other, establishing fewer extremely sizeable pockets. The second part of this process would be using large exterior forces to clean the areas between these pockets, while using the forces inside the pockets to prevent the intra-city Patricians forces a chance to reinforce the defending forces against this large from the outside invasions. Striping their communication network was vital, especially since a small cell phone could alert forces across the States. Therefore, the PP shut down all cell phone towers supporting Houston. Cell phone towers within the States were constantly requiring maintenance, which usually came quickly, as both parties needed their cell phone, thereby allowing both parties to piggyback off these towers. This time was different, since the PP was willingly taking this power away from them as well. The military would use their own field communications networks, which had strong internal safeguards against leaking. The PP also did not want any massive burnings, which could send large smoke signals visible to the nearby Gulf of Mexico.

The forces from Dallas would guard against Oklahoma, Arkansas, and Mississippi, which was a total guerrilla defensive posture, preventing the appearance of a borderline mobilization, which could send a signal of invasion. Austin would attack from the North, Austin from the West. These would be the two massive forces against Houston; with Corpus Christi forces (which included Alice and Orange Grove) preventing escape into the South, especially in Mexico. Mexico no longer trusted the Patricians since their betrayal working with the PP in the Mexican war. The PP additionally deployed naval forces to prevent refugees from escaping into the sea. Laredo provided additional forces to enhance this barricade. The invasion began, while the supply lines kept the front line forces with plenty of killing power, and Houston fell quickly. Their fall came as they fell victim to the feeling of hopelessness, not believing they could break out, and if they did; where would they go, as the open lands to the border were nothing more than opportunities for the PP to execute at will. Hunger took quick hold, as the weakening Patricians lost their strength to fight, and attempted to negotiate their way out of their death trap. The PP avoided talking with the Patricians, because they never kept their promises and instead of using these as delay attempts. This time the PP used these delays to get more forces into these pockets for a harder and deadlier squeeze. Houston, without question, had a problem, as they fell and tumbled hard. The PP completely cleaned them out of Houston, executing anything that wore a yellow hat and their supporting families. The PP's fast and hard push preserved needed domestic supplies, which were no longer needed by the executed Houstonians.

The young newly resettled Alice couples were sent to four separate deployment units, based upon their most destructive combat skills. They were given two weeks before reporting. Fear of Mike not returned overtook Mary, causing her nights to be filled with terrifying nightmares. Each night she witnessed Mike facing extensive torture and execution, after which she would be awake. She would also experience Betty's death as well. Mary became so convinced that Mike would not return that she could not permit him to leave her side. The misery of a strong possibility of a future without Mike and Betty crippled her ability to cope. She felt as if every time she stood on her feet, robust winds would attempt to blow her onto the floor. The part of this experience that Mike could not answer was that her hair would appear to be blowing in the wind, yet no wind was blowing around her. Each person had to be studied in detail to determine if he or she was friend or foe. Under these circumstances, Mary feared she would never again have a male friend and not experience the Carnal knowledge their Church elders taught her. Accordingly, she enticed Mike to perform the love making act they were taught. She wanted to have something to bind them forever, that there would be a method to escape their eternal love and bond. Mike did care deeply for Mary; nevertheless could not see a serious relationship the way the nation was currently. Notwithstanding, this was a chance to be laid, and he could think of no woman with more beauty and taken as a whole, he never wanted to live life without her.

He, therefore, pretending as if it were a great sacrifice, humbly complied with Mary's demand that she seduce him. That was the night that innocent Mary became a mature woman. She thanked Mike for freeing her from the unimpeachable chains of the youth, as; they both agreed that since they currently had this freedom, it would be best to enhance their skills. Mary and Mike enjoyed this copiously and surrendered their most intimate eternal promises. A new powerful glow shined over this couple, as if appearing to be a force blending them into one life. Betty was curious about how Mary got this glow. Mary claimed that she and Mike had surrendered themselves to the Lord. Mary waved for her to stop, as she had heard these sorts of stories previously. She was not ready to share her sexuality with anyone, especially someone she saw each day. Mary also believed this could place pressure on Betty to follow her. Mary now understood how unprepared and foolish she was in this life-changing event. Mary counted herself lucky in that Mike played along with her, so as not to hurt her feelings. Little she knew that Mike was just as naïve as she was. Either way, they were now devoted to each other. That was the highest stage of relationships permitted by law. They would go to the elders, declare themselves, sign a register, and move forward. Families were permitted to hold ceremonies if desired; however, his parents were in Olive Grove and hers along the Lake Corpus Christi. There would be no more ceremonies, just a signed letter from the elders in the registering office. This was more or less for claiming any children in the relationship. This would keep them out of an orphanage. Without question, this news elicited such a loud cheer from

Mary's mother and Grandmother that neighbors on the opposite side of the lake, approximately seven miles away claim to have heard their cheerful glees. Others claim the wind could have helped; notwithstanding, no one ever challenged this claim. Mike's parents were equally happy, throwing a grand party. Secretly, many parents begged and promised large bribes to get their son in the same house and opportunity to earn a right in her bed. Mary was what they all wanted, as so many believed she would be strong enough to bear a child and still fight this ugly war. The skill to kiss your baby with your mouth, while driving a sword into an invader was sought after both in life and their dreams.

Consequently, the day quickly arrived when the four had to march off in the fight for Houston. Fortunately, their fighting would be more about holding a line against any reinforcements entering and any forces attempting to leave the city for rural resupplies. Mary and Betty took close to one thousand arrows each, with the promise of many more available in the inventory. Mary and Betty were provided two crossbows each, in the event one broke, and so they could set up a decoy with a long string pull to appear from being in another position. They were experts at this, even from the point of obtaining an execution from a planted crossbow approximately forty feet from them. The Patricians, while attempting to sneak in on the false position would hide themselves almost beside her, so close that she would slice their throats while they lay on the ground low crawling to her fake position. Mary was a deadly fighter on her own and alone. This caused Mike some concerns, although Mary and the elders could convince him that if she had him around her, it would take away from her concentration and possibly get both killed. The other women in this fighting force had high respect for Mary and if assigned to fight with Mike, ensured his safety was never compromised. They feared that if Mike were killed, she might blame him.

Unfortunately, the Patricians captured some PP and tortured them for all information about this Orange Grove PP. One woman told them that Mike and Mary were in the battle, and they would destroy them. They immediately executed this woman, who with great pride as a warning accidentally told the Patricians how to weaken Mary. The Patricians would go after Mike, believing that if they killed him, Mary would withdraw, as was the normal wartime custom. The Patricians scoured the line until they were able to locate Mike's position, even though the PP had divided her unit into squads and redeployed them throughout the front line. The PP command elders were noticing the Patricians carrying off many of their soldiers as captives and not performing immediate executions. They, therefore, offered fake intelligence to their soldiers, so when they were captured the false intelligence would flow into their ears. Mike held fast to the belief that if the Patricians captured a soldier, their lives would be ended. He constantly vowed the Patricians would not take him alive, a statement he would later prove to be true. The Patricians pretty much ignored his position for two days, causing the PP to pull some troops from his squad and backfilling them on other parts of the line. Then on the third day the Patricians hit his position assiduously, outnumbering them fifty to one. They busted the line hard within minutes, spotted Mike and immediately executed him with gunfire to the chest. They wanted to ensure his body could easily be identified. After the breakthrough, they retreated to their side and dispersed the men back to their positions before they were identified. Ironically, about one-third of the men were executed trying to rejoin their units. Their rush to return propelled them to cross short areas with no cover, therefore, a bullet from a sniper.

Ironically, Mary was not on duty this day. She had been complaining of an upset stomach, and feeling faint, thereby her elders sent her to get medical care. This would be the first day she missed duty in the seven weeks they had successfully hold these lines. Mary averaged six kills per day, many requiring her to get too close to the enemy. Her strong belief was she had to kill these killers before they killed her and her comrades. An enemy with a weapon was markedly dangerous to permit living. Upon arriving at the hospital, the medical staff examined her, afterwards ordering some lab tests, and directed her to rest until they received the results. A few hours later, they informed her she was pregnant. This shocked her and came as a terrible disappointment, and in a position, she never dreamed she would be. Mike and she enjoyed the sex so much they completely forgot about her becoming pregnant. Mary understood the battle rules of the PP that no expectant woman could be in the battle zone. She planned to travel to Mike's unit and inform him that she would be back in Alice awaiting his return. She examined the supposedly updated roster charts and could not find him on any company roster. Mary believed that he was engaged in some undercover work; therefore, she would search back to the last unit he was with, and go see if anyone knew or would promise to give him her message. She would have to travel five miles behind the moving back lines, and therefore, send messages in on the supply trucks. She sent a message in the first day and to her surprise, two Commanders came out to greet her.

Mary held the same rank, yet was considered extremely specialized. The Commanders came out to give her the bad news. Initially, she was extremely angry that she had to do so much research to find Mike. The Commanders informed her the elders wanted to keep this secret, fearing if the men learned of her departure, it could disturb their fighting confidence. After this, Mary remembered being told this in her briefings and then proceeded to the elder's headquarters five additional miles south. The Commanders offered her a horse; nevertheless, she refused it. She had an extreme urge to kill; therefore, she planned to travel in the outlying forests beside the path to the headquarters. Many times, snipers would wait in their positions for weeks waiting for a certain commander to travel across the route. This did turn out to be as productive as she could have hoped, make three executions along the route. She took their Patricians identification chips, a process of cutting deep into their arm and pulling it out, an easy process when they are dead. She gave these chips to the elders as she walked in telling them that three of them could have been these targets. Instead of receiving praise, they scolded her for fighting while pregnant. Mary did not care, since she fully expected this type of response. The elders offered her an escort backward to Alice; however, Mary refused the escort claiming to know a shortcut back to Lake Corpus Christi where she planned to raise her child with her mother and Grandmother. The elders agreed this would be best for her and her child. Therefore, gave her a temporary one-year inactive status. She disappeared into the forests on her way back to her mother's new home, which was more her new home when considering she grew up in the lake.

While walking through the woods, Mary saw a shiny object above the ground and reached down to move the grass away from it. Her hand slipped springing forward in straight into a metal animal trap snapping its sharp teeth deep into her bones. She went to reposition her feet to get a solid footing for pulling out her hand and accidentally stepped into another trap as it snapped the spring-loaded chain pulled her body back, only stopping because of her trapped hand. She was now stretched about as far as possible, preventing her any form of movement. On her fourth painful day, a pack of wild dogs killed her and ate much of her body. Her face was still recognizable, plus her temporary inactive duty papers when a security party was attempting to discover why the buzzards were flying above this area. Upon identification, her body was wrapped tight in a dark-colored plastic wrapping. These wrappings were standard for wrapping bodies found in the woods with heavy decay. The local militia transported her body to her mother's farm per their request. The war for Houston ended just a few days after Mary departed from the elder's headquarters. Mary's mother invited three elders whom she knew personally and Betty with her new dedicated male friend. They arrived at the farm, gave some special words and additional awards. Upon completion of the words, Mary's brother burned the remainder of Mary's body. Everyone was reminded this was to remain a secret, considering most of the fighting currently were squads flushing out any remaining Patricians farms. Mary contributed so much to the Eastern Texas Patricians flushing operations. Additionally, she was attributed much credit for keeping Mexico from invading the dying states and the future of Texas, as it would go back to where it came, an independent nation, with the regretful fate of being a buffer zone between the chaotic remains of what was once a great civilization and Mexico.

# CHAPTER 03

# YORK IS NO LONGER NEW

This terrible war swept across the former union with different outcomes based upon an almost unpredictable environment. The departed revival of York in the new world remained within the hands of the Patricians, nevertheless, suffered its share of misery and destruction. The Patricians' need for corruption and greed for more money did not end when the PP took up positions in neighboring states. Subsequently, the PP took solid positions in Pennsylvania and throughout the New England States, with their largest stronghold in upper Maine. Their primary objective was to reduce the smuggling across the Canadian border. The arrogance of the former state called for the renaming of their territory York as if to take a direct challenge to England. Currently, their race baiting puts them against themselves, as the nation ignored them. York was no longer the intellectual and commercial center of the nation, thereby giving their city with little value except for the burden of preventing a crammed and hungered person with a selfish evil to keep their tempers hot. The overwhelming loss of morality and any sense of loyalty to their community made their laws, not even worth the paper they were printed. The states strong move towards socialization ended with a sudden collapse. Subsequently, the government did not have the productive PP to steal from and give to their puppets. When the freebies failed to flow into their pawn's accounts, blood began to flow as these leaders latterly lost their heads. The PP was wise enough to stay out of this internal chaos waiting patiently for the blood to continue to flow. The PP held the strategic logic that if the Patricians's rag dolls did not see them, they could stay out of their target. If these hostages realized the PP had living resources, they would try to steal them as well. Their former great city once ruled and skimmed the world's finances. Money stopped flowing in this state and with it so did their purchasing power. York had too many people for the PP to challenge in any form of head-on battle. The sole thing that would challenge this territory would need to be based on psychological warfare. Crippling communications would be hard; therefore, the lone hope was to infiltrate it and keep enough hatred and doubt burning preventing the internal unrest to stop. A hungry mass would be uncontrollable for any form of government.

Another critical factor for controlling York was to cripple, as much as possible its transportation network. This was twofold, as the first was to cripple their electrical grid. The PP could survive much easier without a grid, as they had adequate rural space to install solar panels and enough fuel for gas generators. The greatest energy inhibitor was the embargo of all oil products. The Gulf States controlled the southern refineries, as the naval forces that belonged to the PP control coupled with their submarines strove hard to enforce a blockade of Boston, York, Philadelphia, and Washington DC. The overwhelming goal was always to draw the people out of the cities and into the open lands for execution by snipers. The issue that not all lands along the eastern Seaboard were flat, but also rolling hills did not complicate this issue. Instead, it added to the sniper's effectiveness by permitting them to get closer to their targets. The battle for York would be long and slow, with no goal of total conquest.

The PP did strive to establish several large pockets supporting the PP communities already existing within this territory. The PP hardened forces in Maine pushed grueling across the northern parts of New Hampshire and Vermont. They would establish footholds in several of the PP communities with a dedicated mission of confiscating as many Canadian products flowing into York for Patricians customers. There was no solid strategy to determine when these goods would flow over the border, as the relationships were one-on-one with the Canadians and former clients in York. The Canadians continued to pass the goods over the York border demanding payment first before attempted delivery. The York customers understood the risks as they were not willing to finance a support mission to get these products into their hands.

The PP in upper York controlled the border from Vermont to Sodus Point on Lake Ontario, less than thirty miles east of Rochester. Rochester and Buffalo were solid battle zones, with Pennsylvania sending five Armies for permanent duty ensuring, nothing made it south of Henrietta, their corps headquarters. Route 90 was declared a kill zone from Syracuse to Erie, with limited support missions in the Pennsylvania portion of 90. Early in the fighting, some crafty York Patricians conducted operations without their Yellow Caps. The PP launched a massive social media shamming campaign declaring the York's ashamed of being Patricians. The PP tied this into the only Political Correct action and that not to wear their Yellow Caps was their acknowledgement the PP was superior, in that they wore no Yellow Caps. This hit the deranged Yorkers hard, to the point they would immediately execute any Patricians without his or her Yellow Cap, actually going further and demanding these caps be permanently attached to their scalps. This was one of the greatest tools the PP could redeploy repeatedly, and that was the concept of Politically Correct, which, in reality, was Politically Corrupt. As with the overwhelming majority of Patricians were so detached from reality, their responses and reactions were predicted with perfection. This is, without question, a solid card for the PP to hold. Another key characteristic the York Patricians had was they were not prepared to die for their mission, believing negotiation would always prevail. This is where absolute control of communications, especially the destruction of all cell phone towers, was essential. The PP would not negotiate with the Patricians, because they would never hold up to their end and would never compromise.

Instead, they would repair their battle weakness and when an opportunity arose, they would betray every issue discussed and go for the absolute kill.

Patricians used negotiations as a delay and diversion tool. Knowing this, the PP would welcome the Patricians commanders, and ask for a sign of good faith, the soldiers come out in the 'safety' of the opening and take a break, plus have some fun, since technically the battle was over as they were in peaceful negotiations. The PP had executioners hidden around the negotiating room and battalions of snipers surrounding the 'Patricians recreation area.' What made this easy slaughtering possible was the Patricians belief the PP could easily be manipulated. The second the negotiating officials were in the enclosed room, they were stabbed, throats cut, and cross bowed between the eyes or head cut off with a sword. No guns were used. Executions concentrated on techniques to maximize silence, with cutting the throat, and driving a knife from the skin area under the jaw straight up into the mouth and further if possible. This promoted the inclusions of brainers, or medium-sized knives, which need not to be razor blade sharp, but instead must be somewhat thicker, as the thickness would hold the blade in position, while the executioner pushed upward with maximum force. The Patricians troops believing they would be engaging in recreational activities would disperse to the appropriate outside recreational location. The complete execution through gunfire would take about ten minutes, and this is why the PP always had a loud rock song playing on the intercom. They mowed the bodies down and then speared their heads, with was the lone authorized kill verifier by the York PP expeditionary forces.

The primary reason for this was the overwhelming majority of York and New England drug addicts, who would pass out only to awaken later, thereby presenting false dead. This did not do well for the people performing the verifications, which tended to freak out when they witnessed the dead come back to life. The Yorker's drug decency, a process initiated established and initiated by the Patricians for the ease of controlling the dependence of their hopeless masses, was a process the PP elected to exploit. A drug-induced force will behave erratically when going through a withdrawal phase, therefore, the PP initiated an extensive campaign against stopping and controlling the drug trade across the border with Canada. Drug dogs, by the thousands were released in the forests, searching the drop-off points and storage facilities. The

Canadians would sneak the drugs into York, plant the drugs and exit immediately, while at later time agents on behalf of the buyers would retrieve them and place them in their distribution system. The process worked great for a while, even confusing the PP, until the dogs figured this decoy. The PP confiscated the drugs, stopped the planting and then became the purchasers. Canadian drug lords started sending the drugs to the PP, at a much more reduced price, who would place them in drop-off ambush sites. The drug addicts would rush and actually flood these open sites awaiting to make their purchases. The PP would begin selling them, awaiting for the initial one-hundred purchasers to exit, which they did without haste. After this, they would begin the mass executions, usually wiping out thousands of purchasers with arrows and knives. The druggies were always searching for weapons prior to admittance, a procedure the druggies constantly complied, willing to give up their defense in exchange for a reduced risk of another druggie killing them for their drugs.

The drugs were an effective method for drawing these freaks out of York City (former New York City). Another biological and psychological warfare technique was to dump these hundreds of thousands of bodies on the outskirts of York City, providing a haven to the mass reproduction of rodents, who would then take their disease infested bodies into York City. The sheer mass hysteria created by those who attempted to pass through these above ground open and exposed bodies dumping grounds made the citizenry even that much more difficult to control. Pennsylvania deployed an additional ten Armies along the New Jersey and southern York state borders composed strictly of guerrilla warfare units. These forces stifled the Pennsylvania Patricians communities, and prevented the mass exodus of York City residents and drug dealers from relocating in Pennsylvania. The goal was to push them into Connecticut, Massachusetts, and Vermont, whereas these areas could not withstand this population redistribution. To assist with this York blockade, Ohio deployed ten Armies to add needed muscle for freeing Buffalo and Rochester from Patricians control. These cities were completely blockaded, with extensive Artillery fire unleashed both day and night. The goal was to display for Syracuse, Albany and York City what was heading their way. The PP needed this fear factor to elevate drug use, and social unrest and cause as much internal destruction as feasible. The PP controlled the news from these areas, ensuring their propaganda was transmitted where the York media could obtain it.

The initial blockades surrounding Syracuse and Albany were designed to cause limited social impact, such as disrupting food supplies, stripping fuel distribution and the destruction of their electrical grids, which were accomplished by bombing the electrical facilities and generators. A key component of the PP philosophy was to take York away from the Patricians with no desire ever to occupy it. This puzzled the Patricians who believed the PP would pay any price to keep York intact. Thereby, the defensive network they established was designed to inflict maximum damage on any force attempting to take York City. Notwithstanding, day after day, the PP mighty forces did not fall into their extensive ambushes, and instead simply deposited dead bodies of their city's citizens who were able to bypass these defenses. This was so rampart, causing York City to execute thousands of their own citizens who were attempting to break out and obtain living supplies or drugs. A PP military policy advisor once reported that if the PP wanted to break the Patricians defenses for York City, they need only to reverse the thousands of successful breaches by York City residents. York City was surviving and suffering at the same time. To alleviate pressure on this city, Pennsylvania deployed two Artillery Armies to launch thousands of shells into the city. These were designed as a display of what someday could happen and permit the city residents to feel what Buffalo and Rochester were experiencing. Fearing Philadelphia would increase their support, Pennsylvania and West Virginia deployed twelve Armies (six Artillery and six guerrilla) to blockade and prevent any support for York City)

Philadelphia did not have the same fervent desire to fall on the sword for the Patricians as the vast majority of Patricians held cities. They did not agree with the PP, nor did they care what the PP stood against or preached. The issues dividing the Patricians and PP were not worth killing or being killed for according to the city of brotherly love. This viewpoint also precluded them in desiring to engage in any military actions against other Patricians, except for declaring themselves neutral, over even better; they branded themselves as Colonial, holding to the values as originally defined in their city during the late eighteenth century. As could be expected, there were rogue elements within the city that felt obligated to save their brothers in York City. The Artillery Armies surrounding Philadelphia repositioned their fire to rapscallion suburbs and other neighboring cities that claimed to support the Patricians. The six guerrilla units concentrated on gathering intelligence, controlling drug flow, and nailing smugglers who were engaged trading with York City. The PP had to make a strong example of these traitors, claiming they could force the PP to treat Philadelphia the same as, they did York City. No one wanted this misery. Therefore, the PP claimed that these smugglers would be executed in public, along with their families and anyone else the authorities could prove knew about these plans. Like most programs that instill fear and take innocent lives its effectiveness could never be accurately evaluated. The PP continued the program until the war's end, in agreement among the Patricians leadership in Philadelphia, who feared this betrayal by their citizens could lead to the mighty forces of the PP to inflict destruction on their city as they did on several other former American cities.

The value of intelligence gathering could not be underestimated in the York City siege. The smuggling operations helped identify what the city's residents needed and how far they were willing to so as to retrieve them. Even though city officials attempted to smuggle in goods for their constituents, notwithstanding, just as they had done throughout their long history, they screwed everything up, wasted depleting public funds trying this, and completely failed the people of York City. The Fake Press, who no longer had the PP to falsify reports, now turned against the Patricians leadership in their city. Their reports put a light on their disastrous history of leadership and began to cause riots. The city deployed what limited police they had on the Press, attempting to silence them. This turned out to be a rich propaganda tool for the PP as they published it nationwide in an attempt to instill doubt in the presses unwavering and totally foolish bond between the press and the Patricians officials. The goal was to seed some doubt, and provide a talking point for the members from the press who wanted to break free of the destructive chains the Patricians tried completely to bind them. This did put the needed cracks on the wall that would someday result in a truthful press, an element needed if the states were ever to recover. When the press fell in York City, the PP immediately began flooding the waves with their propaganda. These mobile military communications units would deploy, set up their towers and begin broadcasting immediately. They absolutely flooded their stories with false news, coupled with execution stories and tales of misery from other fools who dared fight the 'honorable' PP.

The depressing truth remaining; no one escapes this bloodbath as honorable; they merely escaped it alive. Such a sorrowful course towards the land of the free, when they believed their flag would continue to fly. That flag no longer flew, in even the PP controlled areas. The PP would not fly the stars and stripes complaining this flag represented the corruption and tyranny of the Patricians.

The Carson family operated the Carsonville Hotel on Powell's Valley Rd. in Carsonville Pennsylvania. The family has operated this Hotel for many generations, being popular among many, and even those who were brave enough to visit Little Dick's Deck. The family struggled to work as a team and saving their money to place their four sons through college and pursue other prospective endeavors, considering they had plenty of offspring to keep their Hotel within the family's future generations. Their two oldest sons had graduated with advance degrees in biology and were gainfully employed in a top state Research laboratory. Pennsylvania declared this Research lab as critical for the PP's military operations, a move that puzzled many people who could not understand the potential relationship. Others claimed the Research institution was working on methods to enhance food production. This was, indeed, one of their functions, nevertheless; the PP had additional goals in mind for this institution, one in which Ted Carson and William Carson would be primarily responsible. The overall goal would be to create some biological tools to weaken York City and expedite operations in Rochester, Syracuse, and Buffalo. The state was in the process of establishing the resources and security needed for such an operation. The safeguards would need to be high, so that such technology never was in the Patricians control. Secrecy was such that not even family members could know, and that all employees were housed in special housing built within the lab's secure area and enclosed by a fence. Ted and William were single, and as such lost their Friday and Saturday night mating activities such as movies, dancing, and restaurants. They were more conservative in their relationships with females, having grown up in the Trinity Church, just across the road from their family Hotel.

The PP was searching desperately to find some tools to weaken the Patricians power base within the majority of the cities they controlled. Many hated the current policy of starving these cities and the massive Artillery destruction. With no guarantee, a future government could repair or restore these destroyed cities and that when the masses were permitted to exit their boundaries would spread destruction and lawlessness in other areas; a new solution had to be explored. The PP needed other options. Initially, they considered chemical, yet feared international condemnation or even interference if chemicals were deployed. Nuclear weapons were out of the question, as control over the radiation and residual effects would have devastating effects on PP residents living in the surrounding areas. The PP even attempted the concept of a slow starvation of the cities and hope, peace was made before these people died. The problem with this option was their belief that when these people were finally released, they would seek revenge. Moreover, if the PP were to win, they would have to devote national resources to restoring their health, only to face their later revenge. This was the reason for the war. Patricians would never depart from their delusional drug infected ideologies. They claimed a devotion to death, and the PP was now accepting the sole method to restoring political stability in the former states was to execute all the Patricians.

The Patricians actually began this war by dragging PP members into the streets and executing. The Patricians were so convinced the PP would fail to respond to force with force. The PP was branded as the appeasers. The Patricians would execute an innocent PP in public claiming this execution was in response to the PP's executions, which was a total lie, as no such executions had occurred. These executions continued to the point that one day, when a Patricians group in Miami executed a Cuban American, causing the Cubans completely to destroy the Miami's mayor's office and home. The biased police went after them starting a citywide battle as all PP citizens joined the fight, in an open battle destroying the corrupt police. Bureaucratic Florida State Officials attempted to bypass the governor and activate the state military guard against the now united Hispanic population in Florida. The governor became furious, especially when the bureaucrats attempted to tie the governor up in the courts. The governor did not care and ordered the judge put in state prison for accepting the case and further authorized his state militia to stand down, and then redeployed them to stop the rogue state guards when it became evident they were going to execute the unauthorized raids. The two forces faced off, and against what everyone believed began to fight. The united Hispanic population, surprisingly joined by the state police shifted the tide forcing the rogue militia into a surrender. They were transferred to a new prisoner of war camp established in the Dry Tortugus National Park, located upon an island just west of Key West.

The Hispanic population demanded the execution of this rogue military and the bureaucrat that illegally deployed them. The governor, who was placed in prison by the Department of Justice for imprisoning the judge. This crippled the Florida state government that demanded the release of their judge. The state employees vacated their positions preventing the Federal government from forcing Florida's action. Florida's citizens of all races, with complete support among the whites, blacks, and Asians, joined the Hispanics and borderline Patricians, went to war against Florida's state government, even though they merely found empty buildings. When the Federal government threatened to declare martial law and restore order in Florida, buy some great mystery, all electrical power to any Federal building and military installations. The Federal military stood down, electing to protect their resources and not fight against the American population. The population made their move to Key West, wanting to execute the rogue state comrades held in the Dry Tortugus National Park. Discovering this massive force was approaching them, friends and family of these soldiers rushed boats in order to attempt a rescue. Naturally, the Coast Guard activated a campaign to recapture these prisoners. The Coast Guard issued an order among the prisoners to surrender. Refusing the order, the boats retreated into the international water off the Florida coast, a move that did not have the outcome they expected. Cuban naval forces rescued the prior soldiers and once on the ship and given quarters, the Cubans executed them for crimes against their former countrymen. They pulled the boats out into the Gulf of Mexico, and disposed of the body's in Cuba, by burning or feeding to wild beasts. Cuba never confessed to this execution of justice, being satisfied knowing they had done a great deed. Florida was outraged with the Patricians and began extensive campaigns throughout the states of executing Patricians. The first execution was on a dare televised throughout the state, notwithstanding, once it was accomplished; others quickly followed as the need to revenge became too great to contain. The PP stopped all Patricians executions in Florida, and soon spread nationwide, beginning the Civil War.

Swinging back to Ted and William, their work began with enhancing vegetable seeds to produce increased yields, causing these scientists to believe they were escaping the war. It would take years to perfect this process. Then one day a group of PP leaders visited the Research center. The last President, and only one recognized by the world, Hiplinger moved the Federal government into the bunkers in the mountains of West Virginia. They communicated over a private, non-hackable network with special hand held cryptic devices. Their guidance was relayed to the PP, which operated as their face of the former union. Top level PP officials entered Ted and William's workplace in hopes to change the war. They needed a biological weapon, which must weaken the Patricians city's without a massive destruction of their infrastructure. Any diseases had to work fast and die out quickly. The American government had over 1,000 diseases ready to be deployed, nevertheless; the degree of overall disaster could not be predicted. Simple things, such as an unexpected high wind could blow these creatures into another city. Ted and William came up with an outstanding combination. They would release a flu virus that had a life span of merely three months, yet would kill within days.

Accordingly, it would take three days to manifest itself, which would give the infested person a chance to contact others. The flu created burning in the lower feet, an important added in order to keep these people in the city and not wondering the state savaging. The method of delivery was through the public water. While in the water, this virus spreads at the speed of light. The plan was to pour a vile into a toilet bowl. When the toilet opens its valve to let the water in, the virus swam upstream into the public's water reserve. The virus could enter by drinking, or contact with a surface and then become airborne. It could contact clothing in a washing machine, plus so many other water contact processes. The initial vial dump released one-hundred vials throughout the city, many in public hotels, and other community stores. Even though York City was barricaded, the amount of people going out and coming in each day were extremely lofty. It was so high that York City did not even attempt entry or exit control, leaving the streets open, with the primary fear of being killed by PP snipers. The virus could survive only eight days in the water. Moreover, it could exist an additional eleven days in the air. This flu had a strange reaction when in a human body. Its massive reproduction concentrated in the lungs, feeding on oxygen, and choking on carbon dioxide. The chocking effect was a combination of the dead virus plugging the lungs pours and dripping in the blood attached to the oxygen leaving the lungs. In the blood, it would bind to the walls than the veins releasing chemicals to burn holes into the veins and arteries. This caused internal bleeding. The moisture in the corpse expedited the expiration of the virus, removing any future effect on a living corpse. The first release killed 343,000 York City residents. Considering this was a new virus, and the method the virus degraded in the corpse left the medical authorities in York City completely confused. The randomness of the cases throughout the city provided no clues.

The loss of these people was enough to put the city into a defensive mode. They initiated stricter controls on entry and exit. The PP secured this virus, not wanting to deploy it once more in York City, fearing enough people would have created an immunity to it. Another factor that concerned the PP was that deaths continued to be high in the third week 112,000 and week five 73,222. No significant increase in death rates occurred after this period. The integral deaths from this mystery flu as reported by York City was 528,222, which pushed the city's total population to approximately eight million people. PP officials believed York City was not reporting their population correctly and was not recognizing the massive amount of their citizens who did not return for scavenging for drugs and food. Others reported that with the infrastructure damages York City lacked the ability to maintain an accurate census of their people. Still, another view reported that the city officials did not want to know, considering they could not protect or provide support for this potential time bomb simply waiting to explode. The city had another big problem taking a front seat. They had no electricity nor any fuel oil for their heating pumps. The city was going to freeze this winter. Water pipes would burst, leaving any prospects of repairing it, and if they could be repaired finding a method to prevent another bust. The problem was there was no way without some sort of heat. The apartments could not support wooden fire and heaters. To make matters worse, flu and ammonia hit hard and this time the starving frozen masses whose immunities were weakened by the flu virus unleashed a death vengeance taking over three million people. It divided families, crippled neighborhoods, and sent both fear and pity throughout the former states as their pleas for surrender flooded the nation's networks.

The PP, having the upper hand and honestly believing they could never share a world with Patricians within it. The Patricians were given so many chances throughout history, having set a record of total dishonesty and forcing PP into an appeasement policy if they wanted the United States to continue. When the PP gave up on a future United States, they accepted a war with the Patricians until their bitter elimination. Even in the midst of such a horrifying complete defeat in York City, the Patricians were still completely out of touch with reality. Their concept of a peace treaty, which would save them from absolute defeat, was to offer the PP forgiveness if the Army commanders turned themselves in for a lifetime prison sentence in the city, plus the PP immediately atone for not feeding the York City population by giving them an immediate supply of food. They were also for shipping in all the heating oil and gasoline their citizens ordered and repair the electrical grid. The PP was in total shock as they publish this psychological nut cake demand. The PP reaffirmed their position that everyone still within the York City limits would be executed. They wanted one last attempt to draw them out in the open and turn on their high-powered machine guns. They got their chance, as over 300,000 came rushing out for their freebies, and the bullets did fly, as they mowed down the ones closest to the city's entrance first, creating a blockade of bodies making it difficult for the ones in the open to gain cover, having to climb over bodies to get back in the city. It was a successful day as for numbers, with 263,554 confirmed kills.

The Patricians response was to calculate a delay fee for not surrendering within the prescribed timeframe. Time was now on the PP's hands, as these millions of dead bodies would begin decaying in springtime, spreading diseases and feeding rodents. The PP's then initiated a shotgun parade through the city, using special underground tunnels constructed by the former government. These clandestine tunnels were not secret to the Patricians's. They just never considered them of value. The PP would sneak in and shoot shotgun shells into large windows. They executed this at night, and except for an occasional candle faced nothing but total blackness in the windows. The goal was to instill some fear they could be reached and break the windows allowing the freezing cold to enter easily with more impact. They shot steadily at apartments in the eighth to the fifteenth floor, for maximum impact for the shotguns. Other, longer-range automatic weapons were used for the higher floors, especially as the goal was to break windows and get away quickly. The PP brought guards to watch for the police, who because of the absolute darkness needed some sort of car light for navigation. This program hit as many residential areas as possible. They also set bombs off at fire stations and police stations. The critical component was to break the York City Patricians and their bond with their emergency services. The PP hated shooting at firefighters and police officers, notwithstanding ever since the days in Florida, all officers and fighters were given an opportunity to join the PP or die with the Patricians. The same opportunity was given to the military and Federal administrative agencies. The PP could no longer accept refugees from the Patricians, as it was always said, the Patricians never failed to make you pay for every good and kind deed.

No matter how strong will the PP had, the pain of killing our fellow former compatriots was felt, and no matter how difficult to depress, always found a method to surface through tears and depression. The Patricians would cry out asking how the PP could do this, notwithstanding the PP would cry out the same argument. One death instills the revenge towards another death from the opposite party. The PP was united behind the cause of this war, citing the complete abandonment of justice and open harassment, execution of innocent PP citizens, and total delusional abandonment of the democratic principles. The

Patricians were slaves to their memorized false talking points, and believed that if you repeat a lie repeatedly, eventually people will believe it. The Patricians would constantly lead the argument accusing their opponent of doing what they were accused of doing. An example would be when hiding dealings with the Russians, accuse your opponent of this, and subsequently drag the investigation out with secret special prosecutors, hoping that the public would eventually become tired of this vast waste of money and after that refuse to investigate cases where the obvious crimes were visible, or at the minimum have the special counsel search everything under the sun, knowing that someone has had to have done something, then nail them to the wall, offering plea deals if they lie. Welcome to justice, Patricians style. Remember, always accuse them of what you are doing, have the team remain united with idiot talking points, flood this on the public and after hearing these lies, they will eventually accept them as truth.

No one will ever be able to find a justification for killing another human. We can only hope that justice was served in the process, and future lives would be spared. The Patricians were not going to stop until the completely sold out the former states, and would use any one desire to save the states against them at any cost. The only hope of some sort of society to rebound from the previous union would solely come through blood, just as the union was preserved the first time in blood, and even initially formed from blood through two wars with the British Kingdom. The Patricians were completely immersed in the one-world order concept, as would be ultimately redefined by them once they had a solid grip within it. They struggled effectively to remove a few of the hurdling blocks such as borders and Christianity. The PP would not give up on Christianity, even though the Patricians had passed such amendments (Johnson Amendment) taking away the freedom of speech for Christian ministers, yet demanding freedom of speech for everything against Christianity. The Patricians needed the Christian pulpit to weaken the Americans too smart for their lies. They believed that by silencing the ministers, they could deceive the masses. They were also willing to fight hard to keep this Amendment, and by silencing those who were affected by it, they placed the appropriate safeguards to blend it into the fabric of contemporary law. Their success in this stage emboldened them to join with the atheistic and took God and the Ten Commandments and prayer out of the American public. They believed the Christians would not call them out for their hypocrisy, and therefore, openly demanded the equal treatment of other religions that actually promoted beliefs strictly against our constitution and death to those who did not confirm. One Christian minister claimed the Patricians forgot to read the Old Testament, and that was the part of the Bible this war would be fought with.

Accordingly, the Patricians were promising everything the PP had to everyone in the world. They worked the nations privately one-on-one with the demands of total confidentiality. This was a Patricians ace in the hole technique; keep the other party from talking to each another. Afterwards, if someone does talk, prosecute them and take everything from them, and then deny they said this. Through a total smear campaign, they would totally deface the opposing party convincing the public; they were whirling lies at them. The problem arose that other nations had also seen this published deal. Therefore, everyone knew the Patricians were lying, nevertheless, dare not speak out for fear of facing the Patricians. The lone way to gain favor with the Patricians was to go after the PP. Consequently, the PP stood their ground and refused to honor any crocked deal the Patricians had orchestrated, alleging such deals were not in accordance with international laws. Even though no laws existed, there was no way to prove their non-existence, considering that proof of their absence of existence would not change the outcome. The PP still held the nuclear codes, and boldly professed they would launch these weapons before allowing a rogue government to control the world. Their greatest fear was not so much being ruled by one-world government; it was the methods the Patricians would employ to ooze their corruption into it prior to gaining complete control. This could never take place.

The Patricians had undercover leakers on just about every corner in America. They snooped on everyone at all times. This was one reason most PP decisions were made personally and never spoken of afterwards. Even the flies on the walls would tell on them. William and Ted fell victim to this trap, as many of their coworkers over emphasized their contribution to the York bug. Their coworkers were scared their team impact would be forgotten in history. They did not have the glamorous credentials to get the attention they craved. Ted and William did not feel they did anything exceptional, except for asking a few questions. They later confessed the purpose of their questions were to gain information and not to identify unknown mental avenues. The primary fear the PP had over the publication of this weapon was the Patricians could steal it and use it against the PP urban areas. They collected all the material created by this project and put it in the deepest security possible. By design, no single person was involved in all the stages of development; therefore, at the minimum would need at least ten members notwithstanding to have a remote chance of reproducing the virus. Even at this, they would forever try, thereby causing these scientists a life of fear. Patricians were experts as swooping in and snatching out. The PP currently was concentrating a lot of resources on their high jacking and kidnapping activities. The sad principle the PP was forced to accept was the sole way to keep an abducted Patricians from returning to the Patricians was through execution. The Patricians would never, regardless of the times, they promised to do so, ever release a live PP. When the PP needed intelligence, they would take a Patricians prisoner, perform brutal interrogated, then execute. The continual challenge that existed was the Patricians's belief the PP would not harm them and would not catch their lies. The better interrogation sessions were when the invaders brought back more than one prisoner, thereby eliminating the PP does not execute disbelief with a deadly example.

With the York bug complete, the team was now working on a Pacific bug, with the eye on California. The choice was between Chicago, St. Louis, or LA, San Francisco and San Diego, plus even a shot at Sacramento and Portland. They could not verify a bug released in the Midwest would not find a mode to spread, as the wind patterns in the Midwest could become unpredictable at times, whereas the West Coast offered periods of sustained winds going into the oceans, plus mountains to prevent a mass spread pass the Rockies. They did not worry about Mexico because the Texan nation had driven them far from the border. In fact, the threat that this bug could be hibernating in the vacant buffer zone could offer an additional tool to protect the southern border. The California bugs were still in the early stages of development. PP agreed to allow these scientists to take a short vacation, as long as only one went at a time. They did not want to chance more than one leg of this process would be prime for abduction. This sort of hit the Carson brothers hard, as they both wanted to walk the roads of Carsonville together. Their family did not care, as they would have one at a time, thereby one have one in danger at that time. William and Ted eventually agreed to this security policy, as at worse it could save one of them.

They flipped to determine which one would go first. Ted won the flip and eagerly rushed to collect his military security equipment for the expedition.

Ted bundled up for his trip home. He would travel, hidden under the back of a deuce and half Army truck. The trip would take three days. The truck bed was modified so that Ted could release body wastes while the vehicle was moving. The soldiers asked he not do this in thick traffic or while at red lights. They feared that strange looks from surrounding vehicles could alert the Patricians. The mission plan was to drop him off in Elizabethville and has him ride a family horse the last couple of miles through the forest to Carsonville. They recommended Ted scouted his family's homes to ensure they were not behaving abnormally. As they approached Elizabethville, the Army truck was hit head-on by a Ford pickup truck. The injured soldiers exited their truck to restrain the driver of the Ford truck. They were surprised when they opened the truck door attempting to gain a response, nevertheless, the body fell straight out on the road, with a snake wrapped around its neck. The soldiers shot the snake. The soldiers called their authorities who called the local social guards who agreed to investigate the situation. The inspection revealed the snake was placed in the truck trapped in the driver's seat. The snake bit the driver in his back. The seat prevented the transmittal of its venom, forcing the snake to work through the seat cover and wiggle itself up and quickly wrap itself around the driver's neck in an attempt to choke the driver. This forced the driver to take both hands and attempt to work the snake free. Consequently, the constraints of his seatbelt limited his ability to leverage this tight knot around his neck. It was this time the driver lost control and hit Ted's truck. Initially, the military headquarters suspected this could be an attack on Ted. The challenge to this theory revolved around how a snake killing a truck driver could ever be guaranteed to stop Ted's truck. There has just been no credible method to tie these together.

Word concerning the crash spread quickly around this rural area, causing Ted's father to send his maintenance supervisor to take two horses, ride over to Elizabethville and bring Ted back through the woods. Ted verified he knew this man, convincing the soldiers to grant him his leave. Afterwards, off into the woods, they rode. The soldiers stayed with their truck as it was towed to a nearby country-car repair shop and await its repair. A few hours later, they receive a radio call from their commander requesting status on Ted. His family has reported that neither Ted, nor the maintenance man have reported to the family Hotel. The soldiers report they departed on horseback hours earlier. The commander orders them to begin a search, working from where they last saw him towards the Hotel. Meanwhile, he will deploy two platoons to search the woods. The shop mechanic asks the soldiers to identify where Ted sat in the truck. They show him where he lay in the truck's bed. The shop mechanic guides three of his dogs in the truck bed, allowing them to smell where Ted lay. He then tells his dogs to fetch him. Subsequently, the dogs go running into the nearby woods. The mechanic explains to the soldiers the dogs will show him a short cut. And away they run into the woods, with the dogs barking loudly. Next, they hear a gunshot as one of the dogs goes down. The soldier spots where the shooter is and unloads a magazine on him. He quickly reloads his magazine as both proceed to clear the area. They hear another noise, as the dogs begin chasing in the noises' direction.

One of the dogs bit the running man's leg, forcing him off balance. The soldiers catch him, disarm him and tie him to a adjoining tree. The dogs begin barking at the mouth of a nearby cave. Upon entry into the cave, the soldiers discover the remains of Ted. The notice footprints back into the cave and follow them with the dogs. About twenty minutes later, they discover the maintenance man, and constrain him for further questioning. This man did not appear to have any signs of capture or interrogation, and had a large pocket of cash. They herded him back to the other prisoner, and then forced them to where the shot dog lay. They had quickly wrapped his gunshot injury, before the other dogs had alerted them of an impending danger. They submitted a situation report to their commander, who told them to keep the dog comfortable, and that he would bring a veterinarian with him. They came by helicopter arriving within forty minutes. They secured the prisoners and injured dog and flew back to their base, providing contact information for the soldiers to provide to the patriotic mechanic. The soldiers returned the two healthy dogs to the mechanic and offered to take them back the base. The mechanic asked to follow him. This would simply require them to stop just before the gate, load him and his dogs into their truck, accomplish this mission, and once the mechanic was ready, return him and his dogs to his secured truck. This simple rule had to be enforced. No civilian vehicles could go on post, only military vehicles with the security chip. This chip would continuously scan the vehicle for cargo and personnel. Once the soldiers brought the two healthy dogs, who were given special treats, with their owner to the debrief room, the command group came out and updated them.

The soldiers had uploaded their body cam videos to the group identifying the area where Ted's body was found. The command's intelligence group had dissected the executed Patricians, Ted's body, and was torturing the captured raider currently. They found evidence the captured mechanic was a spy, based on texts on their communication devices with Patricians's superiors. They also secured their body chips and were using a special GPS hacking device to show them traveling in Canada. The attempt was to post them as traitors. The last thing the PP wanted was the Patricians launching undercover operations in their back door. Initially, the maintenance man would not cooperate; therefore, the interrogators brought his wife and two children in and even before telling them what they would do, they immediately told the maintenance man, he had committed a serious national-security crime, and executed his wife by cutting her throat and pushing her body onto him. Subsequently, they told him he had better start talking immediately or his children would be joining their mother, as they went to grab his son. The maintenance man spilled his guts. The Patricians threatened to report his family to the deporting agents and send them back to the country they departed as refugees. He knew if they were sent back it was their death sentence. He, therefore, guaranteed them, he would report when one or both sons came home and ensure they could capture them. The commander looked at the foolish maintenance man, while handing him the report they had received from the Patricians requesting this illegal refugee be deported, and the "Request Denied" stamped on it. They told him he should have known the PP will never grant a Patricians request, and that his stupidity cost him, his children and their lives. The guards took the maintenance man outside, and executed him by firing squad. They next gave the children a painless poison that immediately killed them. The family's bodies and the two executed enemy soldiers were lined up, and a video made of the executions and justice received for the loss of Ted. This video was taken, with Ted's body in the Carsonville family Hotel for a final ceremony, thanking them for their service.

Accordingly, William was heartbroken when he learned about his brother's fate, as were all the members of the Research team, especially as all vacations were cancelled until the West Coast bug was finalized. Fortunately, the mission was not all that damaged, because, as William cited, Ted was the playboy and had a difficult time staying on the task. Without the sibling rivalry and family responsibility, William became deeply immersed in this wartime project, must to the future detriment of the West Coast, as they would discover, that is will rain in southern California. The PP headquarters gained their respect, honor, and glory in the first year of this terrible war. The Patricians initially gained air superiority through several Conus air bases and the commercial airline hub. The former states recalled all overseas militaries, which posed the initial problem was that the overflow would land in Patricians controlled cities. Basically, the Army, Marines, Navy, and about half the Coast, Guards were dedicated to the PP, whereas the Air Force lacked the overall control of their local commanders, therefore, permitting these commanders to declare the party of their base. This only flew when the air base stand alone, as the joint bases with an Army element was shown the light by the Army. A few Air Force Base Commanders were tired and feathered.

The Army made every attempt to take control of overseas Air Force Bases, and if they could not, they would attack them, for fear their carelessness would put these in danger and permit foreign powers to steal American armed technology. There was also the danger that rogue elements in these areas could steal, or sell on black markets, military assets that could endanger America's allies. The skies over America saw numerous air battles. The PP forbid any party supporters from flying on airlines. This opened the door to the one-hundred-percent shooting down of all civilian aircraft. They were forced to do this in order to prevent the Patricians from launching airlift campaigns that undermined PP blockade operations. What many had reported as the greatest action by any American Group was a secret society that was able to hack the American Nuclear security systems and change the codes on the nuclear bombs. This ensured the American Nuclear arsenal would only be used if the continental states were subject to loss of independence and on some occasions, foreign invasion. Surprisingly, they unlocked three nuclear bombs for launch against Mexico during the Texas War. Fortunately, Texas could win the conflict without the use of nuclear bombs, thereby the secret group reinstalled the nuclear locks.

This provided confidence in the party's leadership, who agreed that neither could be trusted. The air war was also dependent on PP fuel, which kept the PP planes in the air, loaded with bombs, which routinely searched for grounded aircraft, in both airports and military installations. The tighter the control over the fuel the more grounded planes to serve as stationary targets. The greatest challenge was blockading the West Coast cities. The blockading of the east coast was concentrated on Massachusetts, high-traffic areas along Long Island, and York City.

A straight air campaign was producing limited results for the PP. They knew extra power was needed if they were going to choke the Patricians, therefore, they assigned the Navy and submarines to stop all sea shipments and shoot down any aircraft flying over their positions. The surprise element produced some immediate results, notwithstanding the PP used this time to issue a worldwide warning that the PP had placed a one-hundred-percent barricade and that any person or group attempting to smuggle people or material through it would be subject to death by military force. The foreign powers joined with the York defensive units and attempted a major show of force. The attacking foreign forces were composed of many African and European nations. When they tried to evade the American PP forces they crashed into each other, and their fire power resulted in hits on their fellow forces. The PP pulled their New Jersey and Massachusetts blockade forces back with the New Jersey submarine forces working the Lower Bay and up to the Hudson River. New Jersey naval ships joined Massachusetts combined submarine and naval ships blasting every port and ship in sight. With the water containing the sunken ships and barges, and the ports destroyed York's ability to receive goods was crippled. The PP Air Force pounded all airports under York City control. They had no controller, since they were bombed off the electrical grid. The thing that continued to amaze the PP were the number of planes that still made it in with perfect timing. Still did not matter because there was a seventy-one percent chance that the plane was not going to leave. The primary two targets were the cockpit and second was the jet engines with a chunk of the cabin.

This battle from the air and sea ended up taking 3.5 million lives and sinking 744 ships or sea vessels, and 20131 aircraft. This included a vast majority of small planes, which would fly beneath the radar. The small planes usually delivered supplies that arrived in a small seaport either in New England or the Carolina's. The frustrating factor of the York City campaign was the ease in getting body counts, notwithstanding the difficulty in impacting the physical component of this smuggling operation. The command group began targeted hits in Baltimore, Washington DC, and Boston. These three cities provided a solid source of resources to York City. The Air Force, pulled their primary intelligence agencies into one new focus. York had to go, and a solid pressure would result in riots. The Navy and Air Force would hit the Airports and Seaports of these cities and also destroy any major bridges. Submarines were used for underground tunnels, which were packed with suppliers. These strikes were specific and to the point. Runways had to be shattered in key places and aircraft hit while over these cities. The more these deadly stings hit over the population aided in the goal of creating the civil unrest. The city concept was so different for the PP as compared to the Patricians. They tried to keep these as functioning units and a base for future anti-PP campaigns. The PP's only permitted about one-half of the population to remain in the big cities, and instead relocated these people to the smaller cities and rural areas. The key was to relocate them to a place where they could be involved in the production of resources needed to maintain the PP society. Army bases traditionally were located a safe distance from a sizeable city, such as Fort Bragg and Fayetteville, Fort Lewis outside of Tacoma, and outside Charleston, South Carolina was a large naval station and an Air Force base, as well as a sister base in nearby Myrtle Beach.

The PP knew that without these military installations, the future of their survival would be at stake. They also knew they could not get all the installations; therefore, they concentrated and secured the ones need for their security. Fortunately, the PP enjoyed a warm relationship with the military. The PP got the information out on which installations they would forfeit. While the Patricians show this a sign of weakness and a testament to their power, the PP supporting military members deserted, making themselves available for duty at PP controlled armed installations. This additional support was needed for the increased nationwide military operations. Every Patricians city would get hit at least three times a week. Initial concentration was on the electrical grid. Considering the sources of this energy was usually around damns or solar power panel sites in rural areas, these sites simply needed a new distribution system to set up where the energy would go to PP controlled areas. The second part was closing any fuel or lines going into the city. Many times, these pipelines had hundreds of security shut off valves, which when shut off would require extensive Patricians campaigns to locate shutoff valves, perfect ambush sites. The PP represented only about 60,000,000 people, whereas the Patricians had over 300,000,000 people. The land occupied was very much different, with the PP controlling eighty-seven percent of the land mass. The PP had to kill, nevertheless, these were too many people to kill, and therefore, psychology warfare had to play in through social unrest, demonstrations, and riots.

The Patricians had too many people packed into tight areas, which could havoc for a few years at most. Therefore, hit and run were a highly important element in the successful defeat of the Patricians. The planes and ships would use long-range missiles when striking targets in secure areas. The smaller bombs were used for opportune targets. These were the targets that appear to come out of nowhere, nevertheless, would be great hits. An example would be construction vehicles around the factory. This could indicate a future underground factory that would be hard to disable. The PP was fortunate in, they had mountain men from West

Virginia and the Rockies, plus most mining operations in the previous States. The PP was devoting a lot of resources to former mines, shocked at the thousands of miles of great undeveloped deep underground mines. These were pretty much ready to go and would be used to move forces and supply pronounced distances using electric vehicles. This was a logistical nightmare with bottlenecks at the entry and exit points considering the depth of these tunnels. The PP was prioritizing the expansion of the entry and exit elevators, which was in no way as difficult as the original installation. They attempted to keep the original lifts and expand the hole to handle at least two more lifts. These lifts would intersect at thirty to forty feet deep with new loading docks created. This was to prevent all loading from being in the open and thus subject to detection and attack. The more activity underground the greater chance of a successful transport.

These tunnels would be beneficial in whatever union was formed after this war. The future on this continent would be life underground. Notwithstanding, the battle in York City was raging; however, within a few weeks, the source transports began to dwindle. The blockade was a success, causing foreign merchants not to risk a shipment, unless the cost of their lost ships and personnel was included in the deal. This naturally made the cost of the goods way too expensive, even though deals were still made. The Navy would start tracking these ships over 1,000 miles from the coast, and thereby move the appropriate level of force to sink the ship. The drastic drop in ships permitted the PP to go for a one-hundred-percent success sinking rate. The air travel was expanding as the drops were as well. The planes were flying much higher and then would attempt a just about straight drop into the city. Accordingly, the PP adjusted the defense and neutralization of these targets by scanning higher and using powerful Artillery to shoot that far up. Missiles were successfully used during the descent, with surface bombs bombing the runway while the plane was in descent, causing a success drop to fail by crashing into a shattered runway. Baltimore, Washington DC, Boston, was suffering from the barricades and angry over the plane machine-gun fire shattering windows of buildings and vehicles. This was essential to reduce the almost zero heat by permitting cold air to come into the residents. The grocery stores were emptying out, as temperatures began to fly in all four struggling cities. The PP believed the Patricians population was not as hardened as their population was. Solid pressure would melt these snowflakes that never had the social apprehension of reality. The PP was working hard for their concept of a society, one where people worked and did not just lay around collecting free bees, or bitch about slavery, which ended less than two hundred years earlier, ironically, because of the First Civil War. The PP now dealt with the brainwashed snowflakes with a bullet into the head, even before they could get a change to vomit their unrealistic talking points.

Accordingly, the attack on York City was now producing massive riots and demonstrations, to the point the city could not contain or control them. These idiots forced their way through the hand tied, and current unpaid police pushing out of the city. Once outside, they got a taste of reality, as the PP bombed, poisoned, and open machine-gun fire, mowing them down by the thousands. The idiots, still refusing to accept the fact that the PP no longer turned the other cheek kept pushing hard, only to end up tripping over the bodies of those ahead of them to catch a bullet in their head. The breakout demonstrations consisted of eight leaks through the city's fences. This week turned out to be one of the largest single week land based combat massacres by bullets in world history with over four million young people killed by bullets. They were carrying a lot of drugs, so much so that it killed rodents that ate them. The Patricians puppets became uncontrollable by their puppet masters. These young people showed signs of malnutrition and effects from poor hygiene. It must have overloaded their memory capabilities when they discovered the lies that had programmed their brains were indeed lies. York City was now nothing more than a skeleton population of senior government bureaucrats. Chiefs without Indians. The PP military began the total cleansing of the city, with a primary goal of totally destroying and administrative tools the Patricians still had. They had surprised the PP almost daily, and the sources of these surprises needed to be discovered. This had to be a total cleaning with smoke bombs being as much as feasible to pull the people out into the streets. Many of the skyscrapers made this impractical.

PP dogs were unleashed in an attempt to catch more people. The subways had to be inspected. Anything that could serve as a legitimate food was removed. There was no way to remove everything that they were eating, as the categories were unthinkable. The sewer systems were disabled, without electricity, flowing water and treatment chemicals. The PP would need to restore this for basic humane reasons, even though there were no plans to resettle here until well after the war. The massive issue now was to remove the corpse that was everywhere. This was a duty assigned to every remaining resident captured, every single day, until their execution. This was not for punishment; it was an attempt to save what was left of the sanity for the PP. The PP also launched a campaign against the rodents, which had almost taken over the city, feasting on the garbage piled high over the city. The living conditions in this city were so terrible that many believe the Patricians march to their deaths, finding escape from their misery through the comfort of a PP bullet. Many of the rodents would be killed by flame throwers, except for those in hard to reach places, where poison gas would be released. After this, the daunting task of pulling the dead rodents out of these hidden crevices began. This task appeared to grow each day, baffling the PP leadership which began to question the need to kill so many. Nevertheless, York had to fall, and the city was simply the beginning. Bodies of humans, rodents, a ton of garbage was bulldozed into the Atlantic and Hudson Rivers, along with all other rivers in the city. Water and sewage were restored as was special generators. Two entire new PP recovery Armies were developed and deployed to this former glory in a task that experts estimated could take ten years to complete. Precautions such as no food in the city were implemented, causing all Army personnel to eat only in special designated areas. This was essential to gain some sort of progression in this threat that would not die and leave.

Subsequently, the attempts to smuggle goods into this former shell of a civilization hub diminished. This authorized the PP to reassign their east coast blockade forces back to New England, and the Patricians holds from Washington DC, down to Miami. The PP learned the hard way that a slow, steady squeeze would also lead to riots and demonstrations, hopefully at a much less carnage cost. The PP was staging Armies in upper Maine for the push to New York's borders. This would be a push from both sides, as a line would be maintained on the New York border to perform a twofold mission, first was to hold the squeeze from Maine, New Hampshire, and Vermont. The second mission ran into Long Island with the mission of keeping New York separated from New England and form a line to hold the squeeze from the west that would come once, Rochester and Buffalo fell. The delay in capturing York City, forced the PP to reassign the Army's involved with these two commands and simplify the chain of command. This began with assigning seven Armies from Ohio to drive and clean the land from the Pennsylvania border to Buffalo. Five of the Armies would launch from Pennsylvania's southern border with New York spread out from Buffalo to Syracuse. The squeeze worked to unite the PP pockets and disrupt New York's distribution network, especially on 86, 90, 390, and 81. The goal of the push was to create a slow, steady panic, as the water goes out, electricity turns off, and traffic ceases. The coordination with the underground PP elements, and process of bringing them back to the forefront was essential to maintaining the newly freed territory.

The remaining Ohio Two Armies came in from the west and pushed straight into Buffalo. They simply had to establish a blockade outside 90,190, and 290, with help from the Coast Guard to disable the ports and unleash an Artillery storm over Allentown and Unity Island. West Seneca was burned to the ground while en route all the way to Buffalo Creek. The purpose was to send a shock into Buffalo, where they could see the burning fires. The few emergency vehicles attempting rescue were stopped by Artillery fire and then all rescuers executed by snipers. This theater called upon the PP to supply a fleet of submarines to Lake Ontario. The PP was successful in gaining control of all eighteen of the US nuclear submarines, through a slick move by a group of top admirals who ordered the submarines back to the east coast for a post-world maintenance upgrade. The actual upgrade was the removal of the nuclear warheads and these chambers filled with normal underwater torpedoes, which were encased in large nuclear bomb casings. The difference was triggering device that would release the twenty torpedoes each one at a time by the trigger in possession of the firing panel operator. For security reasons, the crew believed they were receiving an advanced nuclear system. Afterwards, the crews were rotated to on shore duty, allowing the fresh rotation to board. These crews were dedicated PP as were the new commanders. All orders were issued Top Secret. The reality was that system upgrades were always performed during crew rotations. It was public knowledge that the nuclear codes had been hacked, therefore, rendering them useless. This appeared unusually logical and an efficient command decision. Moreover, considering the sole comfort during such chaotic times was strong leadership.

Accordingly, the PP deployed these subs throughout the Atlantic and Pacific coasts with orders to sink any ship appearing to be smuggling goods into the barricaded cities. The order was to shoot when within one-hundred percent range, a calculation made by the mechanical panel, and afterwards to exit quickly, first down subsequently away from the coast line. For the New York and England campaigns; they would reassign ten submarines, eight eventually to Lake Ontario. Initially, they had sunk smugglers for York City, which contributions during the PP York City campaign were astonishing. These subs had wonderful sonar abilities. They also had a satellite global surveillance system that could warn them of a ship thousands of miles away, allowing them to meet it, greet it, then sink it. The PP declared to Canada that any Canadian ship in US waters would be destroyed. Basically, they told them to stay out. The PP was not going to chase down ships, board them, and conduct extensive inspections while the smaller sister ship would sail right through. Instead, if they saw a foreign ship in the former state waters, that ship was sunk. Canada complained against this sinking, hinting at declaring war. The PP issued a declaration of war against Canada, ordering the Canadians to stay out of the Saint Lawrence River, the Niagara River, and the Great Lakes. The PP would not sink a ship on the

Canadian side of these waters, except for the Niagara River. The PP could not prevent smuggling in this river; therefore, they did not want any ships in it. The Canadians continued to pass by the blockade, with large fleets from Toronto. Their attempts were met with fierce fighting from under the sea.

The Buffalo campaign was a slow but steady house to house style of fighting, eventually involving two of the Ohio Armies originally dedicated to Rochester. The initial problem was keeping the city blockaded. They would eventually run of dead bodies, without hesitation, and like water on a sponge become a part of the city. Geological experts used their advance equipment to search for a tunnel network. They were correctly able to verify that no complete tunnel system was in place. There were a few small ones that a sniper could control, and warning alarms to notify when someone was in the tunnel. Two submarines patrolled the Niagara River from the Niagara Falls to Woodlawn Beach State Park. They were each reloaded with one-hundred missiles per trip up and back. The missiles took up so much apace that sailors actually strapped them to their bottom bunk and rotated shifts, so they could share the same cot. This was solely for the trip to the falls, because of the high demand for firepower each trip, most cots were cleared by the time they made it to the falls. The submarines were careful where and when they sank the ships. They attempted to hit them when they were close to the shore) Canadian and American. This was so they would not fill up the middle of the river and lose their ability to stay deep under the water. This did, of course, allow many to survive, which did not worry the PP. They considered a sailor without a ship the same as a Policeman without a weapon. Especially when the Canadian sailors were caught in the former New York, were easy targets for PP snipers, notably with the limited number of bridges to cross. The PP stocked the river with 200 sharks. With the daily sinking by an average of 343 ships, they had their continuous invitations to great feasts. The PP built special grayish styrofoam solar powered long, thin shaped like a shark, with a large fin that extended above the surface and moved up and down the river, naturally the length determined by Niagara Falls, with half above and half below. These devices had three high-powered batteries that would unleash a deadly shock wave if touched. They also were in synch with the subs, so they could be moved out of their path. The last feature was they emitted a sonar wave that attracted the sharks, who would tag along with them. Accordingly, this tagging along produced the bite when people were swimming across the river.

Subsequently, the Canadians were not so forgiving for Americans who were caught on their soil. The people were treated as Prisoners of War without Geneva status, only something a foolish government could create for its own benefit. Most were executed, while several were placed in concentration camps in the bitter north, above the Arctic Circle. This policy angered the Patricians, who soon sent patrols across the Dakotas, Montana, and Washington State to capture and steal from the Canadians. The PP, without devoting resources that were needed for their campaigns, would catch and execute any Yellow Cap caught smuggling items from Canada. Later agreements with Canada permitted the PP forces to be augmented with Canadians, which placed a great burden on the Smugglers. The PP did not want these supplies to make it to Patricians's cities, while the Canadians did not want their citizens beaten or killed, then robed. This agreement worked out well for both nations, leaving the PP with an opportunity to make a peace treaty with Canada after the war, and for Canada to threaten war if the Patricians took the country.

Subsequently, this action motivated Canada to outlaw smuggling into PP held territories. They cited the over eighty percent kill rate and that this was too great of a danger to risk. It was creating equally important many widows and orphans, which came with it a high social cost. This moved to free up six of the eight submarines to duty blockading the coastal Patricians cities. The goal was to sink at least fifty-percent of the smugglers. This was enough to put a damper on the fools who risked their lives for this what was turning out to be a huge profit. The Patricians were manipulating the financial markets cancelling all PP accounts and transferring those funds into financing their smuggling operations. The PP tried to cancel every account on the Patricians markets, notwithstanding were not capable to do so. They, therefore, created a new market and recorded the transfers of all PP accounts from the Patricians markets, however, were not able to process the fund's transfer. The lone option was to declare in the United Nations, on territory now under PP control that the PP would never honor any debt incurred by the former states nor would they permit any corporation under their control to trade on the stock exchanges. The traders ignored the Patricians claims of ultimate victory and elected to withdraw from the stock exchanges. This naturally forced the Patricians to absorb the great loss in the bottomed out stocks, leaving them with worthless paper. When the stock market crashed, it took with it the Patricians controlled financial system. Banks closed, as did the skeleton crews in many Federal administrative agencies. The Patricians could no longer plunder the Federal government, with their bloody hungry eyes on the Social security reserves. It was not that the money was locked or hacked. The money was floating in the middle of the ocean with no boat to collect it. This would just be possible with the reconstruction of a new financial market, with the assets to back it up. Now that the PP had the remains of York City, only they had the bricks needed to start this rebuilding process. The PP, however, did not want to pursue this until the Patricians had been removed from the face of the Earth.

The York state residents were resourceful fighters from Buffalo to Syracuse. The PP was hoping to avoid another ocean of rotting bodies buried in tons of garbage as they had in York City. Nevertheless, they were hoping to receive another effective tool from William. In the meantime, this campaign was progressing merely feet per day. All told, the PP now had eighteen Armies fighting in this territory, and were beginning to find it difficult to keep them fed and protected the upcoming winter freeze. Ohio wanted to pull their Armies back for the winter. The PP wanted to keep them in the theater, and prevent a possible city breakout, a condition that could cost additional years of fighting house to house and placing the Rural PP citizen's unneeded danger. The PP realized this move would cost much in the future to restore, yet accepted this as an expense to have something to rebuild. This made it much more difficult for the Patricians to trade on the world market. The previous moves by the PP also removed the dollar as the currency the world was based upon. The PP realized the danger of keeping the dollar afloat, and that under the current Patricians abuse, it would fall so far as never to recover. The PP knew they would have to build a solid foundation and leap to a renaissance through steady and strong growth. They did not want to ever again have the world based upon the dollar. Nor would they ever enter a deal not based on dollars, except for a few national-security needs.

Victory in York was vital if the PP were to have any say in the former nation's foreign policy. The Patricians, who were always extremely global had a strong footing in this area. The fall of York City shook that foundation somewhat. Everyone expected Texas to fall, notwithstanding; no one believed the Patricians, and PP would work together to push out Mexico. The Patricians thought it would open doors for them, and instead the PP changed the locks and zipped away. It was the Patricians underground network that was proving to be trouble. The PP spread their guerrilla units throughout several towns in the areas between Buffalo, Rochester, Syracuse, and limited action around Albany. These soldier's lived with PP in their homes, and even occupied some recently available Patricians homes. They blended in and drove throughout the neighboring villages looking for anything. They would savage for the massive Armies in the upstate area. The Armies also bedded down in the neighboring towns and cities, using Federal Buildings and school houses. Naturally, with a war blaring school was out until after the war. Coupled with the snipers from both parties it was too dangerous to allow children to walk around in public, to schools, which within themselves would prove great targets for shook value. With Buffalo at a standstill and blockades, in effect, around Rochester, the PP shifted two Armies to begin an Artillery shelling of Syracuse. The concept was to shake these cities into the realization enemy forces were in the area to destroy them. The concept was, rather than allowing them to enjoy the winter in their homes; they would be forced to guard and protect their cities, out in the cold. Guerrilla units would send squads in order to perform as snipers picking people off in public areas. An effective tool was to prevent them from congregating. The military commanders agreed they needed to divide their enemy before attacking. This steady flow of battlefield executions also enabled the people to secure the dead bodies, removing them from public areas in an attempt to maintain the chaos and panic.

Meanwhile, the Maine campaign kept fighting throughout the winter, finding the high snows an effective tool for monitoring enemy movements and stifling their mobilization. It was easier to identify the occupied homes, as the vast majority of them used wood burners for heat. They would climb onto the roofs, block the chimneys, and wait until the smoke to choke the residents into the open, where they were executed. The greatest battle during the Maine campaign took place in Burlington, Vermont, where 200,000 New Englanders from New York and all the New England States joined for one massive strike at the PP. The PP, monitoring this assembly by air, went through the farms and collected the heavy machinery to block all entrances multiple times throughout this area. The PP had also commissioned two submarines to travel across the St Lawrence River, through the Richelieu River into Lake Champlain and completely blockade Burlington from gap at Ferrisburgh to Route 89 above Highgate and the 2 bridge connecting Grand Isle and Colchester. The submarines furthermore shelled Plattsburgh, Port Douglass, and Essex, among other small towns that had ports or any form of distribution capabilities that could aid the rebels.

The natural gas lines were compromised as well as the electric grids supporting this area. The blockade tightened the already packed fighting force into cold, dark houses, as the food quickly diminished. The PP deployed their sniper units in this city, as they were permitted to roam the city with little resistances. Any fire from a house was an immediate Artillery shell, as the coordinates and visual was provided by the PP's global satellite system. The snipers, wrapped heavy in bullet-proof garments were targets or bait to compromise the Patricians silence. The PP's trained a new media force, since they bombed NBC, ABC, CBS, MSNBC, and CNN, plus the major newspaper outlets. The PP believed these networks were responsible for this war, and charged all who worked in them as war criminals. The snipers cleaned most of them out, and had the remaining hiding and starving in garbage holes. Garbage out, garbage in. The PP's created new networks, such as AAA, BBB, CCC, and ANN. They were currently training in the buildings of their previous networks. Not all were online yet, considering there were conservative networks thriving. The PP planned to use special teams from these beginning networks as contributors, providing unique reports to the conservative networks, at least fostering the notion of a united media around the world. These crews roamed the two-hundred-mile border from Albany to Buffalo for stories showing the fighting in favor of the PP, which was pretty much everything. Infuriating the world, they also reported the post fighting executions. This backfired into the fight until the last man war that now raged from the Atlantic to the Pacific. This was a factor the PP accepted in their stories to the world, as they also reported many of the Patricians war violations. The PP wanted to show they were serious about creating a view the PP would not yield to the corruption of the Patricians. This war's end with one of the two parties buried or burned.

The PP launched raids against all area hospitals, whereas they would execute patients with spears and swords, steal medical supplies, execute nurses and doctors, before unleashing poisonous gasses into the ventilating systems. They attempted to keep the structure of the hospitals in tack for when the PP would in the future occupy them. The immediate effect was to keep the Yorkers in their homes and suffering from the flus, colds, and pneumonias that were killing them steadily. The snipers were killing an average of 2,713 people per day among the four large cities. The PP needed to bleed this resistance as much as possible until the spring time when the fighting was projected to be fierce. Subsequently, by accident, the PP began searching for and depleting the city's ammunition stockpiles. This ammunition greatly enhanced the PP military efforts throughout the complete campaign. It also permitted the PP to increase the destruction of these cities, an action they originally tried to avoid. The PP broke through the borders of Buffalo and Syracuse during the last months of winter. They gained control over all activities, leaving the people to die slowly in their homes. They employed dogs as they searched through the homes while clearing them. The Main force that ran from Vermont to Long Island provided a solid wall that kept Albany in York State. This provided the guerrilla units perfect targets to execute them filling the fields with rotting bodies.

While maintaining their vice grip on the four cities, the PP proceeded with their massive cleanup of the York State rural areas and unite the PP pockets. These pockets provided the essential intelligence needed to flush the countryside of the Patricians. This created some difficulty among the bucolic residents who tended to live peacefully beside the Patricians. They petitioned the PP to create a program for exemption of rural Patricians, who had no history or accusers of anti-PP actions. With the campaigns borders locked, the national council met and heard the arguments for and against some exemption policy. The PP leaders agreed the plastering of the country side with empty houses and rotting corpses could not be of benefit in the long run. After extensive debate, lasting two days, a plan was formulated and executed. The PP was free of Patricians resistances and dealt with situations head-on and expeditiously. They formed the Hendrick Corstiaensen amnesty program for York state rural residents who could prove their rural address for more than five years. Just as Hendrick Corstiaensen, a Dutch settler first settled over the Albany area, his name would now resettle Patricians as PP's in PP controlled lands. Qualifications required the surrender of all property to the PP, recommendations from five PP citizens, and an agreement to relocate separately from spouse and children. The children were separated from both parents. This was for a five-year period, in which at the end, both parents had to submit new recommendations from at least six PP citizens. The father would then serve four years in PP public service, which could include military and law enforcement. Any anti-PP activity resulted in the execution of the complete family unit. The PP set up special units throughout the former states to receive these men and women. They would be given work and pay for that work, at fair-market wages. This money was usually saved for when the family unit reunited. The program was so successful that over 200,000 adults signed up for it. The PP could not believe how fast this program took hold. It was as if overnight, all of York state, except for four small pockets enclosing Buffalo, Rochester, Albany, and Syracuse remained out of PP control.

The PP brainstormed for an urban amnesty program, however, could never agree to the safeguards needed and the potential social risk. The metropolitan Patricians was too brainwashed to ever be trusted. The rural Patricians were furthermore involved in their communities and local traditions, which were the foundations of their first loyalties. The great news was that none of them ever betrayed the PP. These people strengthened PP pockets among strong Patricians areas, a dangerous risk that paid off for the PP. Spring time approached as the last four cities in the former New York State, now called York state by the PP, prepared to meet their demise. The PP decided to level one of the cities for promoting unconditional surrender between the three remaining cities. They decided to level Rochester and unleashed an Artillery storm that soon left the city in ruins. The press reported this great massacre ensuring the world witnessed it. Rochester was selected because it was between Buffalo and Syracuse, leaving doubt about who would be next. Albany immediately surrendered. The PP tried something new; they baited the people with food and transported them to local smaller cities. The press reported what was to be unofficially called the Albany rural amnesty. The people were seen singing and enjoying themselves as they walked to the neighboring cities. This final step was not released by the press as they were all executed. PP citizens would put on the Yellow Caps and shown living happily among the PP in these secluded rural areas. Either way, the PP took possession of Albany, and was quickly able to bring it back on line. They needed a stronghold in the area that would in the future provide a launching station against Boston.

Syracuse fell a few weeks later, yet did not agree to an unconditional surrender. They left the surrender up to each community. This led to a summer of bitter fighting and massive human suffering as the PP left no person living, with the lone chance to earn a few extra weeks of life was for those who cleaned up and burned the dead bodies spread throughout the city. Buffalo was the strangest of the four cities in that the PP tested William's latest city bug also water bound. This bug was much more devastating than the previous York bug. The new bug took three weeks to kill its host and spread by air and touch. These sick people needed extensive medical attention, a task that crippled the city's fighting forces. The city became so weak that when the Ohio Army's, wearing biological protection uniforms entered the city, they saw the rifles laying in the streets beside large piles of bodies. The city did not have enough fuel to burn these bodies, although piles of broken furniture were found nearby. The PP unleashed an Army of flame throwers to burn anything that may have the virus beside it. Fortunately, William had invented a cure for this virus, which was mass-produced and given for all people within one-hundred miles. All fabric was collected and sprayed with a special airborne version of William's cure. The fear was so great for this virus that the victory celebration for the complete control of York state was held in Jamestown, York almost sixty miles south of Buffalo. This was a significant campaign for the PP, as they did what no nation believed they could do and that was brought down the greatest stronghold of the Patricians. The PP was now a major force to be considered when considering the rebirth of the previous union. Many leaders regretted so much bloodshed was spilled for this once proud land. The Patricians had successfully brainwashed what was alleged to be an intellectual powerhouse of the former states. The PP celebration was short lived, as they now had to reshuffle their Armies and submarines to support the raging battle that ranged from sea to bloody sea. York proved one thing, and that was this war was going to be fought to the last man, and would no longer witness the PP turning the other cheek.

# CHAPTER 04

# THE RACIAL DIVIDE

The shocking turn of Florida over to the PP by the Cubans put the Patricians back on their feet. All the intelligence they had created did not even come close to a prediction this wrong. The Cubans did not lie down and allow the Patricians to walk over them. What even sent further waves through Washington, DC, the city of the Patricians, was how Cuba jumped in and executed those who done their brothers and sisters wrong. The Patricians were disturbed by how many Black people were refusing to wear the Yellow Caps. There was a great danger the Black race was realizing the centuries of abuse and bondage the Patricians had made them suffer. They had buried in history, how the Republicans divided the nation in the first Civil War to flood the fields with blood for their freedom. They also buried how the Patricians fought against president Johnson's and his civil rights legislation, even though the Republicans voted overwhelming for his bills, at a rate close to one-hundred percent, while merely a handful of Patricians helped their president pass this legislation. The Patricians immediately launched a nationwide campaign that painted the PP as haters of minorities and at war to strip the other races of their civil rights. When the Patricians confessed to supporting a new world order that would free Americans from borders and open all the world's markets to American businesses. They fell way short on the 'Free Trade' because the other nations would send their goods to America with zero customs, which, for the most part, kept their prices' way below the American products. The Americans, who was selling out their neighbors bought cheaper foreign goods. The increased the unemployment, as the jobs went where the Patricians wanted them, and that is overseas. These foreign businesses absolutely paid the Patricians for the support they provided. Another hidden force was the powers which were dedicated to one united world without borders. Relocating factories to overseas places was simply one important part in this puzzle. The continual 'diversity' push was a disguise for 'to hell with America.' They were surprised to discover that many decided it was time for America to be number one once more.

A mysterious cult lay hidden in the world, a society of wealth that bypassed borders. Their lone power lay in the control of the world's pecuniary resources. Their financial power could launch missiles, put men on the moon, secretly create pandemics, and starve nations. The world was a game board, as they would trade nations, expand projects, and plan how to continue to control the world. They needed checks and balances to keep their ants running in circles. While opponents continue running in circles, they were kept at a safe distance. Another advantage of keeping your pawns running in circles is they remain spinning, not able to maintain focus, as even though the target appears to be running, it is actually staying in place, and as the opponent chases a perceived escaping target, they are, in reality, running into the opponent who disposes of them with ease. Confusion is a valuable weapon; it gives the contributor overwhelming and absolute control, while they continue to observe the reality, while their victim struggles with an overload in sensory input losing all sense of reality. The new counterfeit reality provides the perfect situation for the Provider to gain his or her desired effect. When you cannot determine what you are seeing is real, then supplemental deceitful input create the perception of true reality. An additional powerful tool provided by these rotating truths is the possible explanations, each based on a perceived reality. The opposing parties hold their perceived reality as a truth, with no comprehension of an alternative truth. Any who disagree become their enemies of reality, and therefore, dangerous for their existence. Compromise and co-existence are no longer conceivable.

This world control society which was also known as the Providers controlled the pieces on their planning board. The pieces on their boards were producing unstable variables. As their world moved through different development stages, their input needs changed as well. The industrial age needed people, to feed the factories. These factories created environmental factors that threatened to hamper the human population needed to feed these factories. The initial industrial revolution did not supply all the machinery needed for the different industries; an example was the agriculture needs. Even as late as the 21$^{st}$ century, humans were needed to harvest agriculture products. Each century produced different challenges. The 21$^{st}$

and 20<sup>th</sup> centuries faced a specialized work force, with each specialty demanding a range of compensations, with an agreed minimum needed for those belonging to that society. Even without the human force needed to produce this product, the demand was still there. Unfortunately, with agricultural products if the market does not receive it at a price range previously believed fair, social unrest could occur. The Providers needed to find a solution, which they found easily as it was in front of them. Their pawns from Mexico needed work, at any cost, therefore the Providers pulled the strings to their controlled puppet politicians and essentially removing the southern borders and allowing the abused masses from Mexico in the western States to harvest the agricultural products. They were supposed to go back to Mexico after they finished their work, nevertheless, this is not happening. Even though the work was too severe for the current population, they were willing to do this, which meant they were willing to continue suffrage in order to work their way into this new opportunity. Morality was out of the window, they were here and this was theirs. The greedy agricultural owners did all they could to foster this belief, in the hopes of keeping their pawns on their game board.

The 16<sup>th</sup> and 17<sup>th</sup> offered other challenges, with
the Providers exploring new opportunities to increase
their supremacies. Europe was exploring opportunities
throughout the world. The Americas offered vast land
and resources, and easy prey in clearing any humanoid
ownership claims. The African continent offered
immense opportunities, nevertheless; their social
networks were more militant in structure, making
confrontational exploitation a potentially economical
risky venture. The Providers never considered loss of
life as a reasonable cost unless it involved people they
owned. Methods to gain ownership evolved over the
centuries, culminating in the easiest method in the
21<sup>st</sup> century and that was through credit cards. The
consumers paid for everything with their credit cards.
If they were between jobs, out came the cards. Most
importantly, if they became hungry, they pulled out
their cards and were fed. This is the most important
concept when controlling the masses, and that is to
keep them fed. When they become starving, social
rules vanished. This is the rule for all flesh, such as
even the most domesticated animals will attack and eat
their masters when reaching a critical stage of hunger.
To show the wisdom of the Providers with the creation
of credit cards we can look at the key benefits they

provide. First, the Providers create the need and then the continual upgrades. I can never remember how many times Tide has a new and improved version. Removing patience with an expectation of immediate gratification. In a market where they can merely hope for five to six percent earnings on investments, rate going up or down based on risks. Credit cards could easily earn four to five times that amount, plus the consumer had the buying power to purchase the products flowing off their production lines.

The opportunities in the 16th and 17th centuries were not as difficult to control. The Providers simply concentrated on the Pope, and the Kings. They also mingled with the Muslims only to the extent to keep pressure on the Europeans. An external pressure is always great in maintaining compliance. The Providers could not pass up on the opportunity to feed the European markets with new products from the potentially unlimited resources from the Americas. The problem existed in the killing of the Native Americans, reducing the potential exploitable workforce, and the hatred between these races could not be controlled without complete genocide. This is where Africa came into play. These warring tribes practiced a custom since ancient times, and that is taking slaves from their defeated foes. What changed now was a test for the foundation of a worldwide market. European traders would purchase the slaves from their African owners, ship them to the America's and sold to plantation owners who used them to produce their agricultural products, much of which was shipped back to Europe, who enjoyed the affordable prices, while condemning the plantation owners use of slaves, yet still supporting this network with their financial support. Even though the Native Americans were victims of the European-Americans, they were successfully able to unleash one of the killers upon humanity, and that was tobacco. Tobacco flooded into Europe along with cotton making slavery an important component in this economic process.

The Providers put the slaves in the Americas, using their belief; these slaves would be treated not much different with their American owners as compared to their African owners. Except for the Israelites, few experiences with slavery have turned out favorably. Unlike previous civilizations, the early States were divided in lifestyles and customs, complicated by the great distances between the States. The northern States held on to the more traditional European values, whereas, the southern States evolved their culture around their commerce. The age of revolutions and the decrease in monarchies, twisted a lot of the Provider's holds causing them to jump back, and rethink their plans. The divided States chose to fight a war over the slavery, a process only available because of their economic independence. Either way, this would change the face of the agricultural economy and disrupt the cultural and social network among the States. The four years plus war challenged the foundation of this New World Democratic experiment, nevertheless, came out successful in the long run. This would begin another challenge in history and that would-be housing two races within one border. Initially, this was not a problem, as the whites refused to share their resources with the blacks. Actually, the liberal whites who complained so much about the immorality of slavery were now faced with the requirement to share their public with these former slaves. The true situation was that it was not just a white race; it was many people melting from many ethnic groups into one race. The whites had their hierarchy established by wealth. Still, considering the unbelievable wealth of the Providers, this ensured no extremely few people would ever bunch shoulders with them. The former slaves were forced to jump in line if they wished to become a part of this cold northern situation. The south just did not have the economic basis to absorb the freed slave population.

The Providers had an opportunity to play on this potential division, and that was to lay the foundations for a race card. The whites and blacks were killing the Red man completely ignoring them as human. They both pushed the Asians back as much as they could, fearing them as a threat to the limited resources. Accordingly, a solution had to be found if humanity were to continue. There were those who projected there would not be enough food to feed the world as they entered into the 20th century. No matter how rich the Providers became, time could only be money if they had a workforce to create and consume their products. This is where technology jumped in order to save the day. Machines began to appear that could replace humans. The cotton fields and large farms began operating again, this time much faster and with fewer humans. Cars appeared, using a previously disposed byproduct of oil when producing kerosene, as their fuel. This made the work force more mobile and able to work and live apart. This national wealth created a greater hunger for power. Accordingly, control over this wealth depended upon acquiring votes. The most effective method to capture votes is through creating division within the population. Julius Caesar believed in dividing his enemies before conquering them. Racism was the perfect tool to create this division, considering once a party got a strong grip on a minority; they could count on their votes, even if they had produced no visible results.

The Patricians targeted the Black rate, believing them to be weak financially, not educated, easy to fool and deceive. The problem was their lack of financial resources, although if they got the Patricians in power, the power would create great streams of wealth. The important thing was to create a false narrative, one that could be easier to control. They kept the blacks in the ghettos, fearing that once they began to mingle with whites they would drift towards the PP. The Patricians had positioned themselves as the one who cared about Americans, the ones who were going to take from the rich and give to the poor. It was the giving to the poor that turned into a stumbling block, as they believed it would be to a greater degree for all involved if this money went to them, so they could manage it better. To ensure their control stayed strong they had to keep the blacks poor, while at the same time be able to blame it on the PP. The Patricians had mastered the skill of performing corruption and blame it on the PP. The Patricians would force an administrative agency, all of which they had installed bureaucrats as puppets, to issue a false report on a certain project, and then precisely before it was made public, release to the press how they discovered what the PP had done. The evidence was the fact this action was done, and the PP was just pretending not to know about it. The act of them claiming not to know, was, in fact, a lie. By branding the PP as liars, it placed doubt in the public's eyes that the PP would ever tell the truth. The Patricians would continue to include this charge and the evidence of the lying in their talking points to such a degree that it sounded believable. The Patricians tightened their grip on this minority, created fear of the PP, and walked away with critical financial resources that were badly needed by the people.

The Patricians had established their pathway to power and now desperately wanted to keep it. They would need a twist on the racism and a method to divide the white majority. One method created was called affirmative action, a law which made it legal to discriminate against the majority, while making it punishable for the majority who did not discriminate against the majority. The law required businesses to hire unqualified people based solely on race. This did nothing to harmonize the races. In fact, it created an entitlement feeling in the minorities that the work created and owned by the whites really belonged to them. It existed, give it to me, or I will have the government take it from you. The Patricians had their ways around this. One popular method was to use other minorities for their quotas. Another part of their plan to keep their base divided was called segregation, in which they would move minority children from their districts to the more affluent basically PP neighborhoods. This drove a wedge deep into their hearts, dangling their Patricians puppets in front of them, while even at the same time making their political rivals even pay for their puppet's education. The Patricians were destroying the principles of capitalism, pushing hard for a move towards socialism. They believed that everyone should be treated the same and equal, unless they were successful, at which time they were no longer entitled to those benefits, but instead had to share them with others would have not earned them in a similar fashion. The Patricians put the minorities in the affluent areas, so they could instill the perception this was how the majority lived by taking from them or even worse not eagerly giving them. Notwithstanding, the PP was funding these minority areas unaware of the corruption of the Patricians stealing these funds ensuring the racial tensions burned.

The ability to turn truths into lies can seldom lead to a positive outcome. The Patricians pushed civil rights and secretly took down their leaders, blaming it on the PP. This was the standard method they used to operate. Keep the minorities confused and hungry, being fed only with lies. They would have to throw up a few of their own if they were not complying with their narrative. The Kennedy' provided proof that if you push too hard against corruption, you could land in the Patricians back yard. Such near misses could no longer be risked. They got their puppet back in the White House, one who would keep Vietnam going so his wife could profit from the reconstruction. This is when they began to fine-tune their do an action and accuse the PPs of doing it. They were even able to have a special counselor hire top Patricians attorneys to chase a false Russian intrusion narrative while bleeding the nation of DOJ resources, while diverting public attention from their obvious crimes. Their ability to manipulate and instigate the minorities kept these allusions alive. Twisting small words to create a negative false narrative. The Patricians became so effective at manipulating the blacks; they opened the southern border and brought in approximately eleven million illegal Hispanic immigrants to add to their strongly supported Hispanic voting base. This would provide them an even stronger voting base causing them to mount a tremendous corrupt campaign to legalize them. The Patricians ran into problems with this when the PP's objected to it. In fact, President Hiplinger ran hard on the vision of a secure nation once more, and control over immigration, notwithstanding finding it difficult to implement his promises with resistance from not only the Patricians, but also rogue PP, who would soon get their due reward.

The Patricians opened the competition up now between the minorities. Each minority presented a limited challenge. The blacks were becoming not only established by contributing members of society. This did not fare well among all in their group, as many held those who were moving up were betraying them. The second largest minority group the Patricians grabbed around the neck were the Hispanics. They were able to instill a belief, as they had with the blacks, of entitlement, and that a little thing such as citizenship should not be disqualifiers for their permanent residence. They complained that such a little thing as the country you were born in should not determine your nationality. This was the sort of mentality the Patricians needed in the voting booths. The Patricians passed every law; they could give more to these illegal residents, to include free education, social benefits, and even medical care. The Patricians did not support a strong American Military, even though the Military did hire numerous minority people. This is where the Providers exerted their pressure because they controlled the world, and did not need a powerful America going around blowing up the infrastructures they were using the Americans to finance. The Patricians preferred to provide medical benefits to illegals and deny the much-needed curative care to the veterans who suffered in combat defending the American interests. This caused suffering for both the minority and white veterans. The Military did not appreciate the budget cuts levied by the Patricians, nor did they agree with the Patricians appeasement policies as they permitted Red lines to be crossed and nuclear deals violated.

The Patricians were effective in keeping the race wars boiling between the minority races. They Hispanics were crowded into the ghettos alongside the blacks and forced to fight for limited and dwindling resources. The friction between these groups forced them to create their own Military powers through gangs. The gangs used lethal force to protect their people and to avenge any attacks or destruction of their property. Blood was the lone thing that could permit these subcultures, their foothold and foundation for continued survival. The gangs provided another consequential Patricians function, and this was the distribution of illegal drugs. The drug trade was so prominent to keep these minorities in compliance with their delusional theories. A sober brain was at risk of detecting obvious misinformation and lies. An interesting factor that is often claimed centers the whites against all the other races listed as minority within this union. Not all the races were chained to the Patricians troughs, basically because they had powerful homelands. These included the Asians, with channels in Japan, South Korea, and China, to name simply a few. Another source of the conduits was the Europeans and Muslims. The major difference was that only the non-European Hispanics challenged the established laws and openly invaded the States, claiming the American dream as their dream. Patricians would continue to argue these people were entitled to the American dream, disregarding the painful lack of work for both the whites and blacks. Unfortunately, although by Patricians design, the unemployment rate was disastrous for the blacks. No social climate can survive with so many idle hands who were as entitled to the American dream as any other legal citizen in America. They were left standing among the shadows, their hopes and dreams going to the Hispanics.

Accordingly, the Patricians struggled effectively to mold the Black culture different than that of the mainstream American culture. This promoted the division needed to keep the Patricians the holders of their votes. There actually should not have been that many differences between the Black culture and the white culture, having received their civil rights, plus the civil rights of the white people, (affirmative action and segregation) with just about a half of a century to blend into one culture, just as the Asians, and Europeans, and small groups of the Muslims had done. The natural force between selling Christianity and adopting sharia law was simple, money and plenty of money, which the Muslims had. This would have been beyond the control of the PP if not for a division between the Muslim nations, which saw absolute chaos reign in the 21st century. This will be discussed later in this report, for now it is sufficient to claim that other ethnic groups did mingle into the American culture. It could no longer be claimed this was a white's exclusive club, because blacks were front and center, in sports, in medicine (Ben Carson), TV, Hollywood, and music, to name just a few. They were also strongly represented in education, legal, Law Enforcement, and judicial networks. Many claimed it should be 50/50, even though the blacks represented seventeen percent of the population. The point is that only those who moved into the mainstream neighborhoods absorbed the culture, while the ones remaining in the 'hoods' were forced to unite against the Hispanics, who were eagerly wanting their bite of America and willing to do whatever it took to obtain this.

The pressure of the Black culture remaining in the hoods grew to such a level that something had to give. This is when Black on Black crime exploded. Blacks were killing each other and committing crimes on whomever they could target. The Hispanics had some degree of defense, and at a minimum would strike back at whom they believed to attack them. This of course left many innocents to pay for the crime of another Black member. The point is that the blacks were killing each other, and someone had to pay for this. The Patricians, using their power over the Media, created a false narrative the police was killing the blacks. Fear in the police would further withdraw the Black culture, and it would force them to accept the criminal network, that would now be needed for survival. Any information that was contrary to this false narrative was buried far from the public's eyes. The rate of Black crime was high above that of the other races, with the lowest being among the Asians. Black residents were stealing and killing their neighbors. Many were trying to get the drugs they needed to survive, a process created and maintained by the Patricians, who even warned the PP was going to stop drugs flowing into the country, a promise that President Hiplinger promised during his campaigns. Strangely, no one thought it was the druggies which were rioting as savages to keep their fix, which is a normal survival mechanism to maintain an addiction. The point is that a suspect Black person was a higher risk to engage in criminal behavior than a white (except for Hispanic) person. If the people were going to keep the Black neighborhoods safe, they had to be proactive. Remember, the Patricians had to keep the blacks divided to keep their votes and prevent the ability to challenge their falsehoods.

To keep the power of the falsehoods fed, the Patricians and Media, knowing that the law of averages would have produced a white cop killing a Black person. They needed this to be recorded, thus the previous President Bin Laden gave away free cell phones. This is exactly what a family that cannot afford food needs, a hefty cell phone bill. Simple editing could paint an entirely different picture. The Media did not report the high rate of Black cops killing Black violators, which is attributable to a keener understanding about the factors at play. Additionally, there were far more Black cops killing white people. The crime stats reported an increase of Black on white crime. White people were a safe target, because they could motivate the Media to bat in defense for them. The Media had one agenda, and that was to punish the white cop that was placing his life in danger to protect the Black neighborhoods. The Media got what they wanted, as the police stopped going after the criminals and only responding when there was no way around it. The neighborhoods were dangerous and deadly once more, as the drugs flowed unhindered and the young Black people found a lack of employment opportunities. Just where the Media and Patricians wanted them, especially with the Patricians pushing for beans rather than bullets in the Federal budget. This meant more money for social programs, or basically temporary exploiting the minorities with minimum paying, high overhead, temporary jobs, and less money for the

Military. The PP was taking the minorities money to pay for the Military, when the opposite was, in fact, true. Remember, a strong Military was not needed by the Providers since they controlled all the pieces from the board. The narrative that the PP was making the blacks suffer and sending police in order to kill them were cementing the Patricians vote. They had the Media to repeat this falsehood enough times to make it sound true.

The feeling of being used and treated unfairly was not limited to the Black people, it was shared by all people from a land led by false Media and corrupt Patricians. The nation was being fed a narrative that defied all reality. Any examination into the facts revealed that things did not add. Then, as if by a miraculous event, a white cop shot a Black criminal trying to attack him. The false Media has the nation, raising both arms and begging not to be shot. Alarming that such a lie would take hold and flood the nation, when the witnesses, the vast majority Black denied this happened. It did not matter, immediately after hearing the truth, they would turn around and raise their arms and say, "Don't shoot." Once they had this notion planted, there was nothing that could change their mind, and even though an independent Court reviewed the facts and did not recommend charges be pressed, the blacks turned on the white cop, who was not a part to this process, as they denied it was countless other blacks who refused to lie and told the truth. The Fake Press and Patricians continued to push their lies as the pressure led to riots and the immediate destruction and looting of public property. They believed if they could get their hands on it and steal it, no retribution would occur. When the smoke settled, the police began reviewing tapes and a limited amount of prosecutions began, just enough to keep the insurance companies appeased. The trouble arose that many businesses did not have insurance or could not get insurance based upon previous civil demonstrations. The businesses were no more going to take out loans and great risks to scrape a living in such a risky environment. The result was they could no longer go down in the corner, and purchase convenience items, yet now had to get on a bus and ride across town to purchase these items. The Patricians were quick to blame this on the PP, who was discriminating against minorities by not opening business in their neighborhoods.

Other riots, let loose throughout the country as the Media went to war against Law Enforcement. The Patricians needed to cripple the police's ability to protect not only the minorities but also the PP. Their ability to stop their opponent's speech as true protection of free speech by advancing a new label of hate speech. Hate speech is any speech that does not advance the Patricians policies. Sadly, the brainwashed Patricians masses could not understand this. The drug-induced university snowflakes would never allow anyone to speak before them, unless they were in total agreement. The Patricians's destroyed the university environment, raising the university fees far beyond their reasonable value. The Patricians's further locked their grip on this poor future generation by sinking them in astronomical student-loan debt, which was nothing more than a financial conduit for the student's buried in high debt into the corrupt pockets of university administrative officials and of course the Patricians who funneled public funds into the abyss of university monetary record keeping. The blood that flowed through the university veins was pumped by their professors, who became totally detached from reality. A professor who appeared to support corporeal violence to the sitting president was praised, while a professor who did not echo verbatim the Patricians policy was subject to physical abuse from the students. The university students felt emboldened as the minorities would flagrantly destroy public property and become copy cats as well. The students actually had help from non-student thugs, who wore masks to conceal their identities and would candidly commit violence on anyone who would openly oppose them.

The quintessential force needed to maintain the national racial chaos before the second Civil War was to thrust the Fake news, and to provide the explanation for what was truly happening. Their puppets could no longer interpret events, except for identifying the PP. The lone hope for the young, minorities to survive in the open society was to obtain a productive university education. The possibility of such an education not any more resisted, as they were undergoing a uniform brainwashing process. Now they could stand beside the whites and claim to have the insight into the evils of the PP, yet only to discover the promises of a prosperous future fade as they competed for part-time work at McDonald's. There was no work because the Patricians presidents had given everything away to foreign nations. The jobs all went overseas. The horrors of seeing all young people face a cold, hungry future as, they remained living with their parents, a condition not welcomed if their parents were PP. An epidemic hit the nation that ignored racism and that were drug overdoses. Parents were burying their children. This latest string of addictions found many beginnings in their parents' medical cabinets. These self-entitled with their victim mentality adolescents downed these pills as if there were no tomorrow, only to end up needing more of these drugs and falling deeper into the depths of addiction. The hopelessness of these deceived young people, without regard to race demanded a swift and powerful retaliation. This became a battle cry the PP accepted as they began to muster of the nerve to begin the war to save their children, regardless of race.

The Patricians capitalized on the notion that you do not need racism to divide the races, you simply need the perception of racism to create the environment to become anti-social. An example was in a Virginian city called Char...... e. A white supremacy group was going to join with other groups and protest the removal of a Civil War monument. The local Patricians mayor worked with his police to ensure the two forced could not avoid each other. They planned the routes and pushed the two groups, so they would end up facing each other. The anti-fascist group (that would have made Hitler proud) took out their clubs and began hitting the opposing group, inflicting deadly harm and violence, while the so-called bad people were attempting to defend themselves. The police ignored this criminal behavior, allowing it to escalate, while the Media eagerly fed their hunger for violence. Their greed for blood, mistakenly filmed the actual events showing the masked anti-fascist denying the whites their right to assemble, as was previously approved by the local government. With the violence causing serious injury and the group receiving no protection, they had to do something to survive, thus in haste and foolishness, as is often the case when the feeling of death, a young man jumped in his vehicle and rushed down the street, killing a protestor that fell with a crash with his vehicle. The public immediately went crazy, in that how can white supremacy fight against Black supremacy. President Hiplinger called it like the news video showed it, the Black supremacy anti-fascist came that day to use violence. The local government, set the stage so they could see the white supremacy group suffer great injustice. They promoted the Patricians philosophy that Black supremacy is normal and American, nevertheless, white supremacy is fascist. Therefore, the whites had to live in shame for being white and entitled. If not for the corruption of the Providers and Patricians, this misconception would have fallen war much sooner than it actually did.

President Hiplinger was able to break through barriers that many did not believe possible. He was the first president never to have served in the Military or occupied a public office. Instead of signing the back of government checks, he spent his life signing the front of paychecks for the tens of thousands of jobs he created. He paid and treated his employees extremely fair, so fair that they did not join unions. Even his political opponent wanted to get unions in his establishments, so the Patricians could pull the strings that provided these jobs. His employees refused to go union. This, within itself should have provided the proof needed that those who worked for him knew they had good jobs and job stability. When you have a smart employer, you do not want to shake the waters. Even with this obvious testament, the Fake News and Corrupt candidate dug deep into his history and found something they could twist. They searched hard to find something to shake his great record with minorities, depending solely on illegal immigrants who were afraid they could get deported. Think about it, if you trespass into a store, you should have to worry about more than simply being removed. The concept of illegal should suggest time behind bars. President Hiplinger advanced the argument that it was time to leave the plantation. The

Patricians had run the cities, which were nothing more than prisons for the blacks, many for more than one-hundred years. It was time for a change. How do you fight crime and poverty? Not with free bees but instead with real jobs. Opportunity to become invested in the society as equals. This shook a few of the Black leaders, especially the religious ones to guide their flocks off the plantation. Therefore, just as Moses led the slaves out of Egypt, it was time for many of the Black leaders to lead their flocks into the Promised Land.

Consequently, this did not fare well with the Patricians, who began to yell louder that it was raciest to provide equal opportunities to blacks. The PP was deceiving them, in an attempt to take away their free bees. One candidate even suggested the government gave free college for all and free medical benefits to all. He would make the richest people pay for it, after all, they should pay their fair share. The sad fact was they were already paying much more than their equitable share, and the time to lose everything was not at hand. They would simply move their capital off shore and rebuild in other nations where they would get a fair deal. The Patricians did not worry about this, as the businesses would still fall under the Provider's control. The Patricians did not care what price their puppets would pay, because all they needed to do is blame it on the PP. As long as they kept the PP defending themselves, they could launch new falsehoods through the greatest of all discriminators, the press. President Hiplinger called out the press. The press claimed he was challenging the freedom of the press. He clarified that the press could not be given their own sets of facts. He won American hearts by communicating directly with them through social Media. No longer would the public receive its 'truth' from a lying Media. He could fire off a social Media message and within seconds, over sixty million Americans would know his mind. The frantic press would spend the day spinning their wheels trying to explain what the president said. It was too late, because his followers already knew his mind, as the truth was not Black or white.

Correspondingly, the point in which the Patricians had shifted the definition of racism proved to be a tool they employed with brilliance. An action may be normal between members of different races, yet the trouble makers make this racism by virtue of the tone. It was always a winless situation. Another example, found President Hiplinger while in China learned that three Black players were arrested for shoplifting. The Chinese caught them Red handed on multiple thefts. Accordingly, they were taken to prison. The Chinese take shoplifting seriously and usually lock these thieves up for at least ten years. China is a communist country that protects its people. Items on display in stores are the property of the store owner. It is not a special challenge for the elite privileged. These dipshits had been brainwashed into thinking they could behave in China as they behaved in America. This was disappointing in that they were basketball players for a very prestigious state university. Fortunately, President Hiplinger was a billionaire businessman who knew the art of the deal. He simply leaned over to the President of Communist China and said, "We have a situation where three idiot Americans shoplifted. I sure could use your help in getting them back," or words to this effect. They were in a relaxed and casual situation. Therefore, the Chinese president agreed to free them, and our president brought them back. Asian culture strives not to be like the Westerners, who have low self-control and no respect. These three dipshits shit on the American pride and honor. Amazing that basketball players could not expand their concept of teamwork beyond their playing Court, and become part of the American team. These are basic manners; you do not go into a communist country and shit on them, because they do not have to be politically correct and ignore it. This must have been a shock when they snapped their fingers, and the Chinese ignored them.

President Hiplinger saved these young Black men. For him, it was his sacred duty, and he jumped in for these boys without reservation. He did what a president of the people would try to do. A difference existed; he transpired immediately successful. So, now all he had to do was face the Fake Press and Patricians, who were shaken by this World Stage Class Act. He displayed that he could influence a communist government to release American Prisoners. Several Nations take pride in the American Prisoners they capture, and the hell they can put them through. President Hiplinger overcame the barriers of racism and gained the freedom of three boys who were also a different race. These Presidents displayed race-free eyes and hearts, even overcoming the eastern civilization versus western civilization. Other issues on the table included trade, intellectual rights, and a Nuclear North Korea. The president had many large and somber issues, and he has to take off his serious face and display a begging face. Common sense suggests this weakened his hand. The boys went back to their team, who publicly suspended them from this team.

Believing they were entitled to this defense the boys remained quiet while President Hiplinger traveled to two additional countries before returning home from a wonderful mission. Naturally, the press downplayed it and had a few false stories to seed confusion. One that was interesting was him emptying a carton of fish food to some fish. The Fake Media cut an edited video attempting to paint the president as being rude. The Peoples press caught them and proved this was a false news hit, as they also showed the Japanese president dumping his fish food. Patricians Deception busted once more.

Consequently, the three thieves caught in China returned to America, saying nothing, and just acting normal. President Hiplinger had accomplished a great feat and felt hurt that it was brushed under the rug. If he had not done this, the press would have crucified him as being racist. When he questioned their formal courtesy, the press came rushing back in order to start their racism turmoil. The press fell back on their backs when the three boys came out to thank the president. This was what a socially responsible member should do. Things appeared to be settled, until the trouble makers began by bringing one of the player's father who claimed the president hand done nothing special, and that shoplifting is no big deal. He was a minority that had the minority you-owe-me or I am entitled mentally. President Hiplinger came back hard on this one. He had saved those boys from over ten years in prison. He rightfully challenges the child rearing provided by this Media attention the full and sad examples of a father. His you-owe-me, and it is your job attitude offended the PP. The PP was forced to take an honest picture of the racism in America. This constant demand to provide favoritism for just a few of the minority groups and to deny rightfully fully qualified applicants because they are white.

The Patricians crippled the justice system, especially insane judges, crippled the legislative structure, with total obstructionism and zero cooperation, divided the population through racism, tied the hands of Law Enforcement, turned Federal Agencies into political opponent hit squads, took away the freedom of the press, converting them into delusional liars, plus played the minority and race card to the bloodiest extent imaginable, and then to the most extent possible the sex card and the nail to the cross with religious outright destruction. Keep your pawns and enemies divided so that any dissension can be quickly subdued. The smaller the groups and the multiple qualifications into other groups added to the ease in ability to control. An example is a Christian, Black male, qualifies as a minority as a Black and gender as a male and religion as a Christian. The more deeply rooted in American culture, the more divisive characteristics. Muslims were, for the most part, one race, one religion, and the roles to each sex clearly defined by their law. Another rich source of power for the Patricians was their bonding as one unit with one voice. They voted as one, placing party loyalty over the promises made to their voters. Let the slums suffer, by simply taking the money and then focusing blame on the PP. Another great tool that used the corrosion of loyalty and honor was the Federal Agencies leaking information. The leaks were always in favor of the Patricians. Any leaker not under their control had to be Russian, no exceptions. WikiLeaks helped expose the amount of Patricians corruption, as their refined response was this had to be the Russians working with the PP to harm the Patricians. So, in other words, any information which proved the Patricians was corrupt was not for the public to know, thereby it must be criminals who were releasing this information. Subsequently, the Patricians controlled Federal Agencies actually broke laws by leaking confidential government information, such as President Hiplinger's conversations with foreign leaders.

Consequently, the attack on Christianity was a slow, gradual process in the beginning. First, take prayer out of school. Next, downplay the role of Churches by expanding the social temptations, making compliance with religious morals difficult. The trouble with evil is that once it has you trapped, you can never leave. The removal of basic cultural morality, plus the social campaigns to promote looser morals, and the constant desire for females to get rich quick by teasing, filming, and blackmailing. Just as my mother always said, "It takes two to tangle." The temptation for a taste of power brings forth the most aggressive and compromising people. In the heat of darkness, the trap is set and the male ego to reaffirm their appeal to the opposite sex, and their power ego sets in, and they eat the forbidden fruit. Oh, in what manner they enjoy how they are so far beyond the rules as imposed on others. Then the cat gets out of the bag, usually after they fail to pay the blackmail. These allegations range from outright groping to smiling when they say good morning. Someday, we may have to look how other cultures handle these temptations. The Muslims keep their women covered, from head to toe.

Western Civilizations promote their women walking around almost naked with their breasts, with the legal exception of their nipples, exposed. Swimming suits, where the buttocks are completely exposed, except for a thin string that if for all practical purposes is invisible. As a society, it is unbelievable that so much limited resources were devoted to controlling pornography and prostitution, which promoted the concept of perversion and permissiveness. Afterwards, to be told that the interactions between a man and a woman will be controlled and defined by that specific female with that particular male created such a dynamic sea of quicksand that made even the most primitive of functions appear to be as glimpses into the deepest edges of the future.

Another powerful tool the Patricians tried to take advantage of was the tremendous power that women now held. Just as all the other groups which started to enjoy an increased power, the women took the ball and ran for the finish line. Any slight obstacle that was even perceived to threaten this journey faced the maximum unleash of power they could inflict on any foolish obstructionists. The women now wanted to rule all parts of society. This time, they pushed hard to keep their male counterparts subdued. Society was redefining itself into a culture that no longer needed men. Notwithstanding, men were not required for marriage. Women could marry women. Mother Nature; however, instilled certain safeguards to continue the normal phases of evolution, with the male figure extremely effective in instilling discipline. This is not to say that women cannot instill discipline. It is to say that on the average, spread over many homes, those children with a strong father will adapt and function better than those who do not. Single-parent homes can be a breeding ground for social deviation. Children are like rivers, in that their water flows in the path of least resistance. The least resistance in the social confirmation process will produce the least compliant communal members. Spare the rod and spoil the child, or as in the old days, apply the board of education to the seat of knowledge. That was back in the days when young adults attended college and not psychotic snowflakes. An old tale speaks of a young man in the Wild West who stood with a noose around his neck awaiting to be hanged. He called his loving mother to his side and motioned as she moved her ear to his head. He then proceeded to bite off her ear. She asked him why he did this. He told her that if she were more disciplined with him as a child, he would not stand where he was on that day. Sometimes we must discipline our children and be the bad guy, so society does not have to discipline them for being the terrible guy.

The family unit is the most powerful unit in society. Ironically, children in America had at most two parents, notwithstanding in the most economically trying conditions, one parent. Compare this with many Asian homes having up to four adults, when a family leader such as parents lives there as well. When a child has up to four adults watching him or her, she will pretty much stay in line, whereas a child with merely one adult supervising will look elsewhere for leadership, unfortunately finding it in the wrong places. It was mistaken to blame it on the child, as the old saying goes, the road to hell is paved with good intensions. Another longstanding saying elucidates that any boy can make a baby, but it takes a man to be a father. The role of father as to provide the path for his children to travel during their lives. The father additionally, ensures his children stay on that path. It is a tough job, nevertheless, the greatest job a man will ever have. This role can never be bound by race. Thereby, when the Patricians strove to destroy the family unit, they were weakening Christianity and cementing the base for the Muslims. The Muslims constantly use all their social energy to keep their family unit strong. This includes having the father as the sole decision maker. Such a leadership role lends itself to serious damage for wrong decisions. Cultural forces also come into play, as fathers from different religions hold opposing values. One such decision if female genital mutilating, a decision that Muslim families make to control their young women, such as a same decision never contemplated by a Christian father.

The Patricians were not shy in allowing Hollywood to spread their values, pushing a new world with the harmonizing of the races as the modern norm. Hollywood began taking liberties with the television networks, promoting violence, vulgar sex habits and lifestyles, challenging authorities, and fostering a normal society that could never exist. Additionally, other manufacturers jumped in, especially with console gaming. Here, young people can face battle conditions beyond that possible in reality. This did not matter; the children were being programmed to think fast and respond. They had no time to evaluate the complete situation, or they would die. This conditioning when applied in real-world conditions, would lead to dead bodies. This required special duty assignments until the Commanders could employ them effectively. They were extremely powerful in scouting expeditions into areas where only the enemy occupied. When racism is added to this process, extra pressure and stress led to unpredictable outcomes. Even the weapon holder will fire in both situations; the trigger will remain depressed in situations where a racial fear of retribution is at play. The youth from most races were actively being brainwashed by these games consoles, which interestingly enough, many major manufacturers were Asian, which implied the original objective of entertainment and why most parents were not expressing concern over this subconscious programing process. Scared, existing in a world where what you see and hear is not what you get, being trigger happy with a weapon in each hand and a trained eye coordinated with it, was not a bad thing to have in your survival pocketbook.

Racism took hold in the justice system with the network overwhelmed by the way too many accused. The justice system had to move people in and out like an assembly line. This overload made the detection of corruption almost impossible. The family's funds played a critical role as well, in the posting of a bond opened the jail's door and put the formerly labeled dangerous person on the streets as free as a jaybird. Money always changed the government's view of a previously labeled a danger to society, as instantly a perfect citizen. The legal system fed their sharks, or by some people called lawyers, their first-class financial rewards. Any place you saw a judge, you saw a band of lawyers feeding richly off what the judge was passing their way. One example is the Social Security Administration, who, as a matter of practice consistently disapproved of the initial claim and after that schedule the Court date to where it is usually around three years from the inaugural claim. The incapacitated, if not currently dead, from having no income for such an extended time, must have a lawyer with him for the hearing, who sits there like a bump on a log, while the judge asks a few questions, and afterwards makes his decision. The lawyers who may have spent an hour in the case, plus the hour for the Court date, walks away with around six full months of the disabled person's benefits. Remember, the judge most likely will not rule in favor of the impaired citizen, unless he is accompanied by the financial leach called a lawyer. Before the disabled and most likely suffering citizen is paid, the judge insures the lawyers skimmed his rich bounty of the top. Total corruption.

The corruption flowed into the courts as well. Prosecutors would go through each day with hundreds of cases. The public defendants would have so many clients, that just minutes with each one would exhaust hours upon hours. The courts established procedures for each offense, information only shared with lawyers, and public defendants. The punishment for challenging the system with a not-guilty plea was an absolute financial drain. Even when an innocent person is falsely accused that person could lose the farm on legal fees. The Court added special deals, allowing the person not to contest the charges and for payment of any Mickey Mouse fees, and some probation time went uncharged. The choice is to pay the fee, or pay a lawyer hundreds of times more for a jury trial, and chance the jury will accept your story. Juries do not go against what a police report claims, and the police do not always do the required research or investigation before vomiting their words into a report. They are the judge, jury, and trial at the scene, knowing the jury will fall in line with them. The worst place throughout the world is for an innocent person to be in the judicial system. Getting back to earlier, the attorney knows what to do or say to get his client back on the streets that day. Sign here, and pay at the window. You set before the judge who reads is legally required key points, asks the prosecution if the people agree, and next moved on to the next case. The prosecution has no idea what is going on, as long as his Court gets some money and the judge is not yelling at him; he lets it slide and subsequently looks over at the stacks of case files he has in front of him wondering if he can survive yet another day. There was no Black, white, yellow, brown, or Red in Court, there was only green.

The judicial system was set up for failure by the Patricians when president Corrupt, while between an intern's legs took an action that would place more blacks in prison that what any other president had ever done. He levied long hard prison terms for victimless crimes. Then President Bin Laden, instituted a campaign to release them from prison. The Patricians put them in there and then parade as heroes putting them back on the street, totally unemployable. The Patricians pushed Law Enforcement as the enemy of the minorities, leaving them almost helpless. The minorities came up with their demands against the PP, while the Patricians continued to lay the mines that would slowly cripple them. The Patricians had to keep the minorities starving and foster a notion that the whites had what should be theirs. Crime continued to grow in the minority neighborhoods, as they went to feast upon each other. This is similar to increasing the density of rats in a small confined area. There shall reach a point of total conflict and chaos. This was so unfair for the minorities, many of which who had progressed into the mainstream was assimilating not only successful but also productive. The production process is vital for a growing economy. The Patricians had forced companies to hire who, they said, make contributions to whom they demanded, and employ the production processes they established, and afterwards pay astronomical fees for permission to exist, and after that if by some miracle make a profit, surrender most of it back to the government in taxes. Taxes on everything, more taxes, and then the government through corruption and open mismanagement beg for more money. If you did not gleefully pay these outrageous taxes, you were racist.

Subsequently, the taxation burden exploded of the land of the fee. You only became free after you paid the fee. Wages were taxed by three government levels, (Federal, States, Local), and then Social Security and Medicare. The struggling employee pays enormous tax on each gallon of gas, plus a fee for permission to drive and a license to operate the vehicle to travel to work and home. After this, a sales tax is paid for each item purchased. Subsequently, if the person purchases a home a property tax. A portion of the property tax was used to fund schools. This motivated the schools constantly to beg the communities for more funds, which would come through increased property tax. Pay more for what we provide because of our mismanagement. They cover up the fact that if a homeowner falls behind on their property tax, the greedy government will send the sheriff to remove the overtaxed homeowner from the home and steal the home from its homeowner. Innocent people paying for government mismanagement. The Patricians had established so many methods to suck the blood out of the economy, actually accepting bribes in order to influence government officials to behave as they wanted. Lobbyists bribed legislators to behave as their puppets. The lobbyists knew exactly how to push the right buttons with their chosen people. The Patricians controlled the bureaucrats who ruled the administrative agencies. The PP was not a united party in that they had members who behaved as if they were Patricians. They were beholden to their contributors, who called their shots and ruled them as if they were slaves.

The key thing always to remember is that all who disagree with Patricians are racist. The minorities were lied to, robbed from, and dehumanized by the Patricians who waved big sticks demanding the minorities follow them in faith. This constant, year after year, abuse was building a valve that would soon blow. This gave President Hiplinger more support than previously received by the PP candidate for countless decades. The minorities also accepted his challenge of providing them jobs and opportunities for them to build their communities or mingle into the mainstream. The market would control the migration, just as it has with the mainstream for centuries. An example is university graduate interviews for open positions, and accepts the offers and position wherever it is. Geographically independent. The minorities, along with the other races, who joined the militaries relocated as ordered by their superiors. Therefore, this is not something new. The modern social model declares that progression is made through occupying positions that provide more benefits. The positions are, for the most part, in settled positions, or at least based on a fixed position; therefore, to receive the rewards for this position; one must physically move towards that position. The employment laws required these opportunities to be offered without regard to race. The problems arose that the company's employment was not racist; nevertheless, people cannot be made to like a person simply because it is the law. Assuming the fellow employees was professional, the next challenge came into the community, which was a free for all, depending on the mental capabilities and attitudes.

Communities were the true beds for racism. Ironically, the Patricians, were brutally racist when not in the spotlight. The PP was more accepting of minorities, with all factors the same. PPs in Texas had trouble with Hispanics, notwithstanding, basically only the ones who were here illegally. This can lead support to the notion that since they did not live here, they did not belong here. Different communities have a wide assortment of racial issues. The areas occupied by minorities and elevated crime rates naturally wanted the minorities out with the expectation the crime would go with it. Consequently, there is nothing racist about not wanting high crime in your neighborhood. Without a concerted effort to mingle into the community and assimilate, resistance should be expected. If you want to walk with ducks, you need to think like a duck. Returning to PP controlled neighborhoods, racism seldom was an issue. They were more inclusive and secluded. The seclusion was in their methods of communication and respect for the other neighbors' values. Their communication was the only tool these people had to fight the Patricians's intrusion and attempts to create racial problems. The Patricians's tracked the minorities and unleashed both propaganda and actual home invasions, doing whatever they could do that would punish what they consider betrayers. The Patricians did not think too deep about these KKK style attacks. They bonded the blacks against the whites and other minorities in their community. The community would actually attempt to defend these blacks when they happened. This whole situation permitting the identification of the Patricians as the criminals came from intelligence sources previously anti-PP. By as if it were some miracle, the PP was establishing secret networks. The initial organization used a random machine code generator who would choose with projects to engage. The PP wanted to protect their sources.

The Patricians faced great difficulty in shaking racism from the Christian Churches in the hood. These Churches, when congregated would debate issues and parties to determine which one they wanted and then as a team enacted their decision. This was far different than how they reacted previously, because the Patricians had supporters planted in these Churches to keep stirring trouble. The blacks began to catch how misleading these stories were. The city Churches began cooperating with each other. After some time, they were able to pinpoint these instigators who appeared to be pulling their disturbing stories out of the air. The Churches began to analyze what would happen if they acted on these stories. Their discoveries were not pleasant. This had been a decade-long project, which started when the blacks felt betrayed by President Bin Laden. They were able to determine these variations because they were more vested in the original promise. When they discovered the truth, they reached out to the PP, who analyzed the possible Patricians responses. The uncover intelligence sources believed the Patricians would unleash a wave of terror on the blacks. The PP knew they financially had to support a generic, yet mobile, so as not to tip off their secret intelligence. As the Patricians kept attacking the blacks established a "Proclamation Freedom League." The league wore masks and walking around with weapons. The police added support and protection. The Proclamation Freedom League established branches in all major cities. The Churches were promoting membership. These groups were authorized to attack any Patricians official's public and private addresses.

The Patricians's attempted to use public forces to prevent the Proclamation Freedom League from continuing their operations. Ironically, Law Enforcement complained they needed more funds. The Patricians, with malice towards the Law Enforcement cut their public funding. This unleashed an attack against their city funding departments, who issued an emergency funding for the Law Enforcement agencies and cut all judicial department funding. The courts immediately declared these financial restrictions and ordered their funds immediately. This is when the Civil War began, when the blacks went in and destroyed the city's courts and publicly executed the Patricians judges. The PP listed several honorable judges to receive sanctuary. The wisdom of this move was illustrated later, when these judges, as they were reinstated and ruled in favor of the Proclamation Freedom League. This strategy laid a foundation of trust between the Black leaders and the PP. When they witnessed their young fighters receiving the justice as they believed it should motivate them to become more emboldened to advance further their liberation pursuits. The Patricians pushed the racism charges, and even instigated other minorities to fight against the blacks. They convinced the Hispanics that the blacks were pushing campaigns to force their deportation. This was a narrative the Black community did not want to refute, and elected to fight against the Hispanic attacks. This led to blood on the majority of streets in the crowded middle of these cities.

The PP found themselves in a troubling position in this matter. If they went public, the Patricians would spread out their offensive actions, which might provide some relief to the city campaigns. The PP was not prepared to spread their limited resources to protecting their operations. They would, however, join in campaigns throughout the country against Hispanics, capitalizing on local issues, so as not to create a national concern. The PP also began operations to pull many of the blacks out of the cities and place them in small cities. Initially, many were housed with white families, going with the narrative of just visiting. The importance of smuggling these people out secretly was of national interest. The PP depended upon their undercover agents to alert them on any security breaches, and if necessary, clean up the informants. The PP was forced to begin new things beginning with efforts to develop talking points and every stay with the topic. The Patricians would wiggle for any sort of hesitation they could use to advance their argument. Even if the Patricians discovered what they were doing, there would not be much they could directly do. This of course did not rule out wives and children. The PPs did not want a family slaying contest at this time as they were not convinced the PP would support their end, meaning no response to family members being crucified. The PP had to work meticulously to pull each member into the new fold that was beginning. The local Black church leaders led the crusade against the Patricians, and were wise enough to follow the PP recommendations. The PP believed it was better to attack certain programs, which would force the Patricians to allocate resources for the program, which would benefit the inner-city blacks. It would also divert their attention from other concerns which the PP had in other locations. These policies were employed to create a perception the blacks may return to the Patricians plantation and resume their slave functions. While the Patricians perceived a chance to return, they would mix up their attacks, concentrating more on disguising them as caused by the PP. The Patricians did not understand the PP had integrated all components of these PP sponsored actions, therefore, no matter what the Patricians said, the blacks knew the truth. The Patricians were digging their graves with their own shovels.

A primary issue the PP suffered was their lack of communications security. The Patricians had the large, now international phone companies in their back pocket. Couple with the hidden corrupt bureaucrats in the intelligence agencies, this was almost as troubling as searching for a needle in a haystack. Code words were too dangerous from their ease in detection to the difficulty in remembering. Using people to hand deliver messages always ran the risk of the deliverer being captured. They needed something simple, possibly invisible, and able to apply anywhere. They finally, after listening to their IT advisors, elected to go with computer encryption. Within hours, they could implement this network, using software already installed in the current operating systems. Naturally, many of these machines actually had ports on the motherboard where a small chip enhanced the transmitted security beyond possible hacking. These chips were easy to plug in, as most organizations had a computer geek on board. If not how to videos were available, turning secretaries into computer architects. The final feature about these chips was their extreme low cost, prompting most officials to use personal funds to obtain these chips. In fact, many gave their children the money and had them go around to local retailers and purchase them. This helped to present the image these chips could enhance the game performance on computers. The parents, Patricians and PP, gave up figuring out what their children were up to when it came to their games.

The PP added another special feature, and that was the renaming the Wingdings font to Times New Roman and convert the text into these unknown symbols. The receiving computers would change the fonts to any other readable font, and the message would appear. They also changed the font color to write, thus presenting empty appearing pages. The encryption proved to become a wall the Patricians could not penetrate. The Wingdings and white fonts was to battle against physical espionage. The PP had voluminous communications to disseminate. Another feature the PP attempted to establish was having blacks operate the message terminals. The PP met with unofficial Black leaders who were vetted as not be working with or for the Patricians to establish a united force. The PP eagerly wanted to replace the Patricians throughout the nation with blacks pulled out of the inner cities. This was long overdue as a battle plan needed to reshuffle these populations. Both the blacks and PP were dedicated to fighting the Hispanics. They viewed the

Hispanics as a cancer who, like the Muslims, did not want to assimilate, whereas the Asians, European and African immigrants were eager to immigrate. The PP knew they would have to make their move quickly, and catch the Patricians with their pants down. Having the blacks with the PP would shatter years of misery racism produced by the Patricians. The Patricians were now pushing for Muslim expansion, attempting to rework many religious powers to reposition the Muslims ahead of the Jews and Christians. The Muslims were working with the Patricians with their judge shopping, going after Jewish personal property. They attempted to haul in every Judaic institution using both official public judicial institutions and subversive intelligence agencies. They used their judicial charges to restrain these owners, coupled with corrupt judges put these people in prison with no bail with plans to drag this process out long enough to cause severe financial ruin.

The Patricians campaign unleashed a public smear campaign against the Jews who made Hitler appear as a friend. The loyal Patricians public responded with riots and demonstrations. Fortunately, the PP had informants who alerted them about this injustice. The PP in turn alerted the blacks and Asians. The outrage was such that plans were established for a warlike response. This sort of evil could not be allowed to go unpunished. These groups formed gangs and went after the Mosques, destroying them and then rioting in the Muslim villages. The attacks were comprehensive and nationwide. Consequently, to ensure the PP was kept in the low light, the Christians and Jews led the charges on this. Their religious convictions pulled many of the Christian and Jewish Patricians, as they went straight to the Frontlines in this fight. The PP reminded their followers not to mention they were involved in this. The time had not yet come for them to step in the front light. The important thing now was to keep the Jewish people from further persecutions. The PP presented this as a religious war, forcing the Patricians to retreat and pull back their support, considering the devout convictions was uniting Americans from both PP and Patricians, a union they could not risk continuing, as such unions tend to bond in all things.

The PP planted the right news in the correct places, ensuring the appropriate leaks flowed out into the public. The Patricians were stunned as the footholds were beginning to shake loose. The PP knew they had to act fast; therefore, they rushed into the Pentagon through the leaders appointed by President

Hiplinger. The top Commanders needed to reposition their assets in such a manner as to keep the Patricians unsuspecting. The cover story came a national fear, based on special intelligence, that the Muslim terrorists were planning retaliatory actions against the Americans. They put the overseas installations on full alert. The Commanders elected to pull out of some areas and pull these forces back to the States. The Patricians complained this was not an appropriate response. The Military responded they needed additional forces to protect Americans and pull them out of foreign nations so as not to endanger their people. The PP planted the social pollsters to report public favor for these Military moves. These forces were assembled in South Carolina, a point the Military alleged gave them the ability to respond to dangers along the entire American Eastern States. The Military pulled back the ships and reassigned the Commanders, promoting some junior officers and placing some Patricians puppet Commanders in desk jobs in a new secluded non-essential section of the Pentagon, they labeled as the Military vision for the 22$^{nd}$ century, which was so far in the future to make it redundant at best. They flooded this section with overblown praise such as space age weapon systems and aircraft that could scout our solar system. Totally impossible based upon Patricians believable perceptions of a realism never to be realized. This was enough for them to push hard on finalizing the militaries' Commanders' change of commands. The key positions in command of the fleets and submarine fleets were safely secured. The Army and Marines carefully realigned their leadership, according to their strong PP supporting policies. They were currently preparing to pull back divisions to support any social campaigns that were foreseen.

Another crucial hindrance lay in the unpredictable policies of the nation's police departments, as many were completely funded and controlled by Patricians politicians. This proved dangerous for the Black communities who feared retribution from the police if they publicly supported the PP. The lone solution would be for the PP to establish their own party police force. This would be one of their greatest endeavors as they moved closer to war. The PP had debated the need for total war for almost a decade, yet now with the current overwhelming Patricians corruption and challenge to the bare fabrics of the nation's ties; blood would need to flow. The Patricians were preparing a kangaroo Court system, where they could pull in PP citizens and make them their political prisoners. When the PP discovered these plans in the works, they activated the Black hit squads they had formed and put them in direct conflict with these Fake courts, burning them, killing the judges and their families. The Patricians were so arrogant that they blamed the PP for these anti-constitutional invasions on the public liberties enshrined in freedom. The PP now selected cities to challenge their police forces, with Chicago being the first. Their secret forces assembled in the city hosted by the Black communities, where they settled in unnoticed, afterwards marching with the blacks hitting the police hard, and quickly gaining control of the police force. The police was captured and executed publicly and on video for nationwide distribution. The act of executing police caused concern for many; however, only the police which refused to join the PP were executed and ironically executed by those police who pledged loyalty to the PP. This sent tidal waves across the nation when they witnessed police executing police. This created the appearance of a police Civil War, disguising the PP involvement.

Subsequently, the next stop was city hall, and the Black community led the charge on this mission. They had a vengeance to settle. These citizens were now aware of the corruption that had kept them in the chains of slavery for way too long. The smell of freedom was leading them on a feeding frenzy that was growing stronger by the minute. Computer hacks and IT people invaded the city's secret files and brought to light the terrible things the Patricians had in the works against the minorities. The religious persecution of the Jews was merely the first step in this ladder to hell. The Chicago press was put on notice that any false news would be dealt with deadly force. The PP needed a city to establish as their headquarters, nevertheless, did not want to come out just yet, so they devised the Black Freedom Nation campaign. In this campaign, the blacks would declare their war against the Patricians for racism and oppression. This would keep the PPs out of the limelight, providing the PP the extra needed time to set up a sub-culture in the States. Some areas would be initially forfeited and provide an area to herd the Patricians. Ironically, the PPs were moving the blacks out of the inner cities, providing the future homes for Patricians. They would live beside the Hispanics they attempted to give our nation. The PP wanted to keep the Gulf of Mexico and Great Lakes coastlines and initially provide the Patricians the East and West Coasts, except for South Carolina and southern counties of Virginia. The most important network that the PP's needed to gain control of was the D.U.M.B. (Deep Underground Military Base).

The PP would forfeit the DUMP installations in New York and New England. They would secure the tunnels along the Pennsylvania and New Jersey borders. The most contested and projected to require the greatest fighting will be the tunnel section running through Delaware, Maryland to the Virginia shore from under the Chesapeake Bay. The PP wanted to hold this section, so they could assemble forces for a future invasion of New York City. The wonderful feature of this multibillion dollar government forgotten project is the PP can hide a huge number of forces and move supplies to them. This was a mission the PP, passed to its Military Commanders. The PP met with the Black leaders and their Military leaders. The Army and Marines were pulling back their Military personnel and equipment. The Patricians believed they would be made available for them to support their judicial reforms. It was important the Patricians feel these forces would be under their control. The forces would be assembled near D.U.M.B. entry points in Southern California, and points enroot to Las Vegas. They would also be brought ashore in Georgia, Carolinas, and deep southwestern

Virginia. Once at the assembly points, with force, these divisions would gain control of the entry points. Once they gained control of the entry station, they would move their units underground. Afterwards, they would maintain control if more units were scheduled to enter. If not, they would seal this entry point and move towards the stations in the Midwest areas. They would flow through the stations who had not reported PP control and gain that control.

The blacks played critical role in the PP gaining their foothold. Naturally, there were rogue blacks who were too brainwashed in Patricians doctrine. The blacks would establish the method they would use to eliminate these threats. These actions alerted the Patricians who were calling on President Hiplinger to retaliate. The PP alerted President Hiplinger the time had come to battle the Patricians and protect the PP. The Patricians were currently openly rounding up PP citizens and executing them. The PP put President Hiplinger into the D.U.M.B. network where they would move him and his cabinet to Chicago, and once this fresh capital was secure; he would come aboveground and run the new PP state. The Patricians instituted their Yellow Cap sewn into the skull of their citizens. With their control of the press, they put this rule out throughout the complete country for an immediate compliance. This was secretly hailed as a great gift for the PP. Effectively, this would make it easy to identify the Patricians as targets. The PP, which was made up of a council of one-hundred members spread throughout the nation. Most meetings were on the Internet, and were now in the process of using exceptional phones that would be linked with a special secure Military network. The PP launched a campaign to knock off the nation's Internet. They were also looking at newly formed guerrilla units to sabotage cell phone towers, beginning in Maryland and Virginia and New York City (later renamed York City). Time was beginning to fly, actually just about beside the bullets that were slowly ringing across the nation. The PP had the Navy, Army, Marines, and critical Air Force Bases, plus President Hiplinger who was still the constitutional president.

The nation's manufacturing and retail networks were closed. Trucks stopped moving commercial goods, because radical Patricians were shooting at them. This was forcing the PP to build Military units and deploy them throughout the Midwest and Western States, with the goal of executing Patricians. Once this campaign began, the war was at hand. The Patricians controlled the press and Hollywood. The PP instructed its citizens only to listen to PP approved networks. The PP sabotage units went into action in Hollywood, after three Air Force fighter planes sprayed bullets at selected targets in Beverly Hills and Hollywood Movie Production staging areas. It would take some time to rebuild the studios, and since the bullet spraying was more for a show that they are prone to force, seventeen actors were injured, and merely three killed. Stage 2 of this revenge operation involved the Black units which were training in this area. Special guerrilla units noticed there were only a few police manning the local stations, so they went after them flushing out the stations. With the police under control, the PP released the Black neighborhood to search for any Yellow Cap, execute them, and after that occupy their homes. Once occupied, paint a Red P on the front door, take pictures with cell phone, and subsequently go back into the fight gaining homes for friends and family. When these raids began, the PP Blood Coats went into their first official action. These were special hit squads that would go into an area with trucks of ammunition and destroy all living things within. They wore dark-Red uniforms and Red masks, and had long sword and long knife and razor-sharp arrows and spears. They always sprayed an area with gunfire, then dug in house by house cleaning them out. Naturally, they wore chemical masks and would spray areas with chemicals to pull out stole ways hiding in strange places.

The Blood Coats were concerned initially with cleaning out public areas, and market places. Their mission was to make the community secure for its future residents. The battle for Chicago raged for three weeks, as the Patricians foolishly sent untrained and unorganized forces against it. The PP also had an additional asset in the first few months of the war, and that was the Oreos. This term was used to exemplify the new bond between the PP and the Black community. They were quick to point out they were the Chocolate Oreo, with a brown inside versus the original vanilla cream. The Oreo cookie had evolved through the years with a wide range of colored frosting, which now could lend itself to any race or mood. These were undercover blacks who would pretend to be Patricians but were PP all the way. They could only function in the Military because the Military had their own headgear and refused to wear the Yellow Caps, for what they labeled as deadly targets. These soldiers had a chip implanted in them, that when activated would create a non-painful silent shock through them. They would know it was their activation call. The key for this one-time plan would be to activate them once all the Patricians troops were activated. The PP had control of most Military forces, nevertheless; the Patricians had secretly gained control of those units existing in their strongholds. The PP had to release these units, to buy the vital time to secure the D.U.M.B. Notwithstanding, they did integrate the Oreo into these units. The challenge remained that previously the Oreo was unleashed the Proclamation Freedom League would be also be activated and establish its bases aboveground. Once this was activated the secret card of a Black freedom force would be unleashed.

The importance of this activation could not be overstated. The PP worked hard with the Black communities to ensure that nationwide activation was possible. The PP wanted to know of any trouble areas, so they could supplement those areas with Military force. The more successful this action was, the greater the belief of an affluent war. This campaign would also need some Blood Coats to assist in relocation efforts if the city campaign failed. The Black leaders identified California southern cities, Arizona, southern New Mexico and southern Texas as problem areas because of the high Hispanic populations, which pretty much had the Black communities pinned in. The PP decided to use naval artillery fire on San Francisco, San Diego, Oakland, and Los Angeles, concentrating on the Law Enforcement, marketing areas, and government offices. The marketing areas were to create the bait for the Hispanic to loot, providing the Black communities to make their way out of the city. They were instructed to execute any Yellow Cap or Hispanic they saw while exiting. The goal was to inflict some damage and at least tie these cities up with infrastructure repair, loss of communication with the Patricians control centers. This delay was important to bait the Patricians to spread their Military forces out of which would permit the PP to blockade them. These blacks would enter the D.U.M.B. for relocation throughout the Midlands. Their fighting age males were invited to create larger, more lethal units in the Proclamation Freedom League, with a mission to protect and secure lands for the Black PP. This time around; the Blacks would be permitted to decide how they wanted to live and who they would live among. For this stage, the important issue was to protect them from their angry masters (Patricians) who had the whips and were coming to bring them back to the plantation. The time was at hand; the Oreos were activated, and the Proclamation Freedom League was set in force. The second Civil War was now filling the streets with blood.

## CHAPTER 05

# LET THE BLOOD FLOW

The time came across a land, which began with blood and then through hard work fought the world to save them from evils, notwithstanding evil came flooding in when the Providers turned on the water valves. They knew no chance existed with the PP, so they fed the vampire Patricians, who would sell their mother to make a dime. The PP knew the time of 'No more had arrived.' The true Americans would no more bow to foreigners. The Americans would no more beg forgiveness from foreigners who tried to harm us. No more allowing foreign nations to rob us blind in our trades. No more allowing criminals to walk across our borders and rape our women. No more listening to the lies from the Patricians. No more taking the 'American

Dream,' from the American children and giving it to illegal immigrants. No more watching our children dying from drug overdoses. No more fearing gangs terrorizing our neighborhoods. No more apologizing for being white. No more imprisoning the blacks on the plantations. No more lying to the people. No more corruption. No more robbing the people and giving the money to corrupt politicians. No more sending our jobs overseas. No more starving Americans. No more homeless Americans. No more forgotten Veterans. No more over taxation. No more watching your children fall behind in education from the children of other countries. No more high crime. No more being pushed around by idiots. No more watching idiots occupy political positions. No more lying press. No more being told you cannot pray in public. No more being a second-class citizen because you are a Christian. No more watching the guilty go free. No more complicated, impossible to understand taxes. No more being told lies. No more making sacrifices so those who hate you can become gluttons. No more sexual harassment. No more being told that marriage is not only between a man and a woman. No more being politically correct. No more being told guns is the source of all evil. No more having rights being challenged. No more United States of America. No more Patricians. This no more was so wonderful the PP had to repeat it, No more Patricians.

The PP council opened up their network to over 150 military and intelligence leaders. The PP instituted a new policy which placed an armed guard beside the contact and was instructed, they would execute that individual if they determined they had compromised the network. They reminded these contacts that we will tolerate betrayal no more. The betraying of friends for a false glory or rewards from the enemy were no more. The PP had their Blood Coats in place to do one thing, and that was to protect the PP and their intelligence. This panned out into a house to house and person-to-person war. That was not quite the original objective, nevertheless, the Patricians had their noses in everything that had any money attached to it, with sticky hands to skim a 'fee' portion. The time it would have taken to carve out a section for the PP to occupy, the Patricians would have captured and imprisoned the PP citizens, plus set up defensive and offensive operations along the perceived limited border and effortlessly choke them economically and commercially. This could not happen. The PP wanted to hold on to as much land as possible, and at the same time to keep as many of the Patricians in their targets as possible. The Patricians were moving fast towards the major cities. Except for Chicago, the PPs was moving out of these cities and looking forward to taking control on medium and small cities. The PP was bringing the blacks out of the cities and sharing the homes that were attainable and those that would be unoccupied after a few bullets were put in their Yellow Caps. Unfortunately, not all blacks joined the Proclamation Freedom League, with about thirty-percent staying back. The majority of these were elderly, handicapped, and political. This would work out better for the PP, in that the seventy-percent possessed a greater chance to defend themselves and deploy on offensive actions.

The killing began nationwide when the Patricians issued the order to kill any and all PP. The PP activated all its military resources and distributed the stockpile of armed weapons to all PP citizens who would accept them. Naturally, many of the rugged outdoor men had their own weapons. Either way the fighting was going on almost every street in the former United States. Technically, the United States still existed as the Patricians took over the White House and all Federal buildings in Washington, DC. The PP pulled the President and PP congressional members and their staffs, plus families into the DUMB. They received cover fire from the military. The military kept a foothold in the city, plus attempted to block all roads going in and leaving DC. In this early stage, the adult males were the primary target for units attempting entry into cities. The concept was that women and children would drain resources, increasing any benefits from a blockade. The PP was not able to blockage all cities due to locations and available resources. Cities far from any strategic benefits or out of the way were boycotted after rescuing the PP members and relocating them. The first week accounted for about fifty-percent of the executions. Those who survived this stage pretty well knew how to smell an ambush or crawl while in the house avoiding windows. The PP had spread throughout the rural areas and dug in around fixed positions to create productive ambushes. Telephone poles were efficient sniper positions. The most productive offensive weapons the PP had were its guerrilla units that were going in and actually clearing areas, removing the Patricians. This prompted the PP to temporary redesign its military divisions into small flexible guerrilla units. These units had members who were experts in surviving from off the land.

These units were deployed as soon as they received certification and equipped. They would initially be deployed based upon the density of Patricians not within large cities. The established military units were shelling the cities. Ironically the Patricians believed their corruption had sealed them the military, and were treating the military as they treated the blacks, as being so far in their pockets they were now totally brainwashed by their lies. The Patricians would publicly reveal their control, whereas the PP kept their operations clandestine. These guerrilla units were initially placed under the operational control of the Proclamation Freedom League, whose mission was to pull the PP blacks out of the cities and relocate them in future vital geographic positions needed to be held by the PP. These positions were a sprawling as if one threw sand on a map of the states. They were everywhere, in the hills, along the rivers, along the major highways, and near the communication towers. Moreover, they were within striking distance of any Patricians strategic locations. The PP had dedicated large pools of people towards logistics in assuring these units had all the war power they needed. These pools trained specific forces that would locate gun dealers and ammunition storage and production facilities and place them under tight PP control. The ammunition storage facilities were completely liquidated and restored in the DUMB. Major distributors were ordered to turn over their ammunition inventories for national-security reasons. Unfortunately, a few attempted to pass these on to the Patricians, with an almost zero percent of success. The neighboring public had an insight that the Patricians-leaning distributors were, activating local forces to capture the ammunitions and executing the betrayers in public. The time for games and delay obstructionism were history.

The PP used Air Force bombers and Marine fighter jets to disable the electrical grids, water supplies, and public media stations nationwide attempting to disable the large Patricians held metropolitan areas. Accordingly, Chicago was exempt from these raids as it was currently held by the PP as their party's capital. The PP gained control of the refineries in Washington State, actually securing most of the state barricading King and Pierce counties. The true refineries linked to the Gulf of Mexico were far easier to secure. The PP wisely broke their strong resistance against the Hispanics as a unified group, capitalizing on President Hiplinger's relationships with the Cuban Americans and Haitian Americans. The Patricians immediately went after the Cuban Americans unleashed an attempted blood bath. This failed instantly as Florida, deployed their Proclamation Freedom League to employ sabotage warfare and through well-placed sniper fire to grind to a halt their mobile convoys. Cuba and the

Cuban Americans reinforced by the Proclamation Freedom League effectively fortified the state of Florida as the initial PP state, as reported previously in this account. The significance of this campaign was how it established the first treaty between Cuba and an American State. The PP chose not officially to recognize this relationship, electing instead to thank them for their lives-saving heroic deeds, with a promise of non-aggression. There were enough ideological barriers between the Cubans and Cuban Americans. The dangerous friction existed because of the communist government. The Cuban Americans welcomed and in many cases loved the Cuban people. It was working around those political chains around their necks that weighed down their words and actions.

Consequently, until the Cuban Americans had a strong central government, they needed to work harder to keep American soil out of Cuban control. The Cubans were not interested in obtaining Florida, considering the Patricians was promising them Puerto Rico. The Cubans did not want to occupy the Florida peninsula, believing that someday, American forces would go to war against them, and the amount of needed devoted resources would not produce their desired effect. The truth remained that the Cuban Americans escaped once and would likely do this again as their communist government established its foothold. Moreover, even though the Patricians were agreeable today, history revealed they were not trustworthy allies. Additionally, the PP would, once united, would push them back to the sea. The Puerto Rico deal looked great; it fit their expansion needs. As for the PP, it relieved them from a fiscally irresponsible territory. The PP set up a provisional government in Florida, notifying its citizens to expect a hard future push from the Patricians. The PP could merely hope the numerous campaigns throughout the remainder of their previous nation would keep the Patricians occupied. The PP had over 100,000 guerrilla platoons in action across the departed union. These platoons were equipped and portable, though most merely mobile within a 200-mile circumference. They each had a connection to the DUMB, which permitted this fighting forces to keep well equipped. These platoons also supported local Freedom Fighters. These were citizen squads which fought to remove any Patricians households and positions located within their area. The Blood Coats worked and deployed regularly with the squads to create a powerful deadly cleaning force.

The fall of the United States shook the world, as many worried about their defense treaties and the stabilization of the dollar. Neither the PP nor the Patricians wanted China to replace their dollar. The Providers were pushing forward to replace the dollar with the yuan. The push was too powerful for the Patricians, who were busy transferring American Wealth from American dollars. The PP did not worry about this in that they were pulling American forces and assets back to the Conus. The value of the dollar would not affect the financial activities within the old states. The PP wanted to reestablish the previous states as a new entity, and effect passes all previously liabilities on the Patricians. The total financial liquidation of any former liabilities would reset the basis for the future generations. The government's debt was too great to carry. The Patricians planned to liquidate the PP assets, whereas the PP offered the Patricians assets in exchange for debt liquidation. The PP was careful to separate the land from the assets, speaking strongly that no foreign entity would be given control of previously Federal lands. The Patricians did not worry about this technicality that they planned to surrender all former US territory to the Providers. The PP attempted to spread this plan to the public, emphasizing it as a complete betrayal of the American people. This did have several citizens take off the Yellow Caps and join the PP cause. Public demonstrations were no longer possible, even under heavy protection, as the Patricians could preposition snipers for some easy unprotected community targets.

The Providers were met with immediate concern as the American map witnessed the PP having established a solid foundation for future control of the departed states. The initial blockade actions were instrumental as the PPs informed the world to stay away from the past American states. While the world press attempted to stagnate the spread of this news, in that it was life saving. The PP new the old method of playing the press game of allowing them to take you hostage to get your information out was finished. The PP elected to commence sinking ships heading for the states. The initial day of enforcement the PP sunk 126 cargo ships, while at the same time permitting sixty-four passenger ships passed through after boarding and capturing any possible military hardware. The message got out quickly, as those who lost ships suffered an immediate economic loss, and the insurance companies refusing to pay labeling this as wartime activity. When you hit the billfold, former bonds break, and the press no longer trusted. The ships redirected heading for the Gulf of Mexico, West Coast, and New York City. The PP had to tighten up on the Canadian border. The

PP used artillery fire, striking into Canada disabling the cargo trucks prior to crossing the border. Canada could not officially complain in that they were officially warned not to smuggle goods across the border. The Providers were eager to break across the borders and assist the Patricians put the PP into the history books. The Providers did not understand that even though America was divided in political parties, there were other divisions that were not so finalized. Two such divisions were the desire to keep the foreigners from over taking the American soil and the East versus the western cultures. The Providers unleashed the Mexicans upon Texas, which proved to be a major miscalculation. The West witnessed its PP, and Patricians unite and drive the Mexicans far south of the border inflicting a genocidal wave the North Americans was spared for almost a millennia. Once driven out, Texas returned to its previous PP dominance, as the bloodshed flowed once more securing Texas as the second PP holding.

The greatest showdown occurred within the New England area. Nevertheless, prior to this campaign, the PP needed to secure control of Ohio and Pennsylvania. Although the final time to clean these states would take much longer, the PP was effective in chocking the major cities, such as Cleveland,

Columbus, Pittsburg, and Cincinnati. The primary mission was to maintain these chokes while sending large numbers of guerrilla forces into the New England territories. This was possible because of the DUMB networks that put these forces into the neighborhoods they were destroying. The naval forces pounded the sea coast and York City. These submarines also pounding Cleveland and cripple the Lake Erie and Lake Ontario trading lanes with Canada. Although it took almost one year of constant bloodshed, New England fell. The forward deployed forces, eventually all formed between the New England and York PPs took over the security of their homeland. Millions of Patricians ended in the burning fires until no Yellow Caps remained. Those who initially found secure hiding places either starved to death or surrendered gaining freedom from their terrifying pain through the peace of death. The Ohio and Pennsylvania Armies returned to their original positions to enjoy the fruits of the Freedom Fighters, Blood Coat, and the Proclamation Freedom League, which had forced the Patricians into pockets the PP Armies hit head-on with massive artillery leaving all Patricians within their targets lifeless.

The PP had Chicago, New England, Ohio, and Pennsylvania colony it renamed Freedom Land. The two southern lands kept their original names of Florida and Texas. The PP believed the guerrilla efforts of the Freedom Fighters; Blood Coats and Proclamation Freedom League were terrorizing and crippling the Patricians. The PP placed a priority in keeping their satellites supplied with food and arms, which proved each day to weakening the Patricians. The world needed to see some more visible results, causing the PP to establish two new objectives. The first was to link Chicago with Freedom Land and linking Maryland and northern Virginia. Meanwhile, the remainder of the former nation lived in absolute raging war. The Patricians created motorcycle gangs to raid throughout the nation. The PP had powerful motorcycle gangs as well, that stood strong on behalf of President Hiplinger. These gangs raided Illinois, Indian, Michigan, and Wisconsin. The local Blood Coats would inform them of any resistance cells. The PP used their special closed circuit military communication lines to establish sniper ambushes, which would pick off several of the bikers. A few solid hits that resulted in the bike hitting the road, crashing other bikes, which put the drivers on the grounds and provided the snipers easy open target kills. Additionally, a well-placed bullet into a bike gas tank always provided explosive results, good for several other bikes trailing them to fall as well. The Patricians motorcycle raids rather quickly faded as the bike groups dropped to merely a few members, which were ineffective with the at most hope of survival was to return to their base, as only a few achieved.

Accordingly, thousands of squads were engaged in battle throughout the former states from coast to coast. Most were families fighting to protect their homes. One such family was Bill and Liz, who ran the small Sorensen Truck & Equipment off Hannegan Rd in Whatcom County, Washington State. Their home and business rested on about 1,000 feet outside Lynden. Lynden is less than four miles from the Canadian border and less than ten miles from the Pacific Ocean or to be exact the Strait of Georgia and Semiahmoo Bay. Adding to the features of this business, just 200 feet out of their back door ran the Nooksack River. Their backyard was an open field running all the way into Lynden. The front yard was different as just across the Hannegan Rd rose a thick forested hill. They faced one challenge, which could work for defense, or more probable provide cover the Patricians. This was the small hill packed with trees that rose approximately eighty-feet and ranged between sixty to one-hundred feet thick. Bill and Liz had five boys and three daughters, an average-sized family for a farm family. Two children, one boy Ted and one girl Beth, were still in school. Two of his sons ran the family farm, with its large barn just a little over one-hundred feet from the Equipment shop parking lot. The barn overlooked the Nooksack River. The family merely had a few heads of cattle, couple pigs, and chickens running around their buildings. The boys would cut the hay from the large field behind the barn and house. The family had a sizeable garden, where in addition to field corn, they raised the family's vegetables. Unlike Seattle and Tacoma, which were a few hours south or approximately one-hundred miles, Whatcom County was predominately PP, with Lynden as its second-largest city. There existed now a population just over 14,000, of which 1,542 put on Yellow Caps.

Lynden was about ninety-percent white, including Latino, which accounted for approximately nine percent, less than one percent black, six and half percent Asian or Pacific Islander. The town did not know what to do with the 1,542, as they were brothers, fathers, cousins, neighbors, fellow teammates, and church mates. The large farms pretty much merely traded and attended a few ceremonies with Lynden have a lot of work on their plates. The children naturally attended Lynden High School on Vinup Road, and occasionally gets some skating in at the Lynden Skateway. British Columbia Avenue hosted several churches on the other end of town close to the city's claim to fame in the region, and these were the Northwest Washington Fair and Event Center. The city had a small Airport just down the road from the Lynden Christian Schools. With large mountain ranges north in Canada, and Canadian cities of Victoria and Vancouver hugging the Ocean line, and the three mountain ranges that ran through Washington State, it is easy to understand why even the Nooksack established their Indian village Squahalish at this location. The area offered so much farm land as many of the residents used their free natural gas for their home heating and canning of their food. Bellingham was a direct shot south on 539 less than fifteen miles. Fortunately, there were a few other communities along this route, coupled with the strong support of the Blood Coats 539 were staged with many ambush sites. There were plenty of open areas on the route to prevent and large enemy movements to go undetected. The constant in city fighting in Bellingham kept Patricians movements in the area extremely occupied. As with the entire West Coast, route 5 always posed a danger for Patricians mobilization. The safety valve for this area was its lack of any great economical of financial resources. The communities survived from agriculture trading and providing lumberjacks for the nearby mountain forests.

Consequently, this wide-open land did provide a once valuable resource for the PP, and those were guerrilla squads. Hunting was an extremely popular activity throughout this area, with both boys and girls growing up with a knife in one hand and a rifle in the other. The distinction between town folks and country folks died when the war began. Lynden activated all children, male or female above thirteen into their home guard. These guards patrolled 539, 546, and kept guard on strategic points along route 5. Additional duties included selling produce and excess oil from the farm pumps to Canada in trade for gasoline. The gasoline was stored for use with their generators and emergency. All schools were closed and any adults who needed work, such as government workers, postal, and most retail were now guerrilla soldiers or working in the farm. Everyone had a mission, and learning to kill was not that difficult as soon as everyone learned how to kill and butcher their meat. They learned to sharpen their knives, so they would slide through the animal flesh with minimal effort. The cleaning of the non-edible organs took some time to fine tune. These organs were collected along with all other wastes from the carcass and fed to the town dogs. Their county released all the dogs, leaving no dogs chained. This was a custom that was now widespread through all the areas that were predominately PP. The Patricians were strangely afraid of dogs. The PP usually fed their dogs publicly, allowing everyone a chance to contribute. Accepting a dog will not bite the hand who feeds him, everyone was eager to feed the dogs. The PP community employed mountain traditional recipes to produce their dog food.

Notwithstanding, Lynden experienced its battle with the Patricians, as merely a handful of communities was spared the bloodshed. One rainy spring day as the soft rain sparked in the air as the drops sung their song on the rooftop of the Sorensen buildings. Bill and Liz's children had created a special area in the loft above the barn where it met with the two silos. They had collected hay and used this area as a stockpile for their unique collection of arrows. These children created windows with boarded door-like windows covered with the same aluminum medal panels to match the outside of the barn. They enjoyed congregating in this loft when it was raining, as the cool air chased away the normal hot stuffy air. Since the war was now in full force, any one of their kids who happened to be in the loft during the rains would open the window and use their binoculars to scan the forests that covered the hill across Hannegan Rd. They would also scan the open fields across the Nooksack River, giving additional attention to Hannegan Rd. Many worry about this road in that it eventually ran into 542 and Bellingham and ran parallel with 539. Sam, Jr. and Anne were taking an afternoon break from the showers and their roaming guard duties. Anne was using her binoculars scanning down Hannegan Road. She was teasing her brothers about their success with the neighbor's daughters.

Accordingly, the brothers blamed the war for the reason they had not invited their neighbor's daughters to the Lynden Skateway. Anne continued her teasing until she saw some movement in a field about three-hundred feet down the road. She immediately informed her brothers who rushed to her side, one pulling out their night star telescope. They determined it was at least eight men with Yellow Caps hiding among the few trees near the junction of Polinder Rd. and Hannegan Rd. The farm buildings were occupied by a family that moved in with relatives in Lynden. The farm was left empty, occupied as a rest and eating station when the town worked in the farm's fields. They would have to cross a wide field and then cross the Hannegan Rd bridge where it crossed the Nooksack River, a perfect place for Anne, Jr. and Sam to ambush them. The closest bridge was 539 a few miles west. It was a good distance to find an easterly bridge. The greatest danger was the farm located on the West side of Hannegan Rd just before the Nooksack River. This was the farm that housed the two girls whom Jr. and Sam were eyeing. Presently, the farm children were reconning the streets in Lynden, and the parents were working their back fields. Jr. has identified the locations of all nine men. There was an additional man in this revised account. Jr believes they need to shoot now with their crossbows. The rain is falling heavier currently, so visibility is low, meaning they can pick a few off on the edges. This way, when they make their move across the field, there will be fewer to hit. They each focus on a target with their loaded crossbows and seven spare arrows at their sides. They only have two windows, so Sam will get one while Jr and Anne share the other. They all take a deep breath, while whispering their prayers and unleash the three arrows, hitting two in the head with the third arrow missing its target. Anne knew this was her target and immediately reloaded her crossbow and with a quick focus fired, hitting the man in his back as he was attempting to hide in the tree.

Subsequently, the count now was five. Sam wondered if they would continue the attack or load their dead and return home. The PP did not like to leave bodies behind, nevertheless; the Patricians did not care about their comrades' bodies. Either way, the siblings loaded their crossbows and were attempting to guess what the enemy's next action would be. The wait was not long, as they witnessed four of them low crawling and the fifth one behind a tree with binoculars, most likely trying to determine where the arrows were coming from. Sam reasons this will be tricky, in that the further in the field they go, the harder it will be to hit them, because of the trees running down the river. If they shoot too early and miss, they will run back behind the trees and begin shelling their loft, which cannot stop a bullet. The elected to pick up the remaining crossbows, which were nine, and load them. The family had so many crossbows, because they never threw one away when getting a new one. Maintaining the old ones was a fun cold winter day activity. They each assembled their four crossbows, and with Anne's order began shooting. The first round Jr. had a hit, second round Anne and Sam got their hits. The last round Jr. once more got a hit, his second in this raid. As this man rolled over, Anne and Sam tucked two more arrows in his body. They now began emptying the crossbows into the four corpses to ensure they were dead. Anne fired a few shots at the tree of the man searching for them, forcing him to fall deeper into the long line of trees he was hiding.

Consequently, Anne reveals she can no longer see the scout. This forced Jr. to reason it was time the town was notified and did a section sweep. Meanwhile, Anne was to keep scanning the trees and field behind and front of it and attempt to find him. Jr and Sam reloaded the crossbows and water bottles, slid down out of the loaf and rushed to their farm house to talk on the town walked-talkie alerting the town. Even though six of the seven were killed, the last one had to be stopped so he would not go back to his headquarters and report any scouting intelligence. The odds were they had nothing on Lynden, nevertheless, they could have intelligence on Whatcom County. Approximately one-hundred PP citizens lined up on the two plowed fields about 1000 feet south and began their march north. Most agreed that if the invader tried to pass this field, he would have been spotted by Anne. To be on the safe side, they had the dogs sniff the six dead men, whom the town lined up on the road, and released the dogs, with twenty experienced hunters to do the push beginning with the farms eight legs to its tree wall. The dogs ran through first, then all congregated around on leg in this unique farm-tree barrier arrangement. They had the man pinned, and upon verifying it, called back the twenty field pushers to encircle this area. Meanwhile, Anne was waiting for a view, so she could pop an arrow in his leg or arm. The town wanted to capture him alive, so they could turn him in to the Blood Coats for real interrogation. The man foolishly tried to work his way up the tree, not knowing Anne had him in her view. He finally hit a dead branch where Anne got her view and instantly got his arm, dropping his rifle to the ground below. Several men went up, tied him and dropped him to the ground where their teammates subdued him. They called the Blood Coats which praised the town for taking the extra time and providing them with a possible source of intelligence. They took the dead bodies as well, wanting to do autopsies to determine their food diet and general health for signs of population weaknesses. Determining any food sources could lead to methods to destroy that source, such as crop dusting, as common and routine Whatcom custom. This time they would be dusted with stronger poisons that would endanger humans equally important, notwithstanding, making sure they did not dust any PP livestock or population sources.

Lynden called this event the Polinder Rd Invasion and recognized Anne, Sam and Jr. as the leading fighters against the Patricians. Lynden was now in the war officially, as word spread throughout the area, waking up the area that war could soon bleed up from Seattle and Bellingham. The Patricians had ignored these areas, recognizing the Proclamation Freedom League had resettled heavily thanks to the hard fighting of the Freedom Fighters and Blood Coats. The Oreos were extremely instrumental in killing of Yellow caps who tried to sneak out of Seattle and Pierce County. King County was sealed tight, because of the PP national policy of chocking big cities. The seaports of Seattle and Tacoma were quickly approaching an impassable level of danger in that so many ships were sunk in their waters. This led to the rise of military submarines, with three now scavenging under the Seattle-Tacoma waters loading up this sunken cargo and delivering it to PP secured ports. Of special note, these were not nuclear subs, but long overdue decommissioned older subs. The PP naval forces now believed that the lone way to decommission a submarine is with its failure on the Ocean floor. The Marines and Army had secured North Bay and Aberdeen constructing the ports for these sea dumps. North Bay was secured by a mountainous range just off the Pacific coast and within sixty miles southwest of Seattle and due west of Olympia and less than five miles north of Willapa Bay. The control of these two bays gave the PP a mobile flexibility against the Canadians and Patricians alike. Moreover, the southern tip of the Willapa Baby was less than three miles from the mouth of the Columbia River as it emptied into the Pacific. The Navy kept one large nuclear submarine in this bay for easy pickings of ships that attempted to smuggle products into the River and on to Portland. The rocky waters between Frankfort and Cathlamet were perfect places for the submarine to hide and strategically sink ships in such a manner as to greatly endanger future ships attempting to sail over these damaged ships.

Accordingly, the Canadians initially attempted to drop some fast shipments in support of Seattle and Portland. The PP issued a strong promise that any such deliveries would be sunk and the ports of Victoria and Vancouver blasted with artillery from the Navy and Air Force. Naturally, the Canadians had enjoyed years of ignoring Patricians threats and attempted the smuggling activities, forcing the PP to sink twenty-two Canadian Cargo ships; the sole hesitation was ensuring they were in water shallow enough for PP scavenging operations. The Air Force flew three-hundred sorties over Vancouver, destroying the ports, major factories and government buildings. The PP warned any retaliation would result in attacks on Toronto and Montreal. The Navy fired eighty-two missiles into Victory, destroying all ships in dock around the horn plus Oak Bay and knocked off bridges on Esquimalt Rd, Bay St, Tillicum Rd, Johnson St, Admiral Rd, and Galloping Goose Trail. These attacks woke Canada that the PP had control of the Military punch and under President Hiplinger would use it. President Hiplinger traditionally gave one warning. His administration, now based in Chicago, warned Canada and Mexico, there would be no more warnings.

Anne and her family's victory were short lived when the word broke concerning gunfire near the ball fields at the corner of 8th St and Edson St. This was scary, in that the area still hosted games on these fields, as in hope to maintain some sort of community sanity. These fields were precisely two brief streets from one of the town's primary ammunition storage facility housed in the Lynden Middle School, only on the other side of Main St. This field was a popular place for the elementary kids to sneak off and play. The parents reasoned that since the adults were on this hunt, the children snuck off to play. These grownups rushed for their vehicles, those who had them, who naturally permitted other adults to crowd aboard and the town made a mad rush to the park. As they approached the park, the Blood Coats waved them back, ordering that they proceed with their trained military canvassing method, which meant everyone provided cover for each other. The Blood Coats had arrived and secured the area, pulling out the lone casualty, little Janice Martin, five years old who was playing in her front yard under the family trees. Upon learning the Martin girl was dead; their neighbors rushed to pull them aside to comfort them. Rage filled the crowd as they attempted to find someone to blame. First, they attempted to blame Jr. and Sam for pulling everyone out of town. In response to this, the Blood Coats wanted everyone to bring their children to the front, so they could be executed. They simply wanted to achieve the same results if those seven Patricians had entered the town. This woke the community up quickly, as they struggled to find someone to blame.

The Blood Coats warned that whomever did this was still on this side of Main Street, as they had maintained control of Main Street. Another squad that operated in St Joseph's Catholic Church attested that British Columbia Ave was secured immediately after the gunshots. Ironically, this left areas open the families had rushed back on, many on Hannegan Rd, while some rushed up S 1st St, and others bounced over the alley to go up S 7th St and S 8th St, causing the city to call on the neighbors Front St and Judson St to secure the open fields south of the city. Ironically, Anne, Sam, & Jr. jumped into the family boat and began patrolling the Nooksack River looking for any signs of anyone attempting to cross the river. The hunt was now on. All generators in these neighborhoods were turned on, so that all lights were on. The dogs flooded this area. After three hours of searching, the dogs circled a house at the corner of 10th St and Grover St. The older, smaller house had all windows covered, except for a broken basement window, broken previously, nevertheless, apparently was the attraction that lured the fugitive underground. The Blood Coats ordered the neighbors to continue their search while they attempted to flush the invader or invaders out of the house. The Blood Coats understood they had to act fast, and thus elected to smoke the house. They had to know quickly, so if the house was vacant they could redeploy the dogs. Notwithstanding to the joy of the Blood Coats, two men came rushing out fighting for their breaths. The Blood Coats popped a small pistol bullet into their left legs. This was intended to prevent them from running. They handcuffed them and dragged them across the street to the First Christian Reformed Church parking lot, while the other members of their squad did a thorough search of the fugitive's hideout.

Members of the neighboring homes began to assemble in the parking lot, when Blood Coats came rushing out of the house with documents and rifles. The documents included maps of their mission, to search for and execute PP elementary school children. These documents sent shill waves up the spines of those who read them. The Blood Coats had the dogs sniff the riffles and papers and led the dogs of the town to ensure this invasion force did not have any additional members. Two men brought from their home, their movable basketball hoop, and ran water hoses from the church to refill the base to their portable basketball hoop. The Blood Coats put a noose around the first man and immediately hung him, while castrating him, ensuring his last few minutes of life were shockingly painful. They then asked this man if he wanted to keep his fingers before execution. He pleaded yes; therefore, the executioners told him to tell everything about his mission. The executioners instantly cut off his fingers. Subsequently, the Blood Coats ask him if he wanted to keep his eyes. The man began talking, explaining that the Patricians had launched 148 two-man teams to execute children playing alone, and in areas where few people were currently present. They had everything for this execution of Janice Martin except a resounding enough wind or busy downtown to drown down their rifle's shocking deafening sound. The sound tunneled through the town, like air through a horn. The second outstanding surprising factor was Lynden had a community system established for locating rogue invaders. They immediately guarded chief streets, permitting the Blood coasts to provide guidance to the search dogs.

The Blood Coats thanked the man for his intelligence provided, placed the noose around his neck and hung him. PP law was execution as soon as possible after apprehension of all Patricians. The days of appeasing the uncompromising Patricians were no more. The Blood Coats discussed with the town residents present that this intelligence needed to be sent to President Hiplinger without hesitation. This demoralizing plan to murder children would traumatize many families and distract these parents from their missions. The Blood Coats alerted their superiors' word-for-word from the mission statement. The Washington PP agreed and was going to send an Air Fighter plane to the Lynden Airport where the Blood Coats would provide the crew with the documents they acquired. This process actually witnessed the plane in the Airport in five minutes, with the agents arriving at the Airport just in time. The information was rushed to President Hiplinger, who issued an order that any PP town that suffered a child assassination would receive Air Force bombers bombing the nearest cites areas with a dense population. That city would pay a 200 person execution because of the single assassination. The Air Force was alerted to update their on a plane GPS with population density missile guidance systems. President Hiplinger released this national address, and released on all their communication channels.

Subsequently, The Patricians ignored President Hiplinger's warning in California and Washington DC. The President immediately issued thirty-two sorties on DC and 144 sorties on California, spreading among San Francisco, San Diego, Los Angeles, and Oakland. This was a solid punch by President Hiplinger, effectively working up instability in California DC and prepping them for future campaigns. The attack did hit the White House, which was occupied by

President Poophead, the newly selected President of the Republic of Patricians (ROD) which claimed to be the reclamation of the United States. They lied on their territorial maps claiming Freedom Land, Florida, and Texas. This angered the PP as they put out an order for the immediate execution of President Poophead. In response, the ROD filed a complaint in Brussels, the new headquarters for the United Nations. The United Nations agreed and issued sanctions against the PP. These sanctions had no punch, considering the PP was sinking all ships attempting trade with the former United States, and had expanded this for much of Mexico and Canada due to smuggling operations. The PP withdrew its allocated seats at the United Nations, claiming it was the power base for the New World Order. Any issues they would advance would be immediately ruled on in a negative manner. The PPs official policy was that centuries of dialogs created nothing but confusion and appeasement. The time for talking was finished. They were at war against all anti-conservative agencies who had way too long persecuted conservatives and promoted corruption. The PP was fighting for justice as they saw it.

The PP believed they had to gain control of the Eastern coast before winter arrived. They knew the key to this was to knock out the big cities, such as Philadelphia, Baltimore, Richmond, Atlanta, and Columbia. They already controlled Fayetteville, Myrtle Beach, and Charleston, gained through their massive military presence. The battles began when the Proclamation Freedom League pulled their black neighbors out of these major cities. They were met with disappointment as nearly one-half did not accept their invitations. This did not hamper their operations, as they still could pull practically one million out of these cities. The PP pulled these back to the western side of the Mississippi for training in the California campaigns. This population had suffered from Hispanic gangs that terrorized their neighborhoods and thus had a score to settle with the Hispanics who currently were struggling to gain control of California. This forced Texas to launch strong raids throughout New Mexico and Arizona, attempting to force the Hispanics out of their coastal cities and into the hot deserts, although they were well acclimatized for this. The secondary goal was to cripple the southern coast's drug trade. Chocking the drugs from the former states was a serious objective advanced by President Hiplinger, as he knew the Patricians and President Poophead needed these drugs to appease their population, who preferred drugs over food, and with the shortage of food, the drugs were essential.

Texas had the enormous burden of fighting drugs on the southern border. The Blood Coats and Freedom Fighters watched the country gravel roads and bridges along the Canadian border, shooting all vehicles without the PP flags who crossed the border, evacuated their vehicles as the PP border control drove them to their destinations, usually delivering gasoline and dog food. The drivers who brought the vehicles across the border were formally vetted, and if approved, would drive future PP vehicles to their destinations. Due to the possibility of administrative hiccups, all border people who did not pass immediate vetting was retained, and their point of origination contacted and border pass code verified. Any PP crossing the border had to have a border pass code from their launching point. This worked out great, as those Patricians or Canadians attempting northern coast entry were caught, as with most cases their cargo verified their true mission.

Texas elected to contribute by attacking Atlanta from the south and prevent them from breaking for Savana. Freedom Land hit hard from the Tennessee Appalachian Mountains advancing through the Chattahoochee National Forest rushing into Atlanta through Marietta, Sandy Springs, and Brookhaven. They crippled 285 within two hours of their launch, preventing the Patricians the mobility needed to shift their forces. The Patricians struggled to face this crushing force, permitting the Texans easy access through East Point and College Park in the heart of Atlanta. Prior to the attack, the Air Force shelled all high population density points, leaving Atlanta crippled unable to mobilize their starving reserve forces. Freedom Land depended upon the Navy to shell Philadelphia, and Washington DC. The PP was flourishing with foreign trade through York city. The Air Force hit Baltimore, just minutes before the PP Armies raided these cities. The cities fell easily, nevertheless; a total one-hundred percent execution rate was levied. This forced the use of chemicals and gasses, while the PP soldiers got into their chemical suits. The Blood Coats raided the White House while the Freedom Fighters hit the Capitol building, which was empty.

The Blood Coats successfully captured President Poophead, forced him to release a video to the world of his capture by the PP. While in the video, the Blood Coats cut off his fingers one by one, after that cut off his ears, while he screamed for mercy, and subsequently cut off his feet. Finally, they cut open his stomach and removed his intestines all on the video. They allowed him to bleed out after they castrated him. His screams faded as he fell into eternal sleep escaping the gruesome terrifying pain. The Blood Coats issued a warning that all who took arms against the PP, domestic or foreign could face the same treatment. The world was shocked by this video as outrage demanded Brussels issue a response. The official Brussels response surprised the world when they recommended people avoid taking arms against the PP. The message was out; the PP was against the New World Order, as the world like chickens backed away from this issue. There were three rogue accusations, one coming from Ireland, one from Iran, and one from France. Those three agitators did not wake up the next morning, as their homes and businesses were struck by missiles during the night. President Hiplinger dared anyone else to play the Patricians role. The Patricians did not announce a fresh President, since Vice-President Ieatpoop immediately resigned. The PP used a new technique when striking the cities in this campaign, sticking with house to house smoke bombs and chemical bombs inside apartment buildings. People in vehicles were shot by snipers. After the chemical releases, the Freedom Fighters flooded the roof tops with snipers who shot any person moving inside their apartments or houses. All water was shut off, so that people would be forced to exit their homes.

The chemicals aired out within a few days, at which time the dogs were released. These dogs did not like anything that had the chemical smell with it, and would attack fiercely. Even if they did not attack, their bark and threat to bite were enough to force the survivors out in the open. No prisoners were taken.

The PP did not want to destroy these cities, looking forward to a future resettlement. President Hiplinger issued a warning to all living in the Eastern States East of Atlanta, who was spotted with Yellow Caps would be shot on sight. The PP was, for the first time during this war, was offering amnesty, allowing any Yellow Caps to remove their caps. The warning was that if anyone who removed their Yellow Cap ever supported Patricians activities not only would they be dissected in public; it would be after their family was dissected in public. PP neighbors were to identify their former Yellow Cap acquaintances. These former Yellow Caps would be brought in public and swear their allegiance to the PP, who would then have them sign the party Sign-Up sheet. Afterwards, they would receive hugs from PP who was present at the swearing-in ceremony. The amnesty was highly successful, as entire cities signed up. The PP raided the hospitals in the vacant Philadelphia, Baltimore, Richmond, Atlanta, and Columbia. They collected medical supplies, which sadly were actually in low supply. The number of PP strongholds prior to this campaign was refreshing to the advancing Armies. The Freedom Fighters in these areas were given license to begin patrolling the newly acquired territories. The PP began launching a large campaign to restore the electrical grid in Texas and Freedom Land, which ran from Maine to Florida.

The PP amplified their efforts to clean Washington DC. They reopened Andrews AFB and expanded the security blanket along the East Coast changing the mission from blockading to security. The world already reestablished trading in York city. The PP wanted to move their headquarters back to Washington DC from Chicago. The Freedom Fighters searched fiercely, nevertheless, could not locate any of the Patricians's administration. It was as if they vanished in midair. The PP knew they had not used the DUMB, which was still in PP control. President Hiplinger would return to the White House, after a short visit to Hiplinger Tower in York city, which had naturally been spared any military destruction, except for chemical spraying to kill the Patricians and their germs from this historic tower. Life began to return to the Eastern PP states, as the utilities were once more established.

President Hiplinger added in the amnesty deal for the reformed Patricians a five-year military contract for all adults and children over thirteen years old. The younger children would be provided care for by the parent's community. Anyone caught mistreating these children would be sent in the military for an eight-year term. The amnesty Patricians would serve in the Army, Marine, and naval units, there the organizational structure was strong enough to ensure appropriate and continued vetting. The war was far from finished. The PP wanted to start the rebuilding process to establish a stronger base to continue the battle to save their former party members trapped in large pockets throughout the remainder of the Midwest and western lands. Their pockets were expanding, more for surrender than through fighting. The administrative costs of absorption were mounting to such a point the PP would have to begin executing again just to maintain stability.

A serious and dangerous cancer within the large cities was treated very much different by the PP than by the Patricians. This cancer was gangs. The PP, through the leadership and guidance of the Proclamation Freedom League, identified their neighbors dividing them into passable and impassable. The unpassable were too deep into the gangs to be trusted, while others were addicted to drugs. The impassable was told they would be given all the homes of those who were departing. Their cover was they were going to war. Their families would go with them, so they could fight harder. This appeared to work well within all the cities. Their exodus was during the period when all cell phone towers still remained, considering the PP needed this communication tool as did the Patricians. The blacks called their relatives and friends throughout the country as the grapevine delivered the message nationwide. President Hiplinger addressed the nation through his communications network centered in Chicago. He used television, notwithstanding more important were the radio channels, that the PP hackers bleed the President's message over the stations current broadcast. Present Hiplinger offered all blacks who left the cities, and came to PP held territories they would be given immunity, and a chance to serve with the Proclamation Freedom League. The Proclamation Freedom League actually was self-governing according to their charter, which adopted the prime mission of the PP. The PP handled gangs in their cities through the Blood Coats, who, upon verification of gang membership; these individuals were quickly executed. The PP avoided torturing not wanting to instill a level of fear that would start a gang war. Nevertheless, the PP was involved in many gunfights with gangs, as these fights continued until the PP cities were free from all gang and drug activity. The drug activity was directed towards those whose addiction prohibited contributing social behavior.

Accordingly, once the PP erased the deadly gangs and anti-social drug abuse from their inner-cities, they converted these areas into military bases. All blacks who exited the cities and pledged to support the PP were provided homes throughout the PP controlled areas in every state. Some states the areas were more limited such as California. The Patricians had a much different approach to handling gangs. They used their social expertise to negotiate deals with the gangs with a view towards rehabilitation. The sad fact is that no city successfully rehabilitated any gang members. The gangs used the purview of peace to gain advantage over other gangs so as to kill and steal from them. The Patricians were experiencing difficulty finding food for their city dwellers, because the PP had Blood Coats around every municipality, and along the popular national routes used for shipping or moving commercial products. PP trucks had PP license plates, and the PP flag painted on both the driver's and passenger's doors.

The Patricians also painted their flags of both doors and had their unique plates as well. On the side to be safe, most truck trailers had their party flags painted extra-large furthermore. This was not required, but was appreciated by the Blood Coats, who would continue to monitor a truck until identification was established. They had to be careful about hijacked trucks, because other Blood Coats may have hijacked a truck or trailer and taking the cargo back to a PP controlled area. They would try to paint a red X over the Patricians flag and swap the plates. Another communication tool used by Blood Coats transferring cargo through other zones was identifying themselves on the Blood Coat closed circuit radio channels. The PP always attempted to execute the truck drivers in such a manner to save both the truck and the trailer. They were unsuccessful in the majority of the times, in that the dead driver could no longer maintain control of his rig and would crash it in such a way as to make it unusable. Fortunately, on many crashes the trailer would break loose spiraling along its trajectory.

The Patricians discovered their appeasement of these gangs what reversing on them. The Patricians attempted to recruit gang members for their military, only to discover they would not report. Those who did enter, stole weapons and other ammunition from the military reserves. The gangs eventually declared their turfs independent of the Patricians, enjoying their increased possessions due to the exodus of the Proclamation Freedom League. The absence of the self-policing Proclamation Freedom League left nothing in the cities to disguise the gang's activities. The crippled drug supply created uncontrollable violence within the cities that actually declared war on the city police departments, who were critically undermanned as they were drafted into the Patricians weak military forces, which were defensive in structure, not having the resources to mount any effective long term offensive forces. These gangs declared war on any within their reach, demanding the Patricians stopped withholding their drugs. They believed these drugs were being distributed the others by the Patricians. The gangs went into complete hysterics destroying everything in sight. The absurdity was how far out of the touch with reality these thugs were. They failed to realize the area they were destroying was theirs and that no new reconstruction forces would be rushing in to fix the destruction they caused. This created even more rage as the gangs and Patricians went head to head is all out hostilities. Patricians soldiers reported it was like fighting raging psychotic lions. The gangs killed everyone in their path, men, women, and children. The Patricians targeted the gangs only, sparing the women and children. This caused additional social problems, in that the Patricians did not have the resources to care for these survivors, any of which were drug addicts and well versed in criminal activities.

The PP launched the Michigan, Illinois, and Indiana Campaign. Originally, the PP planned to delay any campaigns, hoping the benefits of their blockade would promote additional unconditional surrenders, which were occurring among smaller municipalities expanding the PP pockets that dominated a high percentage of the remaining American landscape. Detroit and Indianapolis were hit extremely hard by the gang warfare. Detroit suffered years of economic hardship, only recently beginning a budgetary recovery under the genius of President Hiplinger. Detroit enjoyed an unhampered trade with Canada, the lone obstacle being the total collapse of their remaining fiscal reserves due to the PP barricade. Logistically, the Detroit barricade took three times the effort as compared to other coastal cities. The Patricians struggled extensively to pull desperately needed Canadian products in the starving Patricians communities. Traditionally,

Indianapolis was a steady, peaceful Midwest city; notwithstanding, when the PPs got control of Chicago and the southern portion of Lake Michigan, the gangs relocated from Chicago to Indianapolis. The Chicago Patricians, what few remained alive fled to Indianapolis. The Indianapolis Patricians installed a blockade around the inner-city gangs.

Accordingly, it did not take long for the Indianapolis Patricians to discover they were fighting with a special militant gang. This gang stole and stockpiled weapons in Chicago taking advantage of the previous flourishing crime rings. The gangs pushed hard back at the Patricians driving them into West Indianapolis south of Interstate 70. Fortunately, for the Patricians they still maintained control of Indianapolis International Airport. The PP intelligence from locals in the area reported the constant fighting along the gang controlled barricade. Their primary success came in waiting for them to scavenge and pick them off in ambushes. When they proceeded in gangs, the PP used land mines to divide them before having the Blood Coats pick them off with their snipers. Detroit and Indianapolis were turning into crazy lunatic pins, as reports came through the trees were stripped of their leaves, and people were eating drywall. No pets or animals remained in these cities, as even the rodents were extinct. The PP was devoting too many forces to maintaining the blockades, which turned out to be blood baths each day. Therefore, the PP decided to grant mercy and liquidate these cities through chemical warfare. Biological was no longer possible considering the only living things was human, and the areas were so small that the danger of PP contamination loomed. The chemical had to be carefully managed, considering the PP did not want to wipe out Indiana's cattle or Canadians opposite Detroit. They elected to use localized chemicals, and smoke bombs going house to house.

Notwithstanding, the battles commenced. All utilities were cut, to both cities as the order for total execution was issued. Small torch burners were also employed, to repel any frontal attacks. Four large Armies were deployed, two on each city in a north to south attack on both cities. In Indianapolis, they needed one Army focused on the Patricians and the other on the gangs. The original blockade forces fought to keep the city dwellers from escaping, relying heavily on pre-planted mines, with their placements were carefully recorded for after battle retrieval for both cities. Detroit did not want the Patricians to escape into Canada where they could launch future raids. The Navy and submarines patrolled both the Detroit River and Lake St Clair. A warning was issued to Amherstburg, Lasalle, Windsor, and Riverside as the Air Force flew fighter sorties and over two-hundred helicopters hitting Detroit and the water ways ensuring no one makes it over the waters. As a Precaution, Canada evacuated all its citizens within ten miles of this Battlefront enabling the PP to shoot any person moving within this kill all zone. The Navy was able to block the border with Marines within five hours after the battle beginning, permitting the helicopters to concentrate on human movement within Detroit. This was a tough forty-mile line for the Marines to hold, even though, as the Armies pushed south, they could consolidate their shrinking line. When Detroit fell four days later, the PP forces rushed to expand the PP pockets that remained in southern Michigan, on this side of Lake Michigan. The upper panhandle would be fought in the Minnesota, Wisconsin campaigns. Much of the PPs march north was through waving crowds and swerving past mounds of Patricians bodies that were stacked by the Blood Coats.

Chicago and Ohio launched the countryside Patricians cleaning in Illinois and Indiana. This campaign worked different than the Michigan campaign in that the rural campaign prevailed initially.

They pushed through the foothills of southern Ohio through southern Indiana and southern Illinois. Freedom Land wanted these foothills fortified keeping the flatlands open to a return of titanic cornfields. Corn would be the new gold, feeding the PP for the future march to the Rocky Mountains. The world questioned why the PP simply did not reclaim all the land towards the final West Coast battles. The PP already controlled hundreds of large pockets in these states. The rationale became it was easier to fight in these pockets as the snipers and guerrilla Blood Coats had established overwhelming success with high execution rates. The PP controlled the skies, which now lead to the mass production of helicopters. Texas advanced Airbus Helicopters, Bell Helicopter. Arizona secured Boeing Rotorcraft Systems as the Apache rolled out of Mesa, and the Chinook rolled out from Ridley Park, Pennsylvania. Coppell, Texas rolled out the B-2, which became a Blood Coat staple for the snipers and guerrilla forces. Hiller brought back a 1956 YROE-1 one-man Rotocycle to their relocated headquarters in Connecticut, pulling back as many resources from China as possible, reviving a modernization in its bulletproof front shield and mounted machine guns to provide guerrilla air assault power. Helicopters rolled out of classified facilities as well, providing the PP a massive air pinpointed assault force that could work specifically with the small PP pockets reducing the Patricians attack forces to grounds covered with executed Patricians.

The continual chocking by the PP was slowly weakening the Patricians, nevertheless, the decrease was not a quickly as they wanted. The lone possible reason for this decrease had to be due to smuggling. Additional helicopter forces were deployed along the Canadian and Mexican borders. These forces additionally worked on smashing Patricians pockets that could process these smuggled goods. The Mexicans were profiting from a massive smuggling operation, which the PP was currently merely destroying about twenty-five percent of the cargo. The northern border was fairly stable; therefore, the PP launched its Army and Marine forces to capture Wisconsin, Minnesota, the Dakota's, Montana, and eastern Washington and Oregon. This turned out to be merely a three-week campaign, meeting little Patricians resistance. In the meantime, the Air Force shell shocked southern Arizona, New Mexico and California. The Navy fired countless missiles into Seattle, Portland, Oakland, San Francisco, Los Angeles, Los Vegas, and San Diego. Their targets were selected through the newer, more advanced population density radars. The concept was based upon the concept that vital resources would be stored in the proximity of the high population areas. Texas once more invaded Mexico cleaning out the original one-hundred-mile buffer zone, expanding it to two-hundred miles. It did not take the Mexicans long to learn that after a few villages were ravished and completely destroyed, the remaining villages were immediately vacated. This posed a problem for the PP in that they needed executed Mexicans in order to ensure border stability and a reduction in smuggling. Therefore, they brought the helicopters from the northern campaign in Texas going into Mexico by three-hundred miles to shoot every person they could find. This gave the southern command an additional one-hundred miles of safe territory to their two-hundred mile occupied safety or 'no smuggling' zone.

Accordingly, thousands of Hispanic bodies coated the western and southern borders, nevertheless, the smuggling continued. The Submarines and Naval forces were sinking ships from Asia as the smuggling operations intensified. The PP declared a one-hundred percent sink rate of any ship found within 10,000 miles of an American coastline. The PP recalled and froze all American Assets on foreign shores. To cripple the American Assets frozen by other nations, the PP froze all foreign assets on American soil and forfeited on all foreign American debt. Afterwards, they completely devalued against the dollar to less than .03% of its original value, therefore, those holding American capital assets were holding instruments of no value. The Patricians attempted to reclaim the value, nevertheless, did not a strong enough military to enforce it, as most of their areas still lacked electricity and other public utilities. The PP had the punch to get their message across, as any foreign government that dealt with the Patricians faced capital bombings from the PP. Even the thieves at the New World Order backed off after a few bombings. The PP was in the process of reopening factories mass producing martial hardware and training large military forces. The primary objectives of this stage were the mass production of helicopters, missiles and bombs. The PP had all the natural resources; they needed to accomplish this objective. They also kept the pockets well supplied as the final two continental stages to this useless war were being planned. Let the blood continue to roll.

# CHAPTER 06

# FROM SEA TO BLEEDING SEA

Freedom land began shifting its extra forces towards its borders, from the Rockies of the northwest to the Gulf of Mexico and Carolinas of the East. The objective was to find and unite the PP pockets. These pockets were strong simply needing a hard push to shake loose the weakening Patrician who had profited greatly from there limited resources. The battle cries went out to "Free our neighbors," as the PP grabbed their axes, hatchets, and long sharp knives, with their loaded weapons. The battle plans were broadcasted over the local PP closed circuit. The local actions were coordinated through the district PP headquarters who added the helicopter, artillery, and any missile support along with ground troops. The PP had to have the push begin solidity and hard to send the message to the inner forces who were building an impregnable force along the West Coast. Petitions echoed out across the landside as the Patrician begged for amnesty. Unfortunately, the amnesty period had expired and the Patrician could not accept that the PP would do what they said they would do and not what the Patrician told them to do. Two long years of war had failed to convince them the time of memorizing some delusional talking points and spreading lies was long history. We would no longer bow to foreign nations while they stole our factories and children's future. When they attempted to destroy the American culture, the long policy of appeasement finally eroded as the PP rose to reclaim what was theirs by birthright. Many people believed that once the Patrician weaned from their drug abuse and fell from the spell casts by their delusional professors, their puppet masses began to waiver. The American silent majority sent President Hiplinger to Washington. The next elections, so called mid-term elections was the power crushing blow to the Patrician, as their corruption took a hit at the head of that demonic snake. The venality of the bureaucracy and corruption of the courts, and FBI, and the Patrician Intelligence services were the root causes. An abandoned outrage became known to the public with leaks revealed the American Intelligence services were exploiting foreign nations on behalf of the Patrician and their lobbyists. The overconfident Patrician stepped on some Provider's toes, and the Provider's foot was kicking these Patrician in their butts, by exposing much of their corruption within the American system and intelligence on how they were stealing so much and so deep, as if almost invisible in plain sight.

This created a reaction from the public as PP began to demonstrate. Unlike Patrician demonstrations with protection by the police, they were permitted to destroy public property and lambast the PP. When the PP demonstrated the police attempted to stop them as the beginning of armed conflict took hold. The police, recognizing the PP were not going to back away disbanded. The PP then ransacked the FBI, DOJ, along with all Federal agencies throughout the United States. This was be official crippling of the federal bureaucracy, as Patrician judges who created their liberal laws from the courts were dragged out in public and beheaded. The initial shock and running to hide by the Patrician fed the PP momentum as they continued to hunt down Patrician Officials. Many of the Police went rogue when it was obvious justice was being preserved. For some unknown reason, Chicago and its surrounding area became totally PP, as the Patrician who were still alive fled without hesitation. Once Chicago was declared safe, the PP pulled President Hiplinger and reestablished Chicago as the headquarters of the PP. President Hiplinger always defined this as a total cleansing of those who would not assimilate into the American or Western Culture. He forced his new Congress to modify religious freedom to "the freedom to worship as a Christian" and declared that only a child born from an American citizen (mother or father) would be an American, no matter where the child was born. Any child born on American soil from non-citizen parents was given thirty days to exit our nation.

Surprisingly, two sub-elements formed within the PP, willing to fight to their deaths for this new cause. One was the blacks, who declared life on the plantation had ceased and the chains of small freebees just too barely survive. They no longer wanted drugs in their communities, nor did they want to see their children with weapons shooting their neighbors. The American Hispanics citizens formed a sub-force as well in total support of the PP. The PP relied heavily on their Hispanic forces when they freed New York and New England. They were given prime estates and farms as these estates were previously occupied by living Patrician. The PP, as agreed by their Hispanics they needed to be away from the frontline in that non-PP Hispanics could infiltrate, thereby sabotaging the missions. Considering the blacks represented seventeen percent of the population, it would be impossible to uncover any infiltrators. The PP left it to the blacks to monitor their forces. To accomplish this, the blacks would also establish their communities, especially when considering how brainwashed the Patrician had maintained them. Their massive exodus from the inner cities forced them to locate and fight the Patrician for their homes. They fought in large groups so they could carve out their oases among the Patrician lands. The rules were simple, if you killed a Patrician family, you would be given title to their occupied lands. They were additionally permitted to remove all Patrician within their vicinity of possible. Large groups could clean out the entire Patrician in an area and thereby obtain control of the community buildings, such as hospitals, hotels, restaurants, retail outlets, etc. This motivated the blacks and the Hispanics to invade the nicer homes, which most likely housed the more wealthy and powerful Patrician.

Another primary concern was feeding the land forces as they pushed through this unclaimed territory. Usually, such large forces would survive from the bounty of those conquered. This campaign offered another challenge in that the Patrician lands had no bounty to extract, except for household items the PP had an excess due to the now vacant Patrician homes in the Freedom Land. The DUMB network ran through the middle of the territory east of the Mississippi river. The difficulty lay in the northern line from Iowa to the northeast corner of Oklahoma had to be committed for the push to the west coast. DUMB offered dump points running through northern Oklahoma and Nebraska. Colorado had four outlets as did New Mexico with nine dedicated points; Texas would push along the Mexican line consolidating Arizona using six outlets to finalize a line into California and Nevada. The actual campaign proved to be one of the fasted to date. Many of the PP pockets had made peace with their Patrician neighbors, who were borderline Patrician at best. This resulted in titanic PP pockets as the Armies rushed in and completely destroyed any Patrician pockets. The push was so dramatic that it did not end until the PP forces reached I5 from Canada to Mexico. Their Armies divided Seattle, controlling the Willamette River and bridges along Portland, gaining complete victory in Sacramento, dividing Los Angeles, controlling Pasadena, Anaheim, and Santa Ana. They reached the Pacific Ocean at Dana Point taking San Diego and all coastlines to the Mexican border. The Naval forces had pre-staged this final bloody sea by entering the San Diego Bay and shelling San Diego, National City, Chula Vista and the Imperial Beach Pier. The PP sunk every ship along all the ports in the San Diego Bay and Mission Bay. Intelligence had estimated almost one-half of the smuggled goods entering for Patrician consumption entered through these bays. In the Los Angeles area, the PP established control on Catalina Island, Channel Islands National Park and Santa Rosa Island and San Clemente Island. They unloaded an extensive artillery force onto these islands for a not stop artillery barrage on Los Angeles. This permitted the Navy to concentrate in the Gulf of the Farallones and sink smugglers while shelling San Francisco and Oakland. The intelligence rightly predicted an increase in smuggling here with Seattle crippled and San Diego fallen.

The PP had planned to stop their invasion at this point, however, several areas petition to continue for humanitarian issues. Seattle and Portland fell quickly, not able to handle the intense barricade coupled with the constant shelling. Mass suicides left the streets covered with bodies. The PP controlled the entire Pacific coastline from Washington, Oregon and California from Santa Rosa to its northern border with Oregon. The PP controlled the Mendocino National Forest and

Shasta-Trinity National Forest and Six Rivers National Forest. This final push was nothing more than killing off a few remaining Patrician and creating an area where the PP could travel without danger. The petition was approved and mass executions of the remaining Patrician were executed under the treason against the homeland act. The remaining area was nothing more than a token of an area that was nothing more than target practice for the massive artillery bombardment. The PP were exhausting aged missiles and bombs whose delivery systems were too costly to maintain. The newer advanced missiles were being mass produced at rates higher than World War II to stockpile a titanic inventory. This mass production was kept secret; as the PP planned their war would not end until the last Patrician fell. This also prompted massive productions of battleships and submarines, with fighters and bombers. No one in the world could discover these as all satellite spy equipment flying over Freedom Land were destroyed.

The world had to recognize the PP controlled Freedom Land as the true rebirth of the former United States. The Providers would not recognize this, still claiming that the Patrician controlled the former United States. President Hiplinger declared the remaining Patrician lands in Southern California as a no fly zone. Any plane flying over this area was shot down. The PP had the new advanced radar systems covering all the Patrician areas plus a three hundred mile circumference encircling it. The world appealed this decision; however, these appeals disappeared when the PP received the greatest news since the beginning of the war. The updated nuclear codes were given to President Hiplinger, also with all the software used to originally hack the system. The President had his Air Force review the hacking, created the needed firewalls and change the codes before returning them to his remodeled and renovated White House, which now had two additional security levels or floors below the White House. These security levels were in place prior to the return of the nuclear codes. The military and needed hardware were located on one of these floors. This enabled the conversion process and intense encoding within the matter of hours. With this new control, President Hiplinger promised any nation who launched anything against Freedom Land would be immediately nuked.

The Providers quickly recognized that their New World Order would be delayed. President Hiplinger had cabinet far more intelligent than any in history before. They had planted the seeds for complete takeover of all the American banks. The Federal Reserve was completely staffed by PP, as anyone who had ever voted within the previous ten years for a Patrician was executed. The Peoples Party (PP) would no longer even give a Patrician a chance of survival. There future voice would only come from beyond the grave, which for most would be from hell. The PP began reprinting new currency for Freedom Land, as all dollars were collected, serial numbers scanned, currency scanned to file and destroyed. These serial numbers were printed on the new currency. The banks called all loans held by Patrician and capitalized that capital into the new government's fiscal reserves. They also cancelled all home loans, as it was not fair for a PP to pay for his or her home, while others acquired vacant Patrician homes for no cost. All property taxes were cancelled as was income taxes. The sole tax was a value added sales tax, plus for future trade, a 200% tariff. If Freedomites, the citizens of Freedom Land, wanted to buy foreign goods, they would pay for their Federal Government. Freedom Land would no longer recognize the dollar, nor accept them from foreign nations. This left the foreign nations holding dollars with nothing but worthless paper. Even though the battered area in Southern California still recognized the dollar, they had no ability to get money in and out, especially since the PP retook control of the internet and closed off the world from the internet.

The PP gained control of the Internet by initially destroying the sites in Belgium and Finland, and took complete control of the five centers in the former United States. New protocols and addresses were assigned to the new addresses recognized by the new updated Freedom Land Centers. They established a new chip based encryption device, which the receiving device needed as well to communicate with it. These chips were enclosed in a USB device that had thumb print, facial and voice recognition, plus a password. When the user put the USB device in the computer, a screen would appear for the thumbprints, instructions on how and where to stand for the photo and words would appear for the individual to read. After this, an input screen would appear for the password. If any of these steps failed, the USB device would disable the internet chip immediately. This system drew discontent from the public who wanted the Internet, considering they grew up with it. With this in mind, President Hiplinger divided the internet, Level one was dedicated to the government and all official news. The military and law enforcement also used the network. He then established a new one for the general public. Any cable running through the ocean or over the borders were cut and ends capped with one end secured at the location and the other end recoiled backward into a security building and connected to the domestic networks for added speed and any increased demand that could ordinarily cause an overload. The government controlled the website names and addresses.

The PP regarded celebrates as disloyal and sick to the core a rotten element of the Patrician. The public version of the internet absorbed much of the previous content, including previous movies, television series, and educational links. This would prove to be the foundation for the new education system of Freedom Land. One of the new objectives of the PP was to torment and execute as many of the 'Entertainment Elites as possible. There would be no new "Hollywood" style of entertainment, because the PP had declared war on all celebrities, who, unless known to be PP, were executed on sight. The mighty PP Armies were within five miles of Beverly Hills, nevertheless within three miles of Paramount Pictures Studio. This was well within pinpoint accuracy range for the artillery with a special unit placed in Atwater Village just across the Los Angeles River. They also leveled the "Hollywood" sign and shelled Warner Bros. Studios and Universal City and Sunset Strip. Snipers were able to work their way into this section of Los Angeles using the

Santa Monica Mountains National Recreation Area for cover and concealment. Therefore anyone they saw outside moving was executed. These people had abused the democracy and public faith through their greed and hunger for power. The entertainers promoted extensive drug use and created a society against all the fundamental American values. They constantly attacked President Hiplinger and the PP. These demons also praised the Patrician and financed their corruption and anti-government operations. The PP declared no amnesty nor escape for these entertainers. A few tried to fly out in the private jets, only to see a fighter jet behind them that blasted them out of the air. Another futile attempt was attempting to sail out on their yachts. Once they were outside of swimming to shore range, the submarines sunk them efficiently and at a one-hundred percent success rate. The remaining personal boats were sunk in dock, while the aircraft were blasted in their airfields. The PP believed that giving the enemy hope risked making them willing to fight.

Accordingly, with the overwhelming majority of Freedom Land's children the intense demands of the war diminished. When the Patrician were removed, so was the danger of becoming a casualty of the war. This forced the mothers who were behind the lines with their children to once more begin their lives. The family unit remained distressed with the absence of the father. There never was a great fear the fathers would not return, considering the PP suffered few casualties, somewhere around a ratio of 1:121 to the Patrician. No one could take away the possibility, in that stories abounded of families learning their father lost his life. There was of course the normal, is he cheating on me dilemma. The war effort included approximately seventy-eight percent of women above the age of eighteen and younger than sixty, who were single. The women worked in the intelligence gathering fields, assisted with the security functions, food preparation (along with males), engineering, battle plan designs, and among many other duties, which included social functions. The social functions began to appear after the Pacific Coast campaign. A land that once had over 323 million people now hosted less than 120 million people. Of the population thirty-two million people were amnesty Patrician. Their citizenship was based upon assimilation into the PP philosophy. Anyone who petitioned for a Patrician cause was immediately executed.

Accordingly, the PP did not have time or resources for Law Enforcement. The city had the normal Mayor, and each neighborhood had a community leader. This leader basically alerted the Mayor what their neighborhood needed. The Mayor and his staff would either complete the request or explain why they could not fulfill the plea. Rebuilding the nation would be a task shared by all. The PP propaganda preached working to build a better tomorrow today. The slow, yet steady return of the cell phones, land phones, and other social platforms to communicate assisted in the reunification process. President Hiplinger reestablished the Department of Education, which would be different this time around. The new education department would be located in the White House and would provide recorded lectures and material for a course. The instructor would establish the homework assignments as all answers to the questions would be answered on-line with immediate feedback and material explaining the correct answer. Exams were the same way. The Department prepared all the course material for all grades. This was not all that difficult in that the instructors could record their lectures anywhere they wanted. This added some variety the course. Instructors had a resources contact, which would search for material the instructor needed. Another special feature of this program was the immediate feedback the instructor received from the homework and exams. They could determine what the students needed, so they could fine tune their course. The objective was that they learn and comprehend the material. All courses were pass or fail. Students determined what their goals were and the system would assign them the appropriate courses. Each area, usually a neighborhood had an adult monitoring teem that attempted to keep their students progressing towards completing their education. This program was equal for all children in this young nation. Everyone studied in their homes or at local libraries. Local children taking the same courses could do their homework together. Naturally, all children were given a computer with the appropriate chips and authorizations to completer their program, which they were free to amend at their own will.

The educational system on their laptops ran from pre-kindergarten to doctorate, to include medical doctor. The goal was for all children to have the same opportunities, even though they could be required to relocate in order to successfully market their skills. The communities converted the previous schools into public buildings for local use. A popular use of the classrooms was for student clubs, which provided the students a chance to socialize while gaining specialized experience. The renaissance of society would have some awakening pains. The nation needed people, and the one sure method would be through reproduction. Freedom Land planned never to allow any form of immigration. The days of permitting foreigners to reside among them and work to subvert the hosting culture were history. It died with the foolish and appeasing Patrician. In order to create the population needed would require some social norms be adjusted. Only two religions were permitted in Freedom Land and that was Christianity and Judaism. Their leadership would be needed to pull society into a new way of establishing families. Freedom Land needed to Reverse customs of the ancient world, especially among the Jewish people.

The need for more people forced the government to reduce the age for girls to marry to age thirteen. The girl would mate, and marry if desired, and begin reproducing. Usually, the young mother would continue to live with her parents until age eighteen. This would provide the young mother with siblings and parents to assist in raising the young child plus an opportunity to continue her education, which for all students was self-paced as the internet ran 24/7 every day of the year. The father was provided an opportunity to help raise his child with his 'in-laws' if married. Freedom Land did not have a legal system established for marriage, therefore such ceremonies and social bonding powers were left to the churches. Another popular method was the swearing their bond and oaths to each other in front of their church. This was enough to give the mother her mates name and their family its father's name. By the time the young family's parents reached age eighteen, they were permitted to occupy their own home. This usually involved finding a vacant Patrician home and restoring it. If none were available, the family would add a few rooms to their house to provide a private home for their daughter's family. There were many occasions where the father would take his family to a new home in an adjoining area, or an expansion unit on his parent's home. Consequently, there were simply too many previous Patrician homes. The communities worked to restore as many of these homes as they could. They would then pre-assign them to their young future mothers, who would maintain with her family or even friends until her day of taking ownership arrived. People were slow to move into neighboring vacant streets. Notwithstanding, the pre-assignment method was working well, in that it gave the locally time to transition into their new bounty.

Another form of cleaning needed to occur, and that was erasing the names of the executed Patrician from history. No records from the previous United States were kept. Everything started new, beginning with their names. Everyone selected new names and history began with a new clean slate. This meant all previous debts and possessions were deleted. The PP owners could keep their property by recording their possession with the PP

Mayor, who exchanged the ownership documentation for a new Freedom Land Title. The neighborhood or local community leaders established documentation for new PP ownership of vacant Patrician homes and provided this documentation to the Mayors or district counsel for recording the new ownership. The erasing also went to all media that was saved from the previous States. All credits and names were erased. All media was stored digitally, originals and edited. The originals were saved for future releases of the history of the United States (1776-20xx). The important issue was the erasing of all names for people alive when the United States fell and Patrician leaders in the 20$^{th}$ and 21$^{st}$ centuries. Historical figures and national heroes were recorded in history. Several heroes gained special attention, such as President Andrew Jackson, listed as a mental hero for President Hiplinger. Other issues had to be addressed and settled once and for all. The first Civil War freed the black slaves from their owners, while the second Civil War helped free the blacks from their Patrician masters who used their lying tongues to deceive and once again enslave them binding them with broken promises and enslaving them with fear mongering. Freedom Land believed this was a crime that should never be erased from history.

Nevertheless, the fundamental brainwashing of racism, even though the party and people that depended upon this were executed, and the former United States, the bed for this irreversible crime against humanity, was erased or soon to be with the fall of a small oasis in California, from the face of the Earth. Following the first Civil War, President Lincoln feared the undeniable truth that the European whites would not accept the African Blacks as equal. This was not a concept that was bound to the Americas, but also existed worldwide throughout history. This was even evident when Cleopatra brought Julius Caesar's son to Rome, only to be cast away as if they were dirt, and his adopted step son made emperor. President Lincoln bought land in Africa and offered this to the former slaves who were sold by fellow Africans to Europeans and purchased in the Southern markets. Meanwhile, the next 150 years saw an attempt to do the impossible, even though legal discrimination against the majority for the benefit of a select minority. Nevertheless, no action or series of actions was able to remove the weapon of the cry of racism. President Hiplinger formed a committee to address the issues associated with a minority of seventeen percent in the fallen United States and were now without question with the erasing of all non-citizens of Hispanic origin, the primary minority in Freedom

Land. A fact had to be addressed, which was the lack of successful historical evidence in the failure of multiple races existing within the same borders. With this in mind, the multi-racial committee recommended, with no descents, that an independent nation called Freedom Land South would be established for the Negro Race to rule. They agreed that no person of any race would be forced to relocate to Freedom Land, unless no other homes could be located for Negroes wishing to return to their new homeland. The complete relocations and establishment of government would occur within two years.

Freedom Land had abundant homes made available by this mass exodus, as many simply swapped homes. The citizens from both nations assisted in these relocations. A provisional government was established as Freedom Land agreed to keep their forces, both military and law enforcement, until no longer supported or desired by Freedom Land South. They would be removed transitionally, to minimize any negative effects. In a shocking addition, Freedom Land turned over the buffer zone between Mexico and the southern border. Freedom Land South included Virginia, Carolinas, Florida, Georgia, Alabama, Mississippi, Louisiana, Arkansas, and approximately seventy percent of Texas. They had a mutual defense treaty, that an attack on one was an attack on both, unless in a mutually declared war. The support for this new division was overwhelming, as it would prove to remove much of the mistrust, prejudice, and racism that had plagued the previous United States. Freedom Land North agreed to divide the military forces and provide Freedom Land South with all it needed to protect itself. Naturally, Freedom Land North kept a bulk of the forces in that intelligent sources believed that foreign forces would see this as an opportunity to get a stronghold in the Americas and remove President Hiplinger in which many foreign governments believed to be an international criminal. For the most part foreign nations set up diplomatic ties with Freedom Land South, while not recognizing Freedom Land North. President Hiplinger then closed Freedom Land North from the world, removing any diplomats who still remained. In the meanwhile, all military factories were running 24/7 mass producing military hardware. President Hiplinger published the production and mass inventories of this new fighting power, wanting to show that an attack against Freedom land result in deadly damage to the attackers. The development of drones and expansion of robotic elements vastly reduced the need for manpower, which was stretched to its limits at this time. Men were scarce and women abundant. The elimination of a person being bound by a single marriage law was erased for the females who were now permitted to reproduce with multiple males. This saw a massive increase in the birthrate. Large areas of the Midwest and South were developed into large farming companies to mass produce food and large storage areas established. The mountain areas were reserved for cattle, while predators killed, with a few allocated to the zoos. The cattle would roam free, with their companies brand and chip installed. Non-predator game were allowed to exist as well, with the continued hunting season to help feed the poor and provide an additional variety of meat for the grocery chains, considering there were very few poor remaining. Hospitals continued to make medical advancements increasing the public's health. The next five peaceful years saw many advancements and construction. The quality of life for both Freedom lands was at the highest in recorded history, especially was all the dead bodies now collected and cremated. These ashes were used to fertilize the farming areas, thus increasing food production.

One obstacle remained and that was psychological. The PP did what they had to do in order to establish a more equal and just nation. This included the total purge of anything that was contrary or could inhibit that goal. This was Old Testament style. All bad cells had to be removed in order to create a cancer free body. However the amount of bloodshed was greater in any war in history totaling more than 200 million dead. No human mind could comprehend this degree of death. This included the killing of many close friends and relatives much more psychologically disastrous than any war in history and greater to the first Civil War as the degree of weapons and technology for killing had increased to such a great efficiency and a lack of personalization. The push of a button from an aircraft could eliminate large areas. Plus a few grenades and machine guns could wipe out neighborhoods without even looking into the eyes of those who were dying. The forces moved on quickly so as not to see the devastation that caused. This required the PP to seek spiritual redemption, which was no easy task but had to be done. The older people had to work hard with the younger people who were used to do most of the killing. The president would cite long speeches each morning trying to create positive atmosphere needed for this Renaissance to survive. This was hard that the killing was not finished for the long road of rebuilding and reestablishing the new positive attitude needed for Freedom Land.

Notwithstanding; the world was pumping so much negative propaganda to try and disrupt this new nation. The intelligence forces worked hard to block this information; which was like stopping a leak in the boat that was increasing. The education department worked hard on influencing the youth, knowing they would take this information to their family members. Each day was a psychological battle but the PP was making progress. As each day passed, the memories of these battles were fading. The medical department was able to distribute nerve relaxing medications that help to keep the populace calm. This new nation, more than ever, had to remain divorced from the angry world that wanted revenge. The northern and southern borders remain a great threat as foreign infiltrators would sweep in and spread their propaganda. This was a problem that kept getting worse and worse and had to be dealt with. This nation new that the time to use this new vast military technology and equipment was approaching much quicker they had been projected.

Freedom Land was now restless, as fear along the borders increased. It was now time to change North America and protect what been so hard to obtain and rebuild.

## CHAPTER 07

# SECURING AMERICA AND REBUILDING

F reedom land slowly and quietly began to mobilize equipment along the northern and southern borders. Both nations engaged in this process with the South being focused on Mexico and the North on Canada. The PP was our well-established within 100 miles in Mexico so moving this equipment involved keeping a low profile so the locals were not alarm their government. The operation was a success, since most of the equipment could be deployed quickly such as tanks which were now much quieter than in previous wars and required fewer members to operate. The important thing was to establish supply lines that could move the vast equipment and supplies that would be needed for these forces to operate. The

South would mobilize 100 divisions, whereas the North would mobilize 50 divisions. Both nations would rely heavily on air power and naval forces. The South would initially attack using submarines and satellites to pinpoint their targets. The North would do the same for the Pacific and Atlantic borders however the Yukon and Northwest Territories could be conquered by controlling the supplies they needed. Alaska would be instrumental in conquering these territories. The President sent an additional 2000 aircraft to support this land movement; which was in extremely cold terrain. Military minds reviewed all options and presented them to the respective Presidents for their approval. The Presidents wanted these campaigns to go quickly disregarding how many physical structures were destroyed. They had no objectives nor did they need this territory; other than providing a buffer zone to keep foreigners out of their nations. Therefore; they understood that genocide for both Mexico and Canada with the only option. Therefore; the population had to be zeroed out, which introduced the use of biological warfare. This would leave more of the physical structures remaining for future use and expansion plus it would make cleanup a lot easier. Freedom Land knew this could result in massive retaliation from the world therefore they had to be prepared for a possible World War III. The President believed that there would be enough military hardware still available to fight in Europe, Africa, and Asia if needed. Either way, this was something that the PP believed had to happen. The game plan called for the first mass release of the chemicals in the urban areas to be deployed on the first day. This will be followed by aircraft strategically bombing any potential enemy strongholds. The land forces would be deployed after the chemicals were deluded enough for them to survive. Initially the land troops would deploy with chemical biological protection. This meant they needed to be deployed in large vehicles that could handle them. They would wear out quickly if they had to travel by foot. GPS satellites would spy or survey the areas that they were traveling in; geared towards identifying any potential enemy threats. If identified they would notify command headquarters that would transmit the targets locations to submarines. After day two large naval vessels, which could now be revealed since so many of the enemies population and fighting power was eliminated. The first day was a total success from the military standpoint as an estimated 95% of the urban areas populations were eliminated. Additionally an estimated 99% of the military forces were executed. The remaining 1% were not on the military installations during the attacks with most being on leave. This campaign was so different than the purging of America homeland. There were no safe pockets or groups that needed to be saved. For psychological reasons it was imperative that face-to-face contact be eliminated. The goal was to execute and eliminate the bodies. "Large garbage trucks", were used to scoop up the bodies and deliver them to large burning sites. These workers were given hazmat outfits in order to prevent the spread of any disease. At that time there were a number of diseases spreading throughout Mexico. Canada did not have diverse diseases due to the weather. The difficulty with Canada laid in the cultural similarities although these are not as great as it was before the wars. Due to the vast territory, more salvage trucks will be needed to scan the country areas. Fortunately the vast amount of the population lived within a few hundred miles of Freedom's border. The President decided to deploy thousands of snipers to scan the country areas for farms and other living areas. This would take time; nevertheless, deemed necessary. The South soon began to move ground troops for final cleanup. One additional feature was added for both the South and North and that was the total removal of all landmark signs. Proof of the previous society existing on these lands had to be removed. Roads were remarked and renamed. Within two months Mexico and Canada were both history in other nation's books. The education department labeled them as Freedom's buffer territories. Work began to establish military outposts in these areas as warning signs of European and Asian forces were mobilizing. The President issued warnings that Freedom Land was now a no-fly zone and no shipping vessels were allowed within 3000 miles of its borders. Any violations would result in bombing the host nation's cities. World War III was a spark away. The South offered free territory and homes to any Hispanics that resided in the North, considering there were very few Hispanics living in the South. The North also permitted its citizens to relocate in former Canadian homes and cities, many of which were still intact. The large food companies occupied many of the open areas to use for food production. Oil companies also began producing more oil from these vacant territories, to supplement the production of oil from Alaska. The governments used these proceeds to fund government operations, eliminating the need for taxes. The President insisted on no income or sales taxes on his citizens unless purchasing foreign goods. The South built a large wall on the southern border of the former Mexico. Freedom Land considered longer accepting immigration as the possibility of rogue cells existing on this territory.

The world objected to the purging of America by Freedom Land. The United Nations recognized the vast military arsenal that Freedom Land still had in reserves. No one wanted World War III, recognizing how Freedom Land had a 100% purge war philosophy. Instead, they attempted to establish diplomatic relations with both Freedom Lands. The Presidents forwarded intent to eventually accept, citing that was too early at this present time and expressed their lack of desire for future expansion. Expansion would only result in threats to the current nations and borders. These wounds needed time to heal. The Presidents felt that was essential to block the release of information from American or former American societies. They did not want to make the grass look greener from the other side.

Another problem existed in the prolonged time it was taking to rebuild the population. The current population was exhausted raising the many children and rebuilding at the same time. The President began to entertain a movement to allow immigration. The South also entertained this idea. They would accept same race people from Africa and those spread among other allied nations. Many nations now depended on Freedom Land for fuel and energy which created new allies. India now imported natural gas for 100% of its energy needs. Although they were not Christian their religious beliefs did not promote violence and the North had plenty of former Indian citizens who accepted the PP's philosophy and melded easily into the PP's culture. India now had the world's largest educated and technically advanced population, something that the PP really could use. Therefore; large screening departments were established in both the South and North to screen potentially future citizens. China and Japan also began exporting citizens. The South began to accept educated same race people from Europe and Africa. This process took an additional 10 years; nevertheless, life once again began to flourish in Freedom Land. Freedom Land began to export food throughout the world saving many people who would've previously been starving. Large medical schools had been established and now training doctors at an alarming level, many of which would do tours in foreign countries to help treat the sick and stop the spread of diseases. Another area of interest was the spread of missionary work conducted by the many large new churches that the President had established. The President also built high speed electric trains to connect the vast areas of the former Canada to lower states and Alaska. This would allow the quick supply of needed items and the fast mobilization of military forces if required. The belief was that the quicker someone could make it to another urban area the closer the population would feel. The Presidents were no longer elected by voting but were now appointed for life. Both governments felt that voting represented too great of an opportunity for cheating and corruption. The people were given many opportunities to express their views to their congressmen and senators who were accountable to the Presidents, therefore their voices were heard and views actually acted upon. Many of the government's policies and supporting documentation were made available to the public so everyone knew why they were doing what they did and how they reached the tough decisions. The United Nations reported that many other nations were now adopting this philosophy in these procedures recognizing how important it was for the public to know why their government was doing what they were doing. The President warned that Freedom Land would never be the world's police. The world was responsible for keeping their peace and sharing its available resources. The policing of rogue nations was a responsibility of the United Nations who was by the way no longer financed by Freedom Land.

We must all obey the great law of change. It is the most powerful law of nature. Everything changes; nothing remains without change Buddha (B.C. 568-488). The seen is the changing, the unseen is the unchanging. Plato (B.C. 427?-347?) As the blessings of health and fortune have a beginning, so they must also find an end. Everything rises but to fall, and increases but to decay. Sallust (B.C. 86-34). The question for history would now be how long this change would last and how it would adopt to changes. This was a concern for these new nations knowing that the change was inescapable as people and attitudes evolve; yet we can only pray they would never reach the level that it once had and that another great purge would never be needed. That would be the topics explored in the future centuries and may God help us all.

# INDEX

## THE OTHER ADVENTURES FROM THIS AUTHOR

Prikhodko, Dream of Nagykanizsai
Search for Wise Wolf
Seven Wives of Siklósi
Passion of the Progenitor
Mempire, Born in Blood
Penance on Earth
Patmos Paradigm
Lord of New Venus
Tianshire, Life in the Light
Rachmanism in Ereshkigal
Sisterhood, Blood of our Blood
Salvation, Showers of Blood
Hell of the Harvey
Emsky Chronicles

Methuselah's Hidden Antediluvian Abridgment
American States of China
Unconscious Escapades
11-27
Amazing Truths or Foolish Lies
Legend of the Mu (Lemuria)

# AUTHOR BIOGRAPHY

J ames Hendershot, D.D. was born in Marietta Ohio, finally settling in Caldwell, Ohio where he eventually graduated from high school. After graduating, he served four years in the Air Force and graduated, Magna  Cum Laude, with three majors from the prestigious Marietta College. He then served until retirement in the US Army during which time he earned his Masters of Science degree from Central Michigan University in Public Administration, and his third degree in Computer Programing from Central Texas College.

His final degree was the honorary degree of Doctor of Divinity from Kingsway Bible College, which provided him with keen insight into the divine nature of man. After retiring from the US Army, he accepted a visiting professor position with Korea University in Seoul, South Korea. He later moved to a suburb outside Seattle to finish his lifelong search for Mempire. It is now time for Earth to learn about the great mysteries not only deep in our universe but also in the dimensions beyond sharing these magnanimities with you.

Printed in the United States
by Baker & Taylor Publisher Services